THE
WORST
KIND
OF
GIRL

THE
WORST
KIND
OF
GIRL

a novel

SUSAN RUKEYSER

The Worst Kind of Girl

Published by Red Light Lit Press
557 8th Ave., San Francisco, CA 94118
www.redlightlit.com

The characters and events in this book are fictitious. Any
similarity to real persons, living or dead, is coincidental
and not intended by the author.

Library of Congress Control Number: 2025944047
ISBN 978-0-9998895-5-8

Cover illustration by Emily Reynolds
Author photo by Sandra Goodin Photography

For all the worst girls. I'm with you.

THE
WORST
KIND
OF
GIRL

a novel

SUSAN RUKEYSER

CONTENTS

April 2019

When a Man Just Disappears

Paula

"They found another body," Seth called from the motel's lone breakfast table, across from my front desk. "Out past the dry lakebed. This one was on fire."

His overgrown, salt-and-pepper hair was wild from the night before. Too much wine, but also: Ruby in Room 4. He thought I didn't know. He bit into a toasted slice of the white bread I put out every morning, because otherwise he'd eat nothing at all. He thought I did not see what he tipped into his coffee some mornings, including this one. Seth rented by the week, and this was week ten.

"I hope it wasn't on that land I just bought," I said. "I wish these L.A. types would stop dumping their trash out here."

I pushed a rag around the coffee carafes and the case of organic pastries made fresh by Sky, a local baker. She was cute, and I thought she might have a little crush on me, but I had explained I was straight. I felt my curls bouncing as I cleaned. They'd pulled into tighter spirals as the gray pushed out the brown— prematurely, strangers sometimes remarked, but I did not necessarily agree. My hair was coarser, but that was me in general, at fifty. Everywhere but the inside of my arm, powdery soft as an old woman's. I was not old, but I could see it in the distance.

San Bernardino County said hairnets were required, but I was tired of being told what to do.

"Aren't you an L.A. type?" said Seth.

"I'm from Connecticut. Didn't I tell you? I think I told you."

"Probably," he said, rubbing his forehead. "That is a helluva thing to do, light a body on fire."

"Hopefully a dead body."

"Oh, someone would've heard the screams. Maybe not here by the highway, but a little further out? The way sound travels in the desert?"

Something out the window caught his eye and he watched it for a moment.

"People make no sense," he said finally, like I was inside his head and could follow the jumps. "That's why I write plays."

"What?"

"I want people to say the right things at the right time, I guess. My wife called me a control freak. Ex-wife."

Seth knew that I knew he was stalled, maybe permanently, by the embarrassing reviews of his last play, ridiculed for its "straight white male gaze."

"What gaze am I supposed to have?" he asked. "I'm not even that straight."

"Who is?" I replied, every time.

Only once did our friendship drift too close to something else, one late afternoon in his room at the end of the concrete strip that was the Hi-Dez Motel, one block off the highway in Yucca Valley, California. (I bought it a year ago, when my husband John was finally declared dead in absentia, after too many billable hours with a lawyer who called me kiddo because he was five years older). Seth invited me down to Room 6 to share the boxed red wine he got from the gas station across the highway.

"I never noticed how tall you are," he said, pouring me a glass.

We were both about six feet, slim and sturdy. My late husband John was almost 6'5" and made me feel tiny by comparison. I used to love that.

Seth said, "Let's toast to our exes. Mine takes good care of our daughter."

"John wouldn't touch me," I said. "Then he left. Died, I mean."

Seth kissed me, and I kissed back. Then I shut it down, and we were both relieved. Anyway, I had a man: Jasper. Since I bought the Hi-Dez. Once a month, not much conversation. Jasper was more than enough after my life of men.

I said, "Let's drive out to where that body burned."

"Paula, that is dark," Seth said. "Let's go this afternoon. First, I think I've got some writing in me."

He had no writing in him. He was going to take a nap. But that was good; he'd be sober by afternoon. Seth knew that I knew what it was to be middle-aged and disappointed. All the words we had tried and failed to say and write were stuck to our lips and fingertips.

I watched Seth walk back down to Room 6. He'd lost weight in the weeks he'd lived at the Hi-Dez. His old linen shirt hung from square shoulders that looked strong, like shoulders you could lean on, but at my age, I knew better.

———————

The detectives interviewed me at our house in North Stamford, which boasted a posh Greenwich, Connecticut address. That kind of stuff mattered to John. When they arrived, I ushered them into our formal dining room with its seating for twelve. I sat at the big, glossy table we almost never used. I expected the detectives to join me, but they remained standing. Power move.

The shorter of the two detectives asked if I knew where my husband was.

"He's been missing for years," I said, although I knew it would make everything worse.

In those days, I was always hot and cranky and I no longer watched my mouth. My moods shifted like tropical storms.

The short detective said, "Your husband flew across country to hike and camp in Joshua Tree National Park, alone?"

"Alone, yes."

"Were there problems in the marriage?"

"Of course."

"Such as?" asked the other, taller detective. Not my height, but close.

"We've both been so busy," I replied automatically, as I did whenever someone asked if I was okay, if John and I were okay.

Heat crept up my neck and I flushed with it. Sweat ran down my spine, between my breasts. I took one of John's autographed headshots from a stack on the sideboard and fanned myself with it.

"Menopause," I told the detectives.

Both men looked at their shoes.

Then the tall one asked, "You and Mr. Bowen been married a long time?"

"Forever," I said. "Fourteen years."

Both men looked at me.

"We thought we were a good match, but stuff happens," I said. "John is a jock, and I am not. I am a writer, in theory. John lives for his fans and was excited for his promotion from the WBTW sports guy to their first Black news anchor. He never complains about the long drive to Hartford. He enjoys being alone," I said.

Once, I asked John what it was like, growing up with so many white people.

"You tell me," he said.

Toward the end, one of the few things John and I agreed on was the California high desert, so different from Connecticut. We talked about retiring near Joshua Tree National Park, maybe Twentynine Palms or here in Yucca Valley. John and I both vacationed here alone, sometimes, when we needed space, more space than was already between us.

It got worse, after the miscarriage.

Months after that dining room interview, one of the detectives called me. I could not remember if he was the short one, or tall.

He said, "We're not giving up."

He said they had coordinated with San Bernardino County law enforcement, the National Park Service, local search and rescue groups. They had John landing in Palm Springs. They had him renting a car. Then nothing, not a trace.

The detective said, "When a man just disappears, it's usually because he wants to."

———————

At 3:00 PM, I locked up the motel office and went to my room, Room 1, to check on Alan Alda. Alan was my old, sweet-natured, silver tabby, a cat with straightforward needs. He was easier than a man.

Before I knocked on Seth's door, I listened for him tapping the keys of his laptop. I wouldn't bother him if he was writing. But then the door swung open, and there he stood, sober, truck keys in hand.

Joshua Tree and the surrounding towns were known for their spectacular natural beauty, but Highway 62, which bisected the Morongo Basin, was a commercial strip. We rattled east in Seth's old Mazda pickup before turning off the highway and heading north into the desert. Seth turned onto another road and asphalt gave way to dirt that alternated between thick, sloppy sand and ridges that felt like we were driving over someone's ribcage. Seth drove towards the low mountains in the distance, passing my property, my little square of sand and possibility, then other undeveloped parcels marked with stakes and a few small houses and trailers. He drove fifteen miles an hour because too much dust kicked up otherwise. Seth could be considerate.

He slowed to a crawl and stopped. He cut the engine and the sudden quiet was exquisite. It was a bright, sunny spring day, and a chilly wind sighed through the truck's open windows. Seth pointed out the curve of steep rock, all that remained of a prehistoric lakeshore. He squinted across the expanse of sand in every direction, punctuated by scrub: creosote, white bursage, brittlebush, and lots more that I hadn't yet looked up in John's Guide to Mojave Desert Flora. It was one of the few things he left behind that I could use.

I wanted to tell Seth to put on his sunglasses; drink more water and less wine, whiskey, and tequila; look closely; pay attention. I reminded myself that I was no one's mother.

Seth leaned across me to open the glovebox to grab an Altoids tin, repurposed to hold a few joints.

He finally spoke through a long exhalation of smoke: "It's all Bureau of Land Management that way," he said, pointing. Already he seemed more at ease. He passed me the joint. "Somewhere out there is where they found him."

I drew a deep inhale and let the smoke settle through me. "Him?"

"I meant as in 'person'."

"Hmm. Do you have some idea where to look?"

"Some idea," he said.

Seth put out the joint and got out of the truck. He started walking, and I followed him because I was a little high and he said he had some idea.

It was a beautiful spring day in the desert: blazing blue sky stretching forever, wind whipping just a little too hard. Some of the creosote bushes were starting to break out in yellow. Golden daisies bloomed from the brittlebush, and pink flowers burst from beavertail cactus, clumped here and there in the sand. It seemed impossible that anything dark or murderous could happen here. It felt good to be outside in the fresh air and sunshine, away from the motel and highway, the drive-thrus and out-of-town visitors. It was nice to take a walk with a friend. A man who was my friend—imagine that.

Seth had long legs, but he walked slowly. He wandered, while I was ready to hike. I resisted the itch in my legs to pass him. I had resisted that itch since junior high, when I was already my full adult height, mostly legs and long feet. I was bigger than most boys and convinced that pretty girls were small. So I shortened my stride.

Seth said, "Tell me something embarrassing."

We stepped down into a wash and followed the path it carved through sand.

Finally I said, "My first night at the Hi-Dez, after I bought it, I checked out the rooms. Everything looked fine, if old and tired. Each room had the same dark brown furniture. The same tacky bedspreads and patterned carpets, hotplates, and ancient microwaves. But in Room 4, I found a penis."

Seth came to a halt.

"Not a real one. Hot pink silicone. Battery operated. With bunny ears or butterfly wings or something."

"A dick can be a threat, a promise, or a joke," said Seth.

"Are you quoting something?"

"Just myself."

"You should use that in a play, if you haven't already," I said.

"I think you're the writer."

Seth knew that, after John disappeared, I got it in my head to write a novel, not so much drawn from my life as inspired by it.

I said, "I found a garbage can liner and slipped it over my hand. I picked up the penis and threw it away. What else could I do? Then I washed my hands, which I guess I didn't really need to."

"Never a bad idea to wash your hands," Seth said. "But I'd hardly call that story embarrassing."

We arrived at a blackened clearing of sand. "Here, maybe?" Seth said. "This might be where they found the body." He straightened to look around, squinting against the sun's glare. "Or maybe this was a campfire. Helluva place."

I looked down at the scorched sand where something had burned. I sniffed but all I smelled was creosote.

I said, "It must be hard to burn a body."

"And why would you want to? Bodies are sacred," Seth said.

"Sacred? Come on."

"I found my only sanctuary in the bodies of women."

"That line needs some work, but you could probably edit it into something."

"That was from my first play," he said. "It had a six-week run at a little theatre in L.A."

I looked down at the sand. I realized it did not matter if this was where a body was found. What mattered was that people burned, before and after they were dead, and most of the time no one noticed.

"I think this was a campfire," I said. "A human body would leave more of a mark."

"You would think," said Seth.

"You can see forever out here," I said, taking in the desert, miles of scrub and sand, the rocky horizon.

"Forever looks like more of the same," Seth said. "Let's get back. At least we found something, right?"

The drive back to the Hi-Dez took longer. The highway was clogged with vacationers, retirees, military vehicles, delivery vans. There was no choice but to slow down. Seth's radio was tuned to an oldies station out of Palm Springs: "Next up: Pat Benatar!"

"Pat Benatar is oldies now?" I said.

"Patty is my daughter's name," Seth said.

"She's a teenager, right?"

"Fifteen," Seth said, "Shit, no, sixteen."

"If my daughter had lived—"

"What?" he said, turning down the music.

"I was in my first trimester," I said.

"Oh," said Seth, switching lanes to pass a Walmart truck. "I'm sorry."

I shut up then, because Seth seemed uncomfortable, but I remembered:

The day after it happened, I lay bleeding in our bed. Doubled-up maxi pads, sweatpants. John sat perched on the side. We did not touch.

He said, "If only we'd stuck to our plan. No kids."

"They said we can try again."

"Shh," he said.

John was a logical man and none of this made sense. He looked glazed, in shock. Maybe it had not occurred to him, until then, that he was powerless. Afterward, John would not touch me. Could not. Did not. He brushed my hands away, almost angrily, like I had broken some unspoken rule. We lay beside each other without touching, arms at our sides, hands to ourselves, John seemingly resigned to something he had not discussed with me. In the years that followed, things got a little better and then they got worse. And then John was gone.

Back at the motel, there was a dark blue BMW with Arizona plates parked outside the locked office: Jasper. I never knew exactly when he'd show up. He liked it that way. One week a month, he wanted me expecting him anytime. Always in my good underwear, just in case. I slipped my hand up my shirt— yes, the lacy black bra. Not the super sexy push-up but good enough. Every month, Jasper traveled from Phoenix to Riverside, California. Yucca Valley was out of his way, he said, but I was worth it.

Seth recognized Jasper's car, too. He didn't say anything, but I felt his mood darken. He steered his truck into a parking spot.

He said, "What can you possibly have to talk about?" Seth looked gaunt in the deep yellow, late afternoon light.

"Well, we talk about how much we like fucking each other."

"Nice mouth," he said.

Jasper was hot in an executive way. He rolled dress shirtsleeves over muscular forearms. I still was not sure what he did for a living, and it did not matter.

In the office, the front desk between us, I caught the familiar sting of his cologne as he bent to sign for Room 2, the room next to mine.

Hours later, Jasper said, "I promise I will never say I love you, even if you say it to me."

"I won't," I said, and we laughed.

Time had scarred and weakened us, sure. Jasper couldn't put weight on one knee. I needed neck support. But when we touched, we both felt the jolt: so powerful it banished self-doubt and regret. It was lust that healed. It did not matter that we did not have much in common and lived too far apart; that was kind of the point. When I emerged from Room 2, the Hi-Dez was dark and quiet. No one saw how my cheeks burned.

When I accused John of withholding sex, he said, "You're exaggerating, Paula. It hasn't been that long."

He said I looked desperate, and how could anyone find that attractive? I told him I was hurt. I was furious.

"You're so dramatic," John said, a lot.

I found other men, eventually, after John disappeared. I had luck in the produce section of Whole Foods, where everything was perishable and expensive. Men still found me attractive. I thought maybe it was the silver in my hair. It caught their eyes and made them wonder what other ways I might let nature take its course.

I slipped into Room 1, now my permanent home. I had downsized to a single motel room, and not a great one, from a two-story, four-bedroom house in Connecticut, still for sale. After almost a year, I had not received any real offers. My realtor told me it was a tough sell with just a two-car garage and all my stuff left behind.

My niece Gerry moved in to keep an eye on it. She was on leave from New York University to heal up from a bad fall. Gerry was a big girl, tall like me but heavier. I knew her size made her unhappy. I wanted to tell her that I was big at her age, too, and I still was in lots of ways. Good ways.

I started a bath. A text buzzed from Seth: "Dinner."

I opened the door and there he was, holding a clear plastic take-out container with a colorful assortment of sushi, each a singular, sculptural beauty.

"I know gas-station sushi sounds crazy, but I swear it's the best in the Morongo Basin," he said.

"They get regular deliveries from some fancy restaurant down the hill, in Rancho Mirage, I think. The owners are brothers or something."

I reached for the container, but Seth held on tight.

"You deserve better than that capitalist," he whispered.

"I deserve great sex," I whispered back.

"And also more than that."

"Thanks for dinner, Seth. Next one's on me."

He left and I hurried to the bathroom to shut off the taps. The waterline shivered near the top. I sank carefully into the old porcelain tub, thinking about all the Hi-Dez guests who had bathed there before me, everyone trying to get clean or feel better.

Maybe a woman's body was Seth's sanctuary, but silence was John's. The miscarriage drove John further into silence and away from me. A week later, when the bleeding finally stopped, I drew a hot bath and got in and stayed for an hour. I topped off the hot water until it ran lukewarm, then cold. I curled up my long body like an overgrown fetus, overdue for birth.

Tonight, in my bathtub at the Hi-Dez, I did not fold myself up. Alan Alda watched me from his perch on the toilet lid.

John used to watch me like that, just as silent, from across the kitchen table, from across the bed, offering no clues to his thoughts. As if his study had concluded that we were different species, unable to communicate.

———————

It was just about 5:00 the next morning, still dark, when I heard a knock on my door. I was still in my nightgown and robe, on my first mug of coffee. I was about to get dressed and write. I already had the Word document open: In_Progress.docx. So far, I'd set the font to Times New Roman, 12-point, double-spaced. The page was blank.

A fresh-poured glass of water sat beside my coffee mug, a safe distance from the keyboard. In an ashtray I had one pre-rolled joint, purchased at a dispensary down the hill, in Desert Hot Springs, with the help of a friendly young budtender. I planned to light it and write until it was time to open the breakfast buffet.

I peeked out and saw that it was Jasper, showered and dressed for a hike. His bulky chest filled his moisture-wicking tee.

"I'm taking the morning to check out the Park before I turn around and head to my dad's in Riverside," he said. "Come with me."

"I have guests checking in this morning."

"Guess I'll say goodbye, then," he said, tugging at my robe's silky belt.

I pulled him inside Room 1 and closed the door. I said, "I open breakfast at six."

It was not love we made, but it was something.

The Poets and Sky

Paula

I woke to my phone's morning alarm, an electronic version of an old-fashioned telephone ring, because I slept through anything else. I silenced it and looked around the room, my home since buying the Hi-Dez. It was only a matter of time before the house in Connecticut sold and I had to figure out what to do with the contents. I would have to sell or donate most everything. I could not wait.

After I fed Alan and poured my second cup of coffee, I put on my reading glasses and opened my laptop to check my email. Sure enough, there was another message from my realtor back in Connecticut. Gerry wasn't keeping the place in "Open House condition," she wrote, "meaning spotless and tidy AT ALL TIMES, per the agreement signed by ALL PARTIES."

Had I agreed to that? I wondered. I should pay more attention.

The realtor continued, "Most Greenwich homeowners would not be comfortable putting an occupied home on the market." I imagined her mouthwash breath, the concealer always caked beneath her eyes. "In any case," she wrote, "after almost a year, this listing has become stale. I'm afraid I am pessimistic."

She is breaking up with me, I thought.

But no: "I would like to discuss some ideas for revamping the listing so we can Go For The Sold™. These include but are not limited to upgrades like commercial-grade appliances, heated flooring, master bathroom suite renovation, solar panels, home battery, etc."

Sure, I thought.

"Professional cleaning and organizing and a price reduction, certainly," she added.

I hit Reply. I wanted to tell her to just go ahead and slash the price, toss everything in the house—my stuff, my past—into a dumpster. Whatever it took to free me from that house and my old life, which already felt like someone else's. That house, with its Greenwich address, was an imitation of something better built, with pretentious flourishes and too-thin walls, poorly insulated against the weather.

I didn't want to evict my niece Gerry, but I also worried that she could grow too comfortable, living there. Gerry reminded me of myself at that age: messy and self-conscious, pulled toward darkness. I knew my niece was desperate in a quiet, dangerous way. I closed my realtor's email and marked it Unread.

I slurped the rest of my coffee, then poured an ill-advised third cup. I brought it next door to the office. I brewed two large carafes of coffee for my guests and tenants: caffeinated and ultra-caffeinated. From boxes in the filing cabinet, I refilled the sugar and sweetener packets and the little tubs of non-dairy creamer. From the fridge, I got the butter dish.

I wished I could ignore my Connecticut house forever. I would just give it to Gerry, if she wanted it, if I didn't worry that it would become a trap for her, too. I hoped she dreamed of escape.

"Morning," came a friendly voice from the front door. It was Sky, the dancer, with her daily delivery of her homemade, organic baked goodies. She wore her white chef's jacket, as usual, and held two trays, one stacked on top of the other, maneuvering herself inside before I could cross the floor to help. She grinned as she set down the trays beside a display case, next to the coffee. "You're going to love these," she said. "One sweet, one savory: chocolate chip croissants and galettes with asparagus and goat cheese."

"I love goat cheese."

"I know," she said.

With her chef's jacket, Sky wore jeans and dusty boots. Her hair was buzzed short, black and silver.

"Have time for coffee?" I asked. "It's almost ready."

"Not today," she said, and she did seem disappointed. She looked up as the door opened and in walked Seth.

He hadn't come to breakfast for a couple of days. He looked good. Better.

"I'm gonna leave you to it," Sky said, tilting her head in his direction. "Let me know how you like the galettes."

"You're back tomorrow, right?"

"Sure," she said, with a smile that made me worry I'd sounded too eager.

I hoped I wasn't giving her the wrong impression, leading her on. Of course I had noticed women over the years, but men were always… right there. Easy and interested. Or, well, determined. I was wrong when I said men were easy. Men were tough and hard and sometimes dangerous. Men felt familiar.

Sky left, and then it was just me and Seth again.

Seth pulled his slice of white bread from the toaster and spread butter on it. He filled his coffee mug.

He said, "I quit drinking. I need to get back to writing the new play. Or, to my notes for the new play. It's been slow going. Always is, of course. How much time have I spent, the last couple of years, jotting down good lines for some future character? I have no idea who they are. I don't know their story. I sit down there in Room 6, piss drunk, waiting for them to show up and clue me in. No luck. So now I'm going to try it sober. Why not?"

"That's good, Seth," I said. "Very positive. Listen, I have to ask—"

"I'll have the rent soon," he said. "I couldn't get a writing class together this month. I think the stink on my name finally wafted all the way out here from L.A. I'm a straight, white man, the new definition of evil."

"Give me a break," I said.

"My former so-called friends and colleagues act as if they can't quite remember my name."

"Okay, but—"

"I'll have the money soon. A friend recommended me for some diet drink mix commercial that's filming out here."

"I didn't know you were an actor."

"This doesn't require much in the way of acting."

"I was thinking about taking on some freelance design work."

If Seth heard me, he did not react.

"I should have gone to law school," he said, "like I was supposed to. By now I'd be rich."

"Supposed to?"

"In the early '90s, I met a girl—a lawyer, a grown up—and followed her to San Francisco. She wanted me to apply to law school."

"Did you want to be a lawyer?"

"Hell no. And I could not forgive her to luring me away from New York City."

"She didn't believe in you as a playwright, I guess."

"That's true," he said. "I was not about to go back to New York then, with my tail between my legs. So I moved to L.A., where it was sunny, at least."

"Seth—"

"I wish I had what I owe you."

"I know, Seth."

Seth reminded me of my first husband, the sweet, long-haired boy who cracked my heart for the first and worst time. We met in Port Chester, New York, one weekend when I was back home from art school. I'd already had some fight with my mom, and I was out with my best friend Melody. We went to the same dive bar we'd snuck into all through high school. The place was a dump, but that night, the dust sparkled in the dim light. My first husband was a sporting goods salesman by day, pothead by night. He was a boy playing at manhood. He loved me, I think. We had lots of sex.

His guiding principle was to be nothing like Dad. But, to him, being a husband meant something very specific. He told me this after we were married. The day after we returned from our honeymoon, he took a position at his father's collection agency, as if he had admired the man all along. My young husband cut his hair and managed minimum-wage employees who spent their days calling poor people to remind them to worry. He started using a firm tone with me. He always seemed disappointed.

On the last day we spoke, he said, "I'm sorry I have to hurt you."

After Seth chucked his empty paper plate and coffee cup, I watched him walk back down to Room 6. He walked with inexplicable confidence. He was too thin, but his confidence was sexy. From behind, he could be mistaken for a successful playwright or even a San Francisco lawyer—on vacation, maybe.

You couldn't tell, at first glance, what a mess he was inside. You had to look him in the eyes for that.

Before he left, he promised, "As soon as I'm paid for this commercial—"

I stopped him with a wave of my hand. I did not want him to make promises he might not keep. I did not want him to become another man who lied to me.

———————

Once breakfast was cleared away, I rolled the supply cart down to Room 3, braced for whatever was left behind by the family of five that blew through Sky's chocolate chip croissants. I was glad they skipped the asparagus and goat cheese galettes. I'd eaten one and nearly swooned. Food like that was art, and Sky was an artist. That much I knew, even if I'd never learned to cook. I could not tell you how Sky layered and balanced flavors to make food like that. Before I serviced the room, I wrapped up the galettes and tucked them in my mini fridge in Room 1. I thought maybe they were meant for me, anyway.

All in all, Room 3 was not in bad shape. Every sheet was off the bed, every towel was on the floor, and the TV remote was on top of the toilet tank, but I did not find anything surprising or too gross. (My tolerance for both was higher since I started running a cheap motel.) As I locked up Room 3, my cart full of dirty laundry, Ruby stepped out of Room 4. Ruby Orr was a poet, originally from the South and fairly well-known—in poet circles, anyway. She'd won national awards, but no one bought her books. She had blue eyes and elegant features in a wise, worn face. Her white hair was gathered, long and straight, into a thick ponytail that hung down her back.

She slept with Seth sometimes, that much I knew—but why? Why on earth?

"Hi Paula," she called to me. "Don't suppose you have a toilet plunger on that cart?"

"No," I said. "I'll get it from the maintenance closet and come take a look in a few minutes."

"Oh I can't have you seeing all that of me," she protested, laughing a little, but I knew she was serious. "I'll take care of it. Thank you."

After I brought her the plunger and told her to keep it—I had several—I swung by Room 1 to top up Alan Alda's kibble and refresh his water.

Both parties checking in today had notified me of their late arrivals, so I had the afternoon off. I was going to make the most of it.

I drove east, towards Joshua Tree National Park. At the gate, I flashed my annual pass. I followed the road in, dazzled, as always, by the sheer, sweeping, breath-catching drama of the place. From my first visit to this park, years ago with John, I knew I was home. I understood what "home" meant, for the first time. I felt what it meant. With or without John, I knew I belonged there. What else might I discover, I wondered, if I was where I belonged?

I kept my speed down, despite pressure from an RV following too close behind. I scanned the road ahead for tortoises, jackrabbits, desert iguanas, spiny lizards, antelope squirrels, rattlesnakes, quail. There were cottontails everywhere but that didn't mean I was okay with hitting one.

I pulled off into the Hidden Valley campground. The rocks looked smooth, like scoops of half-melted ice cream. Up close they were sharp and granular. I saw climbers on nearby boulders, including the 150-foot monolith Intersection Rock. There were two climbers on it right then, tiny from down here. They turned in each direction, enjoying the view they had earned and I could only imagine. Before I left the car, I checked my backpack for everything I knew I needed for an easy hike—or not even, just a walk away from these campsites, a walk away from human noise and trash. First: spiral notebook, pen. I threw in a back-up pen, on the off chance that one ran dry when I was on a roll with my writing.

Today, I had decided, I would write my novel. Start it, anyway. For real this time. I'd get something down, ideas or an outline at least. That I could do. I could do that much, once I figured out the plot and the characters and what exactly I meant to say.

I checked the rest of the backpack's contents: sunglasses, reading glasses, full water bottle, granola bar, jacket, knife, Advil, Benadryl. One tampon. These days I always carried one, as a talisman. If I always had one, I would never need it. In the last year, I'd felt a shift. No more sudden, sickening heat surges, breaking me out in boob sweat. It was twenty weeks since my last period.

After almost forty years of monthly aggravation: cramps, stains, and ruined plans, mood swings, acne, pregnancy scares, and pregnancy loss, I wanted it over and done.

I never wanted kids. How much time had I wasted, explaining that to people? Except in the end, I did change my mind. Or I thought I should, because I did love John. I tried not to think about it now, how much I did.

I walked until I was alone among the boulders, as far as I could see. It was so quiet, away from people and cars. Insects buzzed and wind whipped, but otherwise there was silence. The impossibly clear blue sky was vibrant and endless. It made my eyes ache.

I drew a deep inhale… held it… and released. I tried to breathe into my belly, like I was taught at that Berkshires yoga retreat I got roped into by one of John's friends' wives. It helped. Before me were fields of Joshua Trees and beyond that, another stretch of rocks, with steeper, jagged peaks. Bighorn sheep might be able to traverse those, or maybe these fit climbers, people who were strong and brave in ways that I was not.

Yet here I was, sitting cross-legged and comfortably alone on a rock in the Mojave, a continent away from the place I came from, detached from everything familiar. No one knew where I was or waited to hear that I was fine. I did not feel brave, just comfortable.

I put on my reading glasses and opened the notebook. My pen hovered over the blank page.

Finally I wrote, "It was bright and sunny." Okay, I thought. That's okay. Don't panic. You have to start somewhere. "Just keep writing your way through the terrible first draft," I'd read on some writer's advice website. I was determined not to self-sabotage, for once.

I pressed my left palm into the surface of the rock that held me, so hard it left a pattern. I felt the sunshine, the silence, and my weight settled into the rock, and the rock settled into the earth. I was at home in this unfamiliar place, as grounded as I'd ever felt. But I did not know how to write what I wanted to say. I wanted to write a novel but tell the truth.

"It was bright and sunny," I wrote, "and also windy."

I immediately crossed out that sentence, then scribbled over it to make sure it was illegible. How embarrassing. I flipped to the back of the notebook, where I had a letter in progress to Gerry. I usually had one going, these days.

These spiral-bound, college-ruled sheets were a far cry from the stationery my mother gave me to write letters home from art school, and which I used instead to write stories I refused to show her or anyone.

Gerry hardly ever wrote back. And when she did, she never shared much personal. For issues with the house, she preferred texting. But after my last letter, she replied with a letter of her own. She filled a page with slanted lines of her small, tight handwriting. It was not the kind of letter you replied to without first figuring out what you wanted to say. It was not the kind of letter you shared with others, but I wondered if my sister Pearl knew how much her daughter suffered. Not just because she was stuck in two full leg casts. Not just because she'd taken a leave of absence from NYU which, Gerry said, already felt like a dream, a noisy parade she had briefly joined, and which now marched on without her.

Long before any of that, Gerry suffered. In awful, ordinary ways, like most of us. Gerry learned that, to some, her body was her worth. Or her worthlessness. She learned that women played supporting roles, not the leads. That she would spend her life apologizing for taking up too much space, attracting too much attention, talking loudly or in a shrill voice.

"I get it, Gerry," I wrote.

Way off in the distance, two vultures circled above something dead. The desert would and did kill, anytime there was an opportunity. Bodies turned up all the time, not always on fire.

I wrote, "My mother (Grandma) was raised in a time when children were expected to be seen and not heard, and although she was well aware that things were different by the time I was a kid, in the 70s, she wasn't happy about it. At home I was always in trouble for talking back and keeping my room messy. I was sent home from school for yelling at boys who interrupted me. But I was not going to smile and pretend it didn't bother me, like I was supposed to.

"Grandma had a little black and white TV in the kitchen that she watched while she made dinner. One night, she had some news program on, lots of men and microphones.

"I said, 'How come only boys get to talk?'

"'Is your homework done?' she asked, and she turned off the TV."

I stopped again. I was losing my train of thought. I drew some doodles in the margins, to give my mind a rest: a quail hurrying across a dirt road, its feathered skirts hoisted. I drew a great horned owl sitting in a pinyon pine and, beneath that, a steaming pile of coyote poop. I hoped it would make Gerry smile. I thanked her for the present she sent for my last birthday. I'd already forgotten what it was. I told her that I wished she would come visit. The desert could help her, I wrote. Like it helped me and lots of other people, wounded and vulnerable people who just needed a little space. Maybe it could feel like home to her, too.

I did not know everything my niece had been through, of course not. But I knew that, by nineteen years old, we all had secrets. Gerry was entitled to hers.

I wrote, "When I was twelve, Grandma enrolled me in an Etiquette class. We learned about the different forks and spoons, which side of the plate you clear from, and how you can say 'No thank you' in a way that doesn't hurt a boy's feelings. We learned the dance moves of our grandparents: the boy leads, the girl is led. She is responsible for keeping daylight between her body and the boy's, who can't help himself. She has to pretend she is not horny. I was already close to my full adult height—in other words, tall. I was taller than the boy I was partnered with. We stumbled because he pulled one way and I pulled the other. He stepped on my long feet and almost cried by the time our waltz ended.

"'You're a big pig,' he whispered, before running away.

"I stopped wanting to dance with boys or anyone.

"The Etiquette instructor taught us the value of 'white' lies that avoided confrontation. I learned to make small talk: 'I had the most lovely time… I'm afraid I must bow out… You have such a beautiful home… How is it that you never age?'"

Where was I going with this letter? I had no idea. I just liked telling Gerry stuff. I thought maybe if I told her enough stuff, she'd hear something that helped.

"When I was fourteen," I wrote, "at summer camp, I ended up in a tent full of boys. I don't remember how that happened. It was definitely against the rules. I was sitting on top of the pink sleeping bag my mom bought at Caldor for the weeks I would spend in the Colorado wilderness.

"No one was sleepy. The boys wanted my body; they wanted its secrets. They did not want me—even at the time, I knew that. But I was willing. And it felt good, all that attention. And also bad. I started to feel like one of those tables at the kids' science museum: 'Touch 'N Discover.'

"The boys said, 'We're just playing,' and it was true.

"Two summers later, I was in Rhode Island for a pre-college art intensive. All day long I was in the studio, sketching and painting. One morning I worked on a charcoal drawing of a thumbtack, a single thumbtack, and the shadow it cast. I fell into such a deep concentration—you might call it a trance—that I did not notice when a nerve pinched my shoulder and my arm seized up. I dropped the stick of charcoal and watched it shatter into pieces too small to salvage. The art teacher came over to see why I'd stopped. The rules of the assignment were clear: draw one object, without interruption, for one hour. No breaks. Give it weight on the page. Your charcoal must not leave the paper. I told the teacher that my right arm was useless.

"'Then switch arms,' he said.

"Just then, we heard two cars collide on the street below, the crash loud through the studio's big, open windows. We looked down but our view was blocked by an awning. I went down to check it out. On the street, I used my left hand to massage my right shoulder, which was still completely numb. The two cars were in bad shape, but everyone was okay, shaken but alive. Someone could have died, though. My heart pounded.

"I realized a weirdo in the crowd was staring at me. He was gross and old. At sixteen, I did not necessarily rule out older guys, but this was different. I backed out of the crowd and tried to head back into the studio building, but he was suddenly right there in front of me, blocking my path.

"'Come here, sexy,' he said, 'I would do you.'

"'Thanks?' I said, and I tried stepping around him, but he grabbed my wrist.

"He said, 'What, are you too stuck up to say thank you? I paid you a fucking compliment.' He lunged at my mouth, but before he could kiss me, another man put himself between us.

"'Get the fuck out of here,' this new guy said.

"The weirdo released my wrist and ran away—literally ran away. I was free and safe and flushed with relief and gratitude.

"'Oh my god thank you, thank you!' I said. 'He was freaking me out.'

"'It's okay,' said the good guy, and then I noticed that he was also a grown up, just not gross like the other guy. This man looked like a dad, like my best friend Melody's dad who always stayed up to make sure we got home safe when we snuck out to bars, and he never once ratted me out to Grandma.

"The good guy drew me into a hug. He said something like, 'It's okay, you poor baby, your heart is beating out of your chest. Let's take a walk. That always makes me feel better.'

"When we got to the far side of the block, he said, 'Come here for a second.' He pulled me into an alley between the buildings and hugged me, again. Then I knew he was nothing like Melody's dad. He kissed my neck and left a hickey I would have to hide. He pushed up my sweater and squeezed my breasts like he was checking fruit for ripeness. He kept saying, 'It's okay, it's okay...' His sweater was scratchy against my bare skin. Finally, he backed away and said, 'You're okay.'

"I told myself I was lucky that he was the one who touched me, not the weirdo. I told myself I could think of it like one of those unexpected erotic encounters Melody and I read about in the Penthouse magazines she snuck out of her dad's hiding place in their garage. I told myself it wasn't a big deal.

"I wouldn't call it assault," I wrote.

Then I drew a line through that sentence, over and over and over.

I wrote instead, "Do you ever wonder who you might be, if your body had been yours from the beginning?"

I thought, if nothing else, Gerry would relate to that.

Before I could talk myself out of it, I folded the letter and sealed it in an already stamped and addressed envelope. I tucked it into my blank spiral notebook to keep it safe as I hiked back to my car, my reading glasses perched on top of my head. I decided to swing by the drive-up mailbox outside the Joshua Tree post office and drop it off on my way home, before I chickened out and decided to sacrifice the stamp and rip up the letter and toss it in the motel's dumpster like it was nothing.

I was surprised to see Seth and Ruby arrive for breakfast together, the next morning. They walked in, awkward with one another, not used to being together in public. Seth wore an old button-down shirt, sleeves rolled to the elbow and collar twisted from careless washes in hot water. He was obviously hungover.

"Good morning, both of you," I said.

"Prove it," Seth replied. He held a mug under the spout of the ultra-caffeinated carafe and pressed until hot, black coffee poured.

"Ignore that grump," said Ruby, smoothing her ponytail. "It's me he's mad at."

At the breakfast bar, Ruby selected a mini box of Raisin Bran and emptied it into a bowl.

"What's going on?" I asked, moving close enough that we could keep our voices low.

"Nothing a little distance won't solve," she said, tilting her head toward Seth. "I love my room here, but I do miss writing outside. Back in Georgia, I always took my notebook on my wood's walks. I wrote countless poems outside. There was one easy path to a waterfall that I loved, especially. I would find a rock to sit on, just out of the spray, and the poems poured out of me. I don't have the strength or stamina for hiking around here, not at my age," she said.

"I just bought a couple of acres," I told her. "North of the dry lakebed. You're welcome to drive out there, if you want. Bring a folding chair and a hat and you can write outside till sunset."

Ruby retrieved the almond milk from the fridge and poured some into her bowl. "Will you send me directions? That is a most generous offer, Paula." She selected a spoon and carried it, with her cereal bowl, to the table where Seth waited and slurped his coffee.

Before she sat down with him, she looked at me and said, "Thank you."

"No coffee?" Seth grumbled. "Must be nice to be naturally energetic."

"Is that how you would describe yourself after coffee, Seth?" Ruby asked. "Energetic?"

The door opened and this time it was the other resident poet, the one who rented Room 5: Fern Frankowski. Tiny, thin, and white, she had brown hair that she'd bleached and dyed a purplish gray, of all things. She struggled with the weight of the door.

When she moved in, Fern told me she'd come to the desert to hide. She was busted on Twitter when several of her published poems turned out to contain lines stolen from other poets—all of them, poets of color. Fern said she was forced off the internet and out of Los Angeles. She hoped to return, someday, maybe with a new identity.

Now she walked up to me and announced, "I have to move out." She was upset; she'd been crying. "I'm moving back to my parents' place in Orange County until this ordeal is over. I am literally being hunted by villagers with torches, screaming for blood."

"Figuratively," I said.

"Duh," she said.

When Fern moved in, she gave me a phony name. But after a few weeks, I guess she trusted me not to blow her cover. She gave me a copy of her self-published poetry collection, *Desquamation*. I did read it. The poems took themselves very seriously. I looked for more recent work, published online, but they were all taken down following the scandal. I knew that, as a writer—if I was going to call myself that—I was supposed to be mad at her. Lots of people on Twitter were mad at her. But I couldn't help feeling some maternal concern. She could have been my daughter, if I was a mother.

She said, "I have a friend coming later today with a truck."

"Today? You're moving out today?"

"It was the only day Sky could help me."

"Sky? The baker?"

"At heart she's a dancer," Fern said. "An athlete, really, a freaking jock. And I'm a poet. We're doomed."

Same dynamic as me and John, I thought—of course I did, for a second. But, to me, Sky seemed more like a writer than this one.

"Sky is your friend?" I asked, still trying to sort this out.

"For now," she said. "She can be yours next."

Seth looked over from the breakfast bar, where he waited for his white bread to toast.

Fern continued, "The rental agreement states that 'reasonable notice' is requested, not required."

She looked as crumpled as used Kleenex. I straightened and pushed back my shoulders and took a minute to appreciate my height, my vantage point. I had a longer view than some people, maybe most. It was just the truth. It did not make me better or smarter. It did not mean I knew what to make of what I saw.

"Oh," Fern said then, "I've been meaning to suggest that you add a plant-based protein to the breakfast menu. If you want to be competitive with the better motels, I mean."

Better? Fern could have been my daughter, and I felt bad for her—a little—but my god she could be an asshole. When she left, the door closed behind her just a little too firmly. We were all quiet for a moment.

"What an entitled bitch," Seth said, buttering his toast.

"I don't like that word," said Ruby.

"What word, 'entitled'?"

"Seth."

"Sue me, I don't like bitches." He sat back down at the table.

"Seth Gladstone, you cannot use a misogynist slur against a woman just because you disagree with her."

"Disagree? Yes, I disagree with some so-called poet stealing other people's words."

"Well, I am a poet—"

"A real poet," Seth interrupted.

"I am a poet and, yes, integrity is everything. But don't we all make spectacular mistakes when we're young? And when we're old, and all the years in between?"

Seth said, "She's not that young."

"I suppose I have always been drawn to wounded creatures," she said to me. "Even dangerous ones. When I was eight, I was riding my bike along our road when I came upon a wandering skunk, looking just about as sad and in need of a hug as any creature I'd seen. I got a nip for my trouble, and then a trip to the hospital, where I got the first of fourteen shots, over fourteen days, directly in my abdomen. My parents scolded me, but all I cared about was that

Animal Control euthanized the skunk. Because it bit me. I was inconsolable. They killed that poor creature, because of me. They didn't even bother to test it for rabies."

Ruby's eyes filled with tears that did not fall.

"Poets," Seth muttered from the table.

Ruby ignored him.

"You are a tender soul," I said.

Ruby smiled, her blue eyes shiny. "Before she distanced herself, my daughter said I was ridiculous."

"Ruby is still married, did you know that?" Seth said.

I hated him, when he was like this.

"Yes," he continued, "he lives—where was it, again? Somewhere in the South. Wherever you're from."

"Georgia," she said to him. "You know I'm from Georgia." To me, she said, "My marriage outlasted hope, like any fact."

"You're such a slut," Seth said, grinning like he was kidding around.

But I could tell by looking at Ruby that she felt that word like a slap. Seth was exactly the kind of angry man a tender poet like Ruby should steer clear of. But I figured she had her reasons. Maybe the reason was sex. I, of all people, could understand that. Sometimes it was the only thing a woman needed, and sometimes it was the only thing she could bear.

"My daughter is a grown woman," she said. "My husband and I have everything on the table."

She wouldn't look at Seth.

"How's the writing going, Ruby?" I asked.

"Well," she said. "I'm still researching parasites and viruses. I'm particularly interested in these mutating viruses being monitored by the CDC. There is so much poetry in them. Did you know that the only way to kill a virus is to deny it a home?"

"No," I said, but I wasn't really paying attention. As soon as she said "viruses," I remembered that I needed to reorder bleach for the supply cart.

Seth reached out to put a hand on Ruby's back and she turned to him. She smiled. And just like that, Seth disarmed a woman he did not deserve. I had always wondered how men did that. I wondered how they managed to do it to me. It was interesting to watch, from the outside.

I watched Seth and Ruby leave the office and head back to Room 6. They were buffeted by strong winds, which had picked up as the morning wore on.

A few days earlier, Ruby told me the new poems were practically writing themselves, appearing fully realized on the page as fast as she could get them down. She just needed to make the time. She promised me that she would not let Seth distract her.

Seth unlocked the door to his room and he and Ruby went inside. He closed the door behind them, and then one of them drew the curtains.

———————

I was at the front desk, responding to email. I confirmed bookings from the various discount travel sites and ordered more lightbulbs, laundry detergent, coffee, sugar, bleach. I looked over my reading glasses to the Hi-Dez parking lot. From here I saw the highway and the exit that led travelers to us: Hart Flat Road. I watched Sky drive her old white pickup into the parking lot. It felt strange to know she wasn't there for me. Sky and Fern—that had not occurred to me. I felt like an idiot. A big, straight idiot.

When Sky stepped down from the truck, Fern was waiting for her. Sky wore a white tank top, bright against her bronzed skin. I tried not to notice that she did not wear a bra underneath, but I did notice.

At first, the two women stood apart, and it was clear that there was trouble. They'd been arguing. Fern gesticulated until Sky pulled her into her arms, just in time, because from here it looked like Fern was about to pass out, collapse into something so thin and white it would blow away on the next gust of wind. Sky helped Fern walk back into Room 5 and then she closed the door.

I pried myself away from watching them, because I had a strict No Creeps policy at the Hi-Dez, and that went for me too. I turned back to my emails. The Hi-Dez would soon welcome new guests from Arizona, Nevada, and L.A., more people just passing through from someplace else.

I did not get what Sky saw in Fern, but that was none of my business. And, anyway, I knew you could never tell, from the outside, how two people made sense.

Some friends, back in Connecticut, heard me complain about John (his work schedule, his absence, and, yes, in the end, that he would not fuck me—although, for a very long time, I kept that to myself). Friends thought they knew our story.

I turned from my email and back to the window where I saw nothing but the past: John and I, the day we met, at a yacht club in Greenwich. It was the mid-90s and I was back in town after living in upstate New York for a while. My sister Pearl took me to lunch. John was there on business, meeting with some suits offering him an endorsement deal. He did not look interested. He was handsome and very tall, the only Black man in a room full of white faces. I watched him get up to walk the buffet line: scrambled eggs with smoked salmon, local organic goat's milk yoghurt with fresh berries, a board of French and Spanish cheeses, shrimp cocktail, caviar on ice. John made friendly conversation with the servers. He did not overload his plate. When he turned to head back to his table, we made eye contact. He gave me a smile that felt intimate and kind. It was the same smile, I would learn, he gave everyone.

Throughout brunch, we checked each other out, to the point where Pearl noticed and rolled her eyes. I liked the way his jaw flexed when he knew I was watching. The way he squinted at his brunch companion's bullshit. I gave him a long look at my neck—it was worth showing off, back then—while I drained my champagne glass. I was tipsy in the daytime and felt playful, even reckless. When he finally extricated himself from his table and headed for the exit, I followed.

"Seriously?" Pearl said, but I kept walking.

At the valet stand, I approached him. "Nothing lonelier than a club."

"Are you lonely?" he asked.

I laughed because, already, I was in over my head.

I said, "My name is Paula. And yes, if you must know, I am lonely. I usually am."

"I'm John. Do you always blurt out the truth?"

"Eventually," I said.

"Is that your sister?" he asked, tilting his head in Pearl's direction. "You seem related."

"Do we?"

"I see it in your faces," he said. "But yours looks sad."

"I'm in between life chapters."

"What does that mean?"

"I want to be a writer, but I don't write. I wanted to be a serious painter, but I design corporate logos. I want to be home, wherever that is, but I'm living in my younger sister's guest room. Stuff like that."

John looked at me with gentle, dark brown eyes like he understood.

"Are you married?" I asked.

"Not yet," he said.

The air between us crackled with possibility.

He said, "I'm looking for something permanent."

I looked at him and saw a good man I could love, who could maybe love me. Even if we did not have much in common. The valet pulled up in a charcoal gray Audi, and John pulled some folded bills from his pocket, a tip for the driver.

"I can be decent company," he said.

I texted Pearl from his car: "I think I'm in love."

"What else is new?" she texted back. "U owe me half for brunch."

He drove us to a secret spot he knew of, between enormous houses that were empty except for staff and groundkeepers. He found us a view of the water that usually cost millions.

He did not try to sleep with me that first day and I decided he must be a good man.

We were happy, for a while.

Sky and Fern propped open the door to Room 5 and proceeded to load Fern's stuff into the bed of Sky's truck. When they were done, I watched Sky pull out of the Hi-Dez parking lot and drive away. I walked down to Room 5, now unlocked with Fern's key left on the table. Everything looked fine, but there were still several cardboard boxes stacked along one wall. Each carton contained twenty-four brand new copies of a self-published poetry collection, *Desquamation*, copyright Fern Frankowski, now banned from Amazon for copyright infringement.

I called the contact number Fern wrote on what passed for a lease at the Hi-Dez, but it went straight to voicemail.

I redialed and Sky answered: "I'll be back soon."

About an hour later, true to her word, she returned and parked right outside the office. I watched from behind the counter as she hopped down and removed her sunglasses, squinting through the window in my direction. I was glad she couldn't see me, because I was staring. Sky seemed like the kind of woman who wouldn't mind. She certainly wouldn't be surprised. Now that she was closer, I saw that her white, sleeveless shirt was an old Donna Summer concert tee, "Hot Stuff" written in pink neon font. Sky was tall, by most people's standards, especially in boots, but of course she was still shorter than me. She moved with a confidence I thought of as masculine.

When she walked in, the bell on the door jangled in its friendly way. I felt a nervous flutter in my chest, like when Jasper first stopped into the Hi-Dez.

"Hey," she said. "Sorry about this. I told her we couldn't leave those boxes behind. She tried to pass it off like she was donating the books to you. The thing is, she can't sell them, or even give them away, now. She's not thinking clearly. I told her she can't make the books your problem. I'll get them out of your hair," she said, and I caught her sneak a glance at the gray tangle springing from atop my head, any which way it pleased, as usual.

"I like your curls," she said.

Oh.

"Can I get a key?" she asked. "I won't be long."

"I can help," I said. It came out sounding strange.

"Thanks," Sky said. "See you there."

I walked down to Room 5 while she moved her truck. I realized I stood in the same place Fern stood, earlier. I turned to unlock the room and then Sky was behind me, waiting. The key stuck in the lock, like every key stuck in every lock in this old place. If this was a few years earlier, when hormones had me raging and sobbing over nothing, I might have broken the key in my frustration. Sky stood so close she made me nervous. I reminded myself to breathe.

Finally the key turned and I stepped back to let Sky pass, but she waved me on ahead of her.

"You first," she said.

When the book cartons were in the bed of her truck, Sky asked to borrow the motel vacuum cleaner. I got it from the office and gave it to her, then turned to leave. But I did not want to leave.

Sky said, "Would you mind staying?"

I helped move furniture out of her way so she could clean, getting the old, patterned carpet looking as good as it could. She regularly nodded her thanks, like someone accustomed to cooperating with others, sharing the work. I watched her push and pull the vacuum, biceps firm with the effort.

Sky vacuumed under the bed and shouted, to be heard: "Fern says she can only write poems in bedrooms, did you know that? Preferably where lots of sex has happened between people she does not know. She says she needs that sexual energy for her writing practice."

"Huh."

"I know you are a writer, too. Do you have a practice?"

"I'm not very disciplined."

"Interesting," Sky said, like a disciplined person would.

"I write when I have something to say," I said.

"Maybe you're just not ready."

"Maybe."

Sky said, "Fern's alleged practice is bullshit. She is a word collector turned thief, passing herself off as a poet."

"She told me a little about that."

Sky turned off the vacuum. The quiet was a relief.

"I shouldn't talk about her," said Sky. "She is going through a lot. But she is always going through a lot."

"You get sick of each other, sometimes," I said. "In a relationship. I was married twice, I should know."

"Twice?" she asked. "To men?"

"Yes, to men," I said. "Sometimes it's too much, being together all the time. Some of us aren't built for that. We overcommit when it's new, but then it's not."

Sky sat down in one of the chairs at the table and waved me toward the other, as if she owned the place, not me. She ran a hand through her sweaty buzzcut. Her dark eyes were framed by thick brows and long lashes. I had not noticed, before, how pretty she was.

She said, "The problem is we overcommit to the wrong people."

"I used to say I was a hopeless romantic."

"Hmm."

"I know."

Sky said, "So I hear you're a graphic artist?"

She'd been talking about me. "I used to design corporate logos."

"I need a logo," Sky said. "But I'm not corporate."

"Is anyone, out here?" I asked.

Sky laughed and said, "Well, the Marines." She pointed vaguely northeast, toward the base.

"So you need a logo for your bakery?"

"Bakery? Ha. It's just me and my county-inspected home kitchen. It brings in a little money, but mostly it introduces me to nice locals," she said. "No, I'm opening a queer roller disco."

She watched me, like she was gauging my response.

"I didn't know people still did that."

"Queer stuff?"

"Roller disco," I said, blushing hot pink.

Get it together, Paula.

Sky grinned. "Of course! We never stopped."

"I loved roller skating as a kid," I said. "My favorite t-shirt had a big, sparkly, iron-on decal of a pair of skates and the words: LET'S ROLL."

"You still have that shirt?"

"Long gone, I'm afraid."

"You should come skate, when we're open."

"I'm not gay, though," I said.

"So you keep telling me." She took a seat at the table. "We're not getting back together, I don't think." She was talking about Fern. "I'm tired of cleaning her mess. I'm trying to open a business here."

"I'll design your logo," I said. "Free of charge, but if you're happy, please tell your friends."

"Of course," she said. "I always tell my friends when I'm happy."

"I'll need more information about your, um, disco."

"During the day, I want it to be more of a queer meeting place. Just a place to be and hang and maybe hold stuff like artist talks and author readings. Maybe by then you will be ready to write. You can come give a local author talk."

"Author? I mean, I'm trying to write a novel…"

I let the words drop, because I knew it was a tired line and maybe also a lie.

Sky said, "Do you have time to discuss a logo right now? We could stay here or move to the front office? Or your room?"

"My—"

"Don't you live in Room 1?" she asked.

"Sure," I said.

She left the truck with its bed full of books and we walked to my room. I knew Seth was in Room 6, where he'd been holed up since breakfast. I wondered if he watched me and Sky from behind his curtains.

"So, tell me a little about yourself and why you are opening a queer roller disco… you don't have a name yet, right?" I asked Sky from across my small round table, which was identical to the tables in all the rooms.

"No name yet," Sky said. "This looks just like Fern's room."

"It's fifty square feet bigger," I said, for some reason.

"I was a dancer," Sky began. "I guess I still am. Being a dancer is something you are, even when you can't jump as high or turn as fast. It's about how you move in and with the world."

"My ex was an athlete," I said. I did not know why.

Sky said, "I danced professionally for almost twenty years, mostly back-up for pop singers. I don't miss the grueling tours, but I do miss the joy. Everything feels so heavy now. Two years of that asshole in the White House—"

She looked at me, so I nodded my obvious agreement.

"I think we're all angrier," she continued, "and more worried, more unsettled. The planet is hot, tempers are hot, we're heading into another hot summer here in the Mojave Desert, and I am not interested in adding anything to the culture or conversation that is not compassionate, supportive, or refreshing as the ice-cold water we used to drink straight from the hose until we started worrying about that and everything else, all the time. I think a lot of us are stuck. We're white-knuckling it through an existential dread so intense, it's almost—"

She looked at me.

"—erotic."

Now, that word I did not expect. I did not trust myself to speak. I wanted Sky to keep talking. I wanted to keep listening to the sound of her voice, honeyed whiskey and campfire smoke.

Sky said, "I think, right now, Americans are hooked on fear like we're hooked on refined sugar, salty carbs, and porn. But at the same time, there are these deeply enlightened shifts happening. There are," she insisted, when she saw my expression. "We are experiencing the end of the old paradigm and the emergence of a new way, a more welcoming and vibrant way, and if we can just hold on through this excruciating transformation, we will be better than we can imagine. But first we have to survive. I want to create a place of relief, where my harassed community can just be, laugh, and skate. Listen to music that doesn't take itself so seriously. Feel some joy."

"And it's for gay people?"

"Not just."

"I can work with that," I said.

"I was hoping."

"It may take me a few weeks to get back to you with something," I told her. "There's a chance I have to fly back to Connecticut for a few days to help my realtor figure out how to sell my house."

"I'm not in a rush. I've got plenty to do before I'll need a logo."

"Can I get your number?"

She smiled and took my phone to add herself to my Contacts. I saw later that she starred herself as a Favorite.

———————

That night, Seth came by the office while I was working late on the computer. Right away I knew he was drunk.

"I saw your light," he slurred.

"That old line," I said.

Seth carried a bottle of cheap tequila to the table in the breakfast area. He unscrewed the cap and took a swig.

I said, "That is a very bad hangover waiting to happen."

"I deserve it."

"Why?"

"I deserve to puke out my weak-ass guts for being exactly the pointless sack my critics say I am. Yes, mea culpa, mea culpa, mea maxima culpa." He gave me a look. "And it's going to get worse."

"What do you mean?" I asked, removing my reading glasses so I could see him better.

"Some stuff is about to hit the fan. About a former student. She was all for it at the time, but now she's saying she was too young, that she felt pressured."

"Shit. When was this?"

"Years ago. Two years ago, almost. It was only a matter of time. I must be the last straight white male to be canceled. Although, I will point out that I am Jewish. She wanted me charged with sexual abuse, can you believe it?"

"Oh."

"It was bad judgement on my part, at worst," he said, taking another swig of tequila. "Everyone is so uptight and childish these days. They won't let me contact her. If I could, I'd ask her why she's forgetting the good times? Like the mornings we spent in bed, watching old movies and drinking espresso? Or the secret meetups in that little garden in Little Tokyo, where I read her T.S. Eliot and Bukowski? It was wildly, stupidly romantic, yes, but now she's made it ugly."

"Seth."

"I want to call her and explain."

"No," I said. "Bad idea. Especially tonight."

He screwed the tequila bottle cap back on and staggered to his feet.

He said, "It's too loud in my head."

For some reason I thought of a boy I knew in college, a flirtatious varsity lacrosse player who majored in Business because, "Why not? I like money." He got me to write his paper on *The Yellow Wallpaper*, of all things. I was okay with him not reading it, because he would not understand it or even try, and he would mock me for loving it. I did not want him to ruin it. So I wrote his paper, dumbing down the language to pass our professor's sniff test. The college boy, who was a nice guy, never did say thank you. But he did let me sketch his beautiful, bare thighs for my Drawing class homework. I remember grinding charcoal into paper, like I could keep this boy, if I could get him down on paper. Afterwards, he called me a slut.

"Where'd you go?" Seth asked.

"Just thinking about college."

"You ever have a thing for a professor?"

"No," I said. "But I would have fucked my high school Journalism teacher, if he'd asked."

"That lucky bastard," said Seth. "I have to go; I'm expecting company."

Ruby, I figured.

I had guests checking in early the next morning. I'd cleaned Room 3 earlier, but I still needed to make up the bed. Behind the motel office was a shed with a commercial washer and dryer. I unloaded and folded a load of fresh, warm sheets while standing outside under a black sky thick with stars. The warmth was nice against the evening's chill.

I was settling a fitted sheet over the mattress when I heard a door slam.

Ruby shouted to someone, "What are you doing?"

"I came back to get my books," said a voice I recognized: Fern.

"Your books are in Seth's room?"

I killed the light and moved to the window, hidden by the mostly drawn curtains. Yes, I was spying. Eavesdropping. Hiding in my own motel.

Fern stood just outside Room 6, wearing a baggy sweater with a crossbody purse, her pale, thin body lost somewhere inside.

She said, "I came back for my books, and Seth was here."

"So you slept with him?"

What? I thought. Fern slept with Seth? Wasn't she with Sky? And wasn't Seth a man, one she'd barely spoken to, around the motel? Seth was drunk on cheap tequila and incapable of making any choice, let alone a good one.

What was wrong with Fern?

"I could hear you with Seth, just now," Ruby said. "From two doors down. You put on quite a performance, Fern. You must be every dull man's fantasy."

"Way to be sex-positive, you bitter old second-wave feminist."

"I gather you intended that as an insult? It's hard to know, given your imprecision with language."

"You're just jealous," said Fern. "Just like a Boomer to think people belong to each other."

"You are fundamentally disrespectful, aren't you? You know what does belong to people? Their ideas. Their words."

Ruby was faced away from me, but I could feel her fury.

She said, "You fancy yourself a poet. Do you know any poem? I mean, really know it? Tell me."

Fern said nothing. She shifted, looking cold and self-conscious as she dug in her purse for something, presumably her car keys.

"Imagine if we spoke the same language," said Ruby. "Poetry, I mean."

"Whatever," Fern said, still digging.

"I know as well as anyone: we all make mistakes. We all choose wrongly sometimes and live to regret it. Everyone deserves compassion, yes? Especially when we're young."

"I'm almost thirty, if you're attempting to be patronizing."

"I'm attempting to be kind," said Ruby. "You are about my daughter's age."

Fern knelt to the ground then and dumped out her purse.

"What are you looking for? Why didn't Seth see you to your car?"

"He's passed-out drunk, like the world's worst lay that he is," said Fern. "I just want to go to my mom's house, but I can't find my keys."

"They must still be in his room," said Ruby. She knocked on Seth's door and, when she got no response, she knocked again, harder, and finally Seth came to the door, shirtless and squinting from a pitch-black room. Ruby pushed past him and walked inside. She came back out right away with a clutch of silver keys.

"Are these yours?" she asked Fern, who nodded. Ruby said, "How about we do something completely unexpected? It's not that late. Let's you and I go for a drink. We'll look at the moon and talk about anything but Seth."

"No thanks," said Fern.

From the doorway, Seth said, "Get lost, both of you. Let me sleep. It's the only time I get a break." He slammed the door behind him.

"A break from what, exactly?" Ruby called through the door.

"Myself!" he shouted back.

Fern got in her car and drove away.

Don't knock on his door again, I willed Ruby from where I stood in the dark, peeking through curtains. Go back inside your room with your dignity intact. It was always easier advice to give than take.

I heard Ruby go back inside Room 4 and I exhaled with relief. But then she was out again, holding her own car keys. She muttered, loud enough for me to hear: "Well, I am getting a damn drink."

Back in my own room, at the bathroom sink, I studied my face in the mirror, shadowed with cold, unflattering light. At fifty, the years I'd spent alive were written all over my face. Every belly laugh, every grimace and sob. I thought about Fern and Ruby and myself, women of different ages but similar loneliness who also wanted to be left alone.

It was kind of surprising that I was not among the residents of this motel sleeping with Seth. I would have been, at other times in my life. Seth was handsome, in a tragic way, and he felt things overwhelmingly, including lust. He was smart and confident, and when I was younger that would have been enough.

When I was younger—Gerry's age—I liked strangers' bodies best, each unfamiliar heart protected by its own ribcage and not my concern. I needed strangers' hands to ground me, confirm that I existed when I got to wondering. I wanted men as terrible as I deserved.

With John, I thought I had leveled up. I was done with all that; I had love. I no longer believed I was terrible. But then he pulled away; then he disappeared.

Jasper saved me because he never lied to me. He did not let us get carried away. He did not have the power to hurt me, but of course I loved him a little.

An Imagined or Remembered Melody

Paula

When Sky arrived the next morning with her delivery, the office was empty, so I told her what I saw the night before between Ruby, Fern, and Seth.

"Fern and Seth? Seriously?"

"I was pissed on your behalf," I said. "After you came back here to clean her mess!"

"I enjoyed myself," she said, fixing me with a look.

My chest felt like it had trapped one of those little bats flapping around the Hi-Dez parking lot at twilight.

Today, Sky did not wear her usual white chef's jacket, but a button-down, oxford pinstripe. The stripes were tomato red instead of the more traditional blue. She looked kind of preppy, and I liked it—I was from Connecticut, after all. I noticed the sleeves ended in tattered cuffs Sky rolled up over her lean, strong forearms.

She removed the plastic wrap from her trays and put them under the display cases. One held Mediterranean muffins with sundried tomatoes, olives, and feta, and the other, iced cinnamon rolls. She sat down at the table.

"It was sort of a parting gift," Sky said. "Helping Fern move out, I mean. Afterwards I told her we were done. It was time. Past time," she said, looking at me.

"Oh."

Sky said, "Fern and Seth? I'm still trying to wrap my head around that one."

"Did you know she liked men, too?" I asked, coming to join her at the table.

Seth was going to be too hungover to show up for breakfast, and I was glad.

"I figured," she said.

"I don't know what Seth was thinking. For what it's worth, when Fern left, she did not seem particularly satisfied."

"Well, that is a shame," Sky said, with a laugh. "Listen, I wish her well. We had some fun, but our hearts weren't in it. For starters, she is too young for me. And she is obsessed with trying to prove she's not ordinary. But she is ordinary."

"Ouch."

"I mean, it's true. I think that's why she stole those poems. She was convinced her own words weren't enough. She wasn't enough."

"Let's talk about something else."

"Okay."

"Is Sky your real name?"

"Yes. But it's not the one my parents gave me. Back in Tampa, I was Sofia. Sofia Silva. I renamed myself after high school when I started to get jobs as a dancer."

"It never occurred to me to rename myself," I said. "My dad wanted a boy. He wanted to name me Paul, for Paul Newman. When I was born, he settled for Paula."

"Do you dance?" Sky asked, and she held out her hand, like she expected me to waltz around the Hi-Dez front office, beside the breakfast buffet, no music but the cars and RVs along the highway.

"I'm a klutz," I said.

She kept standing there with her hand outstretched, so I stood up and took it. Was I really doing this? I felt awkward, slow dancing with a woman. Dancing at all. I was inches taller than Sky. I willed myself to stay light and flexible, prayed that my long feet found the rhythm and did not trip. I willed myself not to lead. My unruly body was still morning stiff, and I did not trust it.

Sky swayed us to an imagined or remembered melody.

She said, "I was always athletic," and spun me so that my curls flared out like a skirt, but I wore jeans. "My first dance teacher told me I moved like a boy."

"I'm sorry," I said.

"Nothing to be sorry about; I didn't care. I was on a co-ed competitive dance team all through middle and high school. We were pretty good. We competed all over the Southeast. I learned most of what I know about people in those years. Then, I got paid to dance. Then I was old."

"Ha," I said, because however old she was, I was about the same age.

It occurred to me that Seth might pull himself together enough to come by for toast. I did not want him to see me dancing with Sky. It wasn't embarrassment… well, maybe a little. It was not shame.

"I told you, I have two left feet," I said. I stopped dancing and returned to my chair at the front desk.

"I get it," Sky said, "not everyone likes to dance. Not everyone is ready to dance."

She came over to my desk. Her dark, sparkling eyes were a dare.

I asked, "So then what did you do? After you stopped touring."

"I went home to Florida," said Sky. "I taught kids to dance. Or rather, I accompanied them as they discovered dance. Now tell me about you," she said.

"Oh, I don't know. Once upon a time I wanted to be an important painter, but I had no talent. Or not enough. I did have a knack for graphic design, though. Specifically, I could distill a lot of corporate nothing-speak into an attractive logo that communicated 'bold strength and integrity,' or whatever."

"That sounds hard."

"Nah, it's an easy trick."

"I can't wait to see what you come up with for me. Listen, I have to go. I have two more drop-offs this morning."

She looked disappointed, which is how I felt, too. I stood up to see her out.

"Don't apologize for making a living," I said.

"I'm hemorrhaging money on renovations," she said. "I'm over budget on everything and bogged down in permit applications. I'm just saying, I appreciate every dollar that comes in."

"Everyone loves your food," I said.

"Oh yeah?" Then she said, "So what's the deal with Mr. BMW?"

I laughed. "You mean Jasper?"

"Are you—"

"Just once a month," I said. "He comes by on his way to see his elderly father. He just happened to stop by the motel one day. We have chemistry."

"So it's just physical?"

"Not just. He's a good person. He shows up, every month."

"That is a low bar, but I get it. Sometimes you just need a friend to help get your legs back under you."

A friend. I thought about the Whole Foods produce section, where I shopped for meat.

Sky left, as she'd said she had to. As always, I was sorry to see her go.

———————

Later, after breakfast and guest checkout, I pulled my sketchbook from under the front desk. It was blank, but I was ready. I thought about Sky's logo. I thought about Sky. I thought about her plans and how much I liked listening to her stories, her voice. There was just something about it. She always seemed to be having fun. She looked at me like she had a secret. I wanted to tell her: "Say it, Sky, whatever it is. Please."

My phone rang with a familiar number: my realtor in Connecticut.

She said, "I know she's your niece, but…"

She said Gerry had the place looking like a cross between a frat house and convalescence home. "She sleeps in the den, are you aware?"

"She's recovering from a serious injury," I said. "She can't do stairs."

"Well, she can put her dishes in the dishwasher," said the realtor. "And honestly, the house is still too cluttered with your late husband's bric-a-brac. We talked about this."

"His professional awards, you mean?"

"It's just kind of depressing, because he's… you know."

"Yeah."

"Perhaps they'd be safer with you in California?"

"Nothing of his was safer with me."

"Sorry?"

"I don't think he would want me to have them," I said.

"Maybe Mr. Bowen's children?"

"He didn't have any," I said. "We tried once, but—"

"You'll have Gerry clean up, then?"

"I'll come do it myself. I hear you. It's been too damn long. I just had to get out of there. I had to run away, but I can come back now. You deserve to sell this house and get your commission. I'll clear the rest of the clutter and get the place clean. Get it ready for sale, for real this time. I still have some frequent flyer miles... I'll book a ticket, is what I'm saying."

That night, when I went home to Room 1, I saw that the realtor had sent a follow up email. The subject was "Exotic Pet??" and it began, "Mrs. Bowen," which did not bode well. She knew I went by Paula Winger.

"Dear Mrs. Bowen, Thank you for your promise earlier today (by phone) to return to Connecticut to help expedite this process. Unfortunately, after we spoke, I tried and once again failed to schedule a showing of your house. Your niece (Gerry) denied me access AGAIN. This time, she said she was attempting to rehabilitate an exotic pet in your kitchen (??) and could not be disturbed. I hope you can understand that this is a competitive, prestige real estate market, and your house is already facing the challenges of a small (two-car) garage and a location that is—if I may be candid—not ideal. It is not exactly Greenwich."

Wow, I thought. She is really pissed.

The email concluded with, "Please allow me and Greenwich Estates Realty to sell your house and Go For The Sold™ by recommitting to the terms of the agreement signed by all parties, which I have attached to this email for your review. Mrs. Bowen, I would encourage you to take this opportunity to ask yourself the question, 'Do I WANT to sell my house?'"

Oh god, I thought. Yes, yes, YES, I want to sell my house. I want to be free of that life, that house, all my lives and houses before now.

I hit Reply and started typing: "I will fly back next week, I promise. We will get this sorted out."

The next morning, I booked my plane tickets over coffee. I got the supply cart and loaded it with clean, bleached sheets from the dryer, cold from sitting all night. The couple in Room 2 left at dawn. I heard them pack up their SUV, careful not to slam doors. They left without saying goodbye. I should have anticipated all these wordless departures when I bought a motel, but I did not.

I spied Ruby as she slipped from Seth's Room 6 to her own Room 4. Goddamn it, Ruby.

"Morning," I called to her, but Ruby did not hear me, or she pretended not to.

Later, I cleaned Room 2. I scrubbed the sink, tub, and toilet, wiped down the table and chairs and the inside of the microwave and fridge. I removed the trash and put fresh liners in the garbage cans. I vacuumed the carpet and stripped the bed. I struggled to push the cart away from the room, heavy with so many wet towels, and Seth emerged from Room 6 to help.

He helped me get the cart back up to the laundry shed, and then he asked, "Are you busy today?"

"Not really. That was the only room that needed servicing."

"Well then, you are invited to bear witness to a formerly promising young playwright turned middle-aged sell-out. I'm filming that diet drink-mix commercial today. They still haven't told me what role I'm playing, but I suppose it doesn't matter."

"Sure," I said. "I'll take my own car."

The shoot was down in Desert Hot Springs. They set up in the open desert, beneath wind turbines that sent shadows looping across the sand. Snow-capped Mt. Jacinto rose up in the distance, semis barreled east and west on I-10, and a steady stream of cars and trucks passed us here on the shortcut from Palm Springs to the Morongo Grade, which twisted up through rocks to Yucca Valley and beyond. The sky was bright blue, and the heat was searing, even in early May. The commercial was supposed to be some sort of candy-colored, pop-up rave in the desert, attended by an assortment of gorgeous, young models. The director told them to pretend they were having the time of their lives, high on club drugs and good vibes. The director said, "Just, you know, dance."

There was no music, so they looked insane.

The DJ booth looked like it was constructed of weathered desert trash: railroad ties and truck parts, rusty metal beer cans and a wagon wheel. In truth it was all painted plywood. Seth stood inside the booth, pouring red diet drink mix into gold Solo cups and handing them out to partiers. They were all much younger, of course. Seth and I had talked about how bewildering it was, sometimes, to realize we were the old farts, now. Wasn't it last week we were the young dancers? Well, some of us never danced. But we did spin, delirious, through our twenties, enjoying the party with or without music. And then suddenly here we were, fifty years old or worse, mid-way to nothing great. Now we were uncool and the party was not for us. Some of us looked like moms and dads. Seth was a dad, but he did not look like one. No, at this party, he was the creepy older guy, handing out red drinks in gold Solo cups. Seth looked over at me and I saw how nervous he was. I gave him a thumbs-up.

The director asked for everyone's attention as he described what he wanted for the next scene, where the dancers would toss their cups into the air, showering everyone in a red rain of diet drink mix that would make them laugh uproariously. He wanted them ecstatic and smiling and dancing and having fun, fun, fun! They would add confetti and glitter in post.

"It'll look like a fucking bloodbath," shouted a man standing behind me.

I had not noticed him until then.

"I'm sorry, did you have something to share with the group?" said the director, clearly pissed. "Who are you, exactly? On my set?"

"I'm Max, the tent guy."

Seth squinted in our direction.

The director said, "When I have a question about tents, I'll be in touch. Fifteen minutes, everybody. We'll use orange flavor, not cherry."

Seth called, "Cowboy Max? Is that you?"

"Seth Gladstone, as I live and breathe," said the man, who moved around me to go shake Seth's hand.

Seth laughed at that, and I could feel his relief. "Max, I'm glad it's you, seeing me like this. You were never a snob."

"Fuck no," said Cowboy Max.

When, finally, they were done, Seth came over to me and Max. By then I was trying to ignore Max, because he'd started to flirt. I felt the chemistry too, sure; I always felt it. But I was tired.

"Cowboy Max! How the hell are you?" asked Seth when got over to us. He hugged Max with genuine affection. "Last I heard you were the resident playwright for that theater group in L.A.… what was their name?"

"Who cares? We put on good shows for a while. Then it was over, and I forgot the details. That's how you live with no regrets, my friend," said Max.

"Max here is one of the most talented writers I've ever met," Seth told me.

"And now I sit in the desert and collect stuff," said Max. "And rent it out. Today it was tents."

"What? Seriously?" said Seth. "You had a great career."

"I'm telling you, brother, I got saved out here."

"You believe in God now or something?"

"Only I spell it nature," said Max.

"Frank Lloyd Wright," Seth said. "I recognize that quote."

"You got it, brother. Nah, it just occurred to me, on or about November 8, 2016, that my fellow countrymen had lost their damn minds and could not be counted on to behave rationally."

I was deeply sad and profoundly pissed. I said fuck it. To all of it, our entire hyper-capitalist, work-till-you're-dead, hoard-your-money, consumerist culture. That was bad enough, but now we're gonna hand ourselves over to fascism? To some racist, misogynist, fucking clown they recognized from TV? Just… no thank you. I decline. I prefer not to."

"Melville," said Seth.

"Yes, Seth, very impressive," Max said. "I escaped to the desert to ride out Donald Trump's misbegotten presidency."

I said, "I've heard worse plans."

Cowboy Max looked at me. He said, "I bet you have."

The wind picked up as the last of the equipment and trash was packed into the film crew's rental van. Seth and I walked to where we'd parked, and Max followed us like he might climb into Seth's truck, or my SUV.

Max said to Seth: "My credo is, be fucking nice." Then he gave Seth a bear hug and slapped him on the back. "To yourself, first and foremost."

"You do seem happy," said Seth. "If a little whacked out."

"No doubt, brother, no doubt," Max said, laughing until he fell into a coughing fit. "How else to be, though, in this terrible world? Wacked-out but happy. Surviving."

Seth asked, "Hey, did you end up marrying that girl? What was her name?"

"No," said Max. "I would have been a lousy husband. Luckily I realized that in time. I wouldn't do that to her, or anyone I loved. My goal now is just to have a complete romance: beginning, middle, and end, without any ugliness. An entire relationship without one single, regrettable word or action. I want to know that it is possible. That's what success would look like to me, brother."

When Max walked away, Seth said, "Apparently the desert fried his brain."

But I could tell that Cowboy Max got to Seth. Reminded him of something. What did success look like to Seth, I wondered? Not like whatever that was today.

I said, "Let's stop at a dispensary and get some weed before we head back up the hill."

"Fuck yeah," said Seth, echoing his happy friend.

Things Break Easily in My Big Hands

Gerry

The night I found the chinchilla, I was on crutches, snooping around the new mansions behind Aunt Paula's subdivision. I looked into empty rooms where nothing had happened yet. Life could still be pretty, inside and out.

It used to be thick, marshy, Connecticut woods back here, but they stripped it to dirt, trucked in sod and saplings and built six distinctive homes for no one. A banner staked at the entrance announced a Spring Open House, with pony rides and a petting zoo.

I figured that was where the chinchilla came from.

He lay on a bricked driveway, wet from the sprinklers. He looked like a tiny squirrel with huge ears. Fur twisted in dark curls. It took some doing, with both my legs in casts, hip to foot, but I managed to pick him up. I tucked him into my messenger bag.

Back in Aunt Paula's kitchen, I laid him on the counter. I tried to dry him with a towel, then my hairdryer. An internet search showed me what he was supposed to look like. Chinchillas were beloved for their beautiful, dense fur. Farmers raised a hundred of them for a single soft coat. Or they were sold as cuddly pets. Beneath the fur, he was a scrawny, pink-skinned rodent. You weren't supposed to see that.

He was not dead, but he was close.

I was excused from NYU for the remainder of the semester. That was it for my Freshman year. For eight weeks, my legs would be in plaster casts that I wasn't supposed to walk on, really. Hauling myself around like this on crutches was exhausting and it hurt, but that felt right. It felt like what I deserved: chaffed armpits, blistered hands, legs that would never be the same. Every night, in Aunt Paula's house, I was asleep before my head hit the pillow. I was too tired to dream.

The hospital set my bones and sent me on my way. A nurse handed discharge papers to my mother. I knew Mom was freaking out about how her big daughter would possibly fit into her cute new condo. She'd only had it for a few months by then. It was up in Norwalk, with a view of the water, finally something just for her. She bought it the second I left for college. Dad was still living in our Greenwich house, a Cape Cod Colonial, but he'd started a major renovation and told me it wasn't safe for me there, in my condition.

Mom had always wanted something different, more modern. I think she was mad that Dad didn't notice how much happier she was now.

Maybe Dad did notice, but he did not care. Or maybe he cared a whole lot.

Mom made as much room for me as she could. The loveseat in her living room unfolded into a bed of sorts. I could not bend my knees in those casts, so getting up and down was hard. I spent most of my time awkwardly, heavily horizontal.

"I just need to get used to you being here again," Mom said.

Sometimes Aunt Paula called to check up on me.

"No, really," she would say, when I said, "Fine."

Aunt Paula was cool. She knew about needing escape. She said I could have her Greenwich house to myself and keep tabs on her good-for-nothing realtor. Keep the HOA off her back. They didn't like vacant homes. They were already worried that their houses looked shabby, compared to those brand-new mansions next door. I texted updates to Aunt Paula and every once in a while she sent me a long letter, full of dark, heavy stuff that I guess she didn't feel like sharing when we spoke by phone. Sometimes the connection was terrible because she was out driving in the desert.

"The HOA sent a notice," I said, hoping she could hear me over the road noise. "They're planting two more weeping Cherries at the main entrance."

"Weeping what?"

"Cherry trees."

"Ornamental," Aunt Paula said, her voice full of scorn. "'Ooh, look at the pretty pink flowers.' But it's a freak! A Frankenstein tree, two trees grafted together, one on top of the other. We're such an arrogant species, aren't we? Always thinking we can improve on nature."

I didn't care about trees, but then I only saw them at night. Aunt Paula told me her neighbors turned in early and I would have the sidewalks to myself after dark. I told her that people stared because I was big. Tall, but it was more than that. I was hefty. Large. Thick limbed with a dense trunk. The kind of tree that blocked the light and made people angry. I was a big girl, the worst kind of girl you can be.

In the hospital, the cop said my dorm room window wasn't supposed to open all the way.

"Did you force it?" he asked.

"I needed some air," I said.

"How did you fall?"

I shook my head, like I couldn't remember.

I could have killed someone when I fell from that second story window. I could have killed myself. I was not dead, but I was close. In my hospital bed, I burned with pain the narcotics could not reach. Humiliation squeezed my heart until I gasped for air. My pulse looped.

The chinchilla wasn't interested in the lettuce I ripped up for him or the carrots I diced. He would not rouse himself to sip water from the dish. He was utterly still, at peace or in shock.

Next door, Mr. Patel went out back for a cigarette. His smoke hung in the air. When he was done, he flicked his cigarette into brush, away from his azaleas. I watched until the ember went dark.

I was scared of fire. I imagined the air sucked from my lungs, my flesh melted to bone, my entire big body reduced to weightless ash.

I wanted that so much it scared me.

Before NYU, there was a doctor who would not help. He said my hormones were normal. No pituitary tumor. My weight was acceptable, for my height, which appeared to have levelled off.

"You do not qualify for bariatric surgery," the doctor said. "And, Gerry, you are not a giant. Leg shortening is very rare. Extreme. You do not need surgery. You're just a big girl."

Oof.

"Fashion models are tall," he said.

That old line. He gave me a kind, reproachful look, the kind my father gave. Then he stood to leave, and that also reminded me of Dad.

Hours later, the chinchilla hadn't moved. His fur was still damp. I texted Aunt Paula and she gave me the name of an emergency vet who once saved Alan Alda.

"Lethargy, diarrhea, cloudy eyes," the vet repeated. "There's only one thing I can do for him. But it won't be long. Keep him home."

I told that New York City cop I opened my dorm room window because I could not breathe. I was sure he had already interviewed my roommate and her boyfriend, a cute Hellenic Studies major who knew I'd slept with at least two of his friends. Before it happened, they sat together on her bed, licking ice cream and each other's mouths, dripping on her pastel paisley bedspread. It was early April, too cold for ice cream.

On my bed, across from them, I tried to focus on the textbook in my lap, something about learning how to learn, but I could not think about anything but ice cream. My mouth watered. I wanted to ask my roommate for a lick, but I knew how that would look, how I looked already.

I could not go out for my own ice-cream cone because I hated eating in public. I hated eating in front of other people, period. I wanted to be a girl who licks an ice cream cone right in front of a boy, like my roommate. I imagined her sticky hands on him, and his on her. What they did when I wasn't sitting right across from them. I wanted that for myself, right now, again. I wanted another boy to distract me.

I could not breathe, and I just wanted to be alone for one freaking second. I stepped up onto the window seat, below the tall casement windows, which were already cranked open to let in the breeze. They weren't supposed to open all the way, but things break easily in my big hands.

Okay, sure, maybe some small part of me wanted to disappear. To leave a hole, big as me. I just wanted to stop longing for ice cream and everything else I did not deserve. I wanted to free up the space I took, more than my share.

If only that surgeon had cut me down to size.

By dawn, the chinchilla was dead. I tucked him back into my messenger bag and made my way on crutches to those empty mansions next door. In one of the never-used backyards, I spotted a young, flowering red maple, the base circled by stones. Hobbling across the lawn, I spooked myself when I thought I saw a man reflected in the glass patio doors, but it was just me. I pulled back a corner of sod and dug a hole.

I whispered, "He was more than his fur. He was forgotten, but I'll remember."

Then I picked up one of the stones and put it in my bag. It was heavy and pulled at my neck. I liked how I had ruined that perfect circle of stones.

I needed to hear something smash.

I made my way to the glass patio doors. I threw the rock, hard as I could, and it hit, right in the center. I thought the whole pane would shatter and collapse, but it just splintered, branching off in every direction. It was not as dramatic as I had hoped, but it was enough.

Later, back inside Aunt Paula's house, on my way to bed, I saw Mr. Patel toss another cigarette. This one also failed to catch.

Halfway to Flight

Paula

I was back in Greenwich for about a week when I woke up completely disoriented. Where was I? Not the desert; the air was different. I was back in my old bedroom, where I'd slept next to John for fourteen years, longer than I should have. It was a bright spring morning in backcountry Connecticut, everything green and noisy with birds. Sunlight poked in through the cheap, plastic blinds I'd meant to replace for years. John always wanted wooden shutters.

"They'll feel like bars on the windows," I said.

"You're so dramatic," John said. "Get whatever you want, then. Just make a change."

But I did not make a change.

A headache stabbed at my temples, from the humidity or the pollen, maybe, or that drink at the yacht club last night with Pearl and Gerry. I wasn't much of a drinker anymore, especially since I discovered that I preferred cannabis. But here in Connecticut, with Pearl, it was back to booze. We met her at the club; I drove us in Gerry's old Hyundai hatchback. Gerry took some time wedging herself into the passenger seat, which was reclined to almost horizontal. Both her legs were plastered straight for just one more week. She was ready to be free. I think maybe the last eight weeks of fighting to do every single, simple thing finally got to her. Maybe she realized she needed to take better care of herself.

My brother-in-law, Clay, bought the used car for Gerry when she moved

53

into my house. Gerry said she didn't deserve a gift like that, especially now that she was a college dropout. But her dad insisted, saying he did not want her stranded.

I heard Gerry moving around downstairs, turning on the coffee maker, opening the fridge. I picked up my phone and flicked away the news headlines, bad news breaking so often I was numbed to it. I recoiled from the sight of Trump. His voice made me flinch. Avoiding him and whatever hateful nonsense he had spewed this time was an act of self-preservation.

I looked at the last text I got the night before. It was from Sky. We texted back and forth a lot now, suddenly. She texted me an idea about her logo and, next thing I knew, we were texting back and forth all day, every day. Suddenly we were close.

So this is happening, I thought.

The last thing Sky texted was, "Sweet dreams."

I am falling for a woman.

We talked about everything, over text, replying when we could: family, politics, food, art. She wrote about how she chose to move across country, away from the familiar, to a desert she did not know but which felt like home. It was something we had in common.

I asked, "When did you know you were gay?"

And she replied, "When I saw the movie *Little Darlings*."

"Kristy or Tatum?"

"Yes," she texted back, with a laughing face emoji. Then she wrote, "I like 'talking' to you."

I felt a thrill shoot through me. Something in me had shifted. It felt baffling and yet also natural, easy. Of course I noticed.

"When u are back in town," Sky wrote, "I will show u the warehouse. It used to be one of those antiques malls. Gonna turn it into my dream."

My feelings for Sky did not surprise me as much as I might have thought.

I got out of bed and walked to the window. Outside, the old red maple leaned too close to the house. The realtor recommended that I take it down before a prospective buyer made it a condition of the sale, but I told her I couldn't do it. Who was I to kill something that actually belonged here? Same with the pignut hickory, which dumped split husks every fall before bursting into glorious yellow. The realtor called it a "messy" tree.

I tied the belt of my old robe, which I found hanging on the back of the bathroom door, right where I'd left it almost a year ago. It was terrycloth, not silky like the one I had at the Hi-Dez. This robe felt strange on my skin, like it belonged to some other woman.

I walked downstairs, the staircase's familiar creaks and sighs welcoming me back. The banister and the floors were dusty; everything was dusty. In a corner, I saw an old, battered, catnip-stuffed banana, a toy Alan Alda left behind when we moved to California. No wonder the place wasn't selling. I should've done a better job of cleaning before I took off. I did not blame Gerry. She was hurt.

As I approached the kitchen, I saw Gerry propped on her crutches near the counter, back to me, shoving something into her mouth and furiously chewing. She did not turn around until she swallowed and wiped her mouth. Gerry was my height, maybe even taller, and heavier. She was solidly built with strong features.

She never ate in front of other people; I'd noticed that. Had my sister? Pearl had her own stuff with food and weight. My little sister was almost fifty years old and still wished herself smaller. She lived by so many rules.

"Gerry," I said.

I'd forgotten how easily my niece startled, like she was always braced for attack, always halfway to flight.

"I'm sorry," I said, gently placing a hand on her back. She felt solid and warm.

"Coffee's almost ready," she said.

The machine gurgled and dripped more hopeful brown drink. The kitchen filled with the reassuring aroma.

I pulled out my favorite pan and got some butter melting, and then I cracked and scrambled some eggs. I readied a slice of bread for the toaster. I felt Gerry watching me.

"Want me to make you some eggs?" I asked. "It's the only thing I cook."

"I already ate. I'm not hungry," she said.

"It's okay if you are."

She looked at me but said nothing. We both knew her mother was disappointed in her. To Pearl, fatness was failure. A big girl was a walking confession: "I have no discipline. I don't care about finding a man." Pearl kept herself thin to prove she was in control, that she was fine. But she and Clay lived apart, and her daughter Gerry, their one child, was desperately unhappy.

I slid my scrambled eggs onto a plate with rye toast and brought it to the table, where I'd set my mug of coffee.

"Come, sit down," I said to Gerry, gesturing to the empty chairs.

Gerry took a seat to my left, at an angle, and I had to turn to try and make eye contact. But she kept her eyes down, on the coffee mug she gripped with both hands.

She said, "So… last night was weird."

"Ya think?" I laughed. "First of all, let's talk about the look on your mom's face when we rolled up to the valet stand in your old car and spent the next ten minutes getting you vertical while everyone waited for their Bentleys and Teslas."

Gerry laughed and I saw her finally relax a little.

At the club, I gulped down my Tequila Sunrise, which my sister declared a "vacation" drink, and I caught an immediate buzz. Pearl nursed her gin and tonic.

"Stiffens the lip," she said.

To sober up, I gobbled appetizers off silver trays circulated by waiters in tuxedos. I recognized some of my parents' friends, the old snobs of my childhood. There were lots of new faces, but everyone looked the same. I felt like I had snow blindness, all those dazzling white faces and tablecloths and dentures and diamonds. White yachts bobbed outside the club's floor-to-ceiling windows, which were thrown open to draw the cool, salty breeze. I heard sailboats rocking in their slips, tugging at their ropes.

"At least Mom is not a Republican," Gerry said.

She sat in John's old chair, at this table that did not feel like mine. Not anymore. Gerry still pretended she was not hungry.

I spooned more scrambled eggs on toast and took a big bite. The way Gerry looked at my plate, I knew that, for her, food was a shameful, toxic love. It used to be like that for me, too. Maybe for lots of women, for lots of big reasons. I chewed and swallowed and sipped my coffee.

"Your mom is a careful person," I said. "She can't forgive failure in others because she is ashamed of her own."

"Yeah, right, like Mom ever failed at anything."

"Oh, honey, of course your mom fucked up, at times, like everybody. She made bad choices. I'd say one of them was believing there was going to be some reward for behaving herself."

"She has no right to judge you."

"But I think that's my role in this family. I am who Pearl measures herself against when she is feeling insecure. At least she didn't try and fail to be an artist, you know? At least she didn't get divorced."

"Yet," said Gerry.

"They'll work it out," I said, not sure I believed. "Your mom gets it wrong sometimes, but so do I. I've failed at lots of things. At least Pearl still has her dignity."

"For whatever that's worth."

"Exactly," I said.

"Mom said fat women should be funny if they want to get away with it. They have to be able to tell and take a joke. But I'm not funny, and in fact I'm pretty sensitive. I think maybe I should just be quiet."

"About what?"

"Everything."

"No, Gerry," I insisted. "No."

Gerry took another swig of coffee, although by then it was surely cold.

She said, "Sometimes I wish you were my mother, Aunt Paula. I know that sounds weird."

"Let's ditch the 'Aunt' part, okay? I'm just Paula. As for your mom, she loves you. She just doesn't know how to handle a daughter who doesn't follow the same rules she does."

"She hates that I'm big," she said.

"Big enough to challenge her bullshit. Stop apologizing for who you are, Gerry."

"You know she says shitty things behind your back, right?"

"And to my face," I said.

"She says you do everything wrong. I bet she says the same about me."

"She might. Who cares?"

"I do."

"There's your problem."

Gerry got up and dumped her cold coffee in the sink. She hesitated for a minute, as if she might get herself something else to eat, but then she sat back down.

"I get it, Gerry," I said, "We get each other, maybe. That was why we always ended up talking at family parties at your house. Remember how we were always together outside, when everyone else was in, perched on your mom's tasteful, Colonial antique-replica chairs?"

"Dad bought those chairs," Gerry said.

"They were so hard my ass went numb."

"I liked your stories. I remember you told me once that each man represented a turn in the road of your life."

"Did I say that? That's giving them way too much credit."

"I always thought you were so cool and brave."

"Back in Connecticut, with Uncle John, I did not feel brave, let me tell you."

"But you moved to California all by yourself."

"I had Alan Alda."

"Well, you seem happy lately, is all I'm saying. I see you texting somebody. You have that look. Is it that guy Jasper?"

I got up to bring my plate to the sink. I stood with my back to Gerry and rinsed it slowly, carefully, more than was necessary before loading it in the dishwasher.

I said, "It's a woman, actually. Her name is Sky. She's a dancer and she's opening a roller rink in Joshua Tree. Well, she calls it a queer roller disco. I'm kind of... interested. In her."

"Oh," said Gerry. "That's cool. Was that kind of a surprise, though?"

"Kind of. A good one," I said. "Imagine! Seriously, Gerry. I want you to imagine good surprises coming for you, too."

I came back to the table and sat down. Morning light flooded my old, familiar kitchen and it felt cozy. I was nostalgic for this house, for this life, sometimes—it was true. Even though I remembered the bad times, I missed the familiar. I missed feeling sure and settled, hopeful that one day I might get through to John and we would remember why we used to think we belonged together.

It soured between us, but for a while, it was love.

"I wish my mom liked me," Gerry said.

"Gerry, why don't you get away from Connecticut, the whole Northeast, maybe, once your legs—"

"Mom says, 'Bloom where you're planted.'"

"Pearl does love a platitude. Some of us need to ride the wind a while before we find our place to bloom, you know? And not all of us have green thumbs. Did your mom ever tell you I lived on a commune?"

"What? No."

"Let's go to the beach. I'll tell you all about it. I need to get myself outdoors. I'm not sure my body understands yet that I've left the desert. It feels like half of me is still out there, and the rest is lost in transit. I need to ground myself at the coast."

"I can't walk far on these crutches," said Gerry.

"I will help you."

I drove us in Gerry's Hyundai through the two-lane roads of my hometown, which I barely remembered after just a year away. In my periphery was a blur of evergreens and bricked driveways, glimpses of mansions set back from the road, in which lurked my teenage self, the ghost of young Paula, still staring moodily from an upstairs window. She thought about how this town was not real life. Who wanted to live among so many rich white people?

Young Paula thought about how many boys her age, teenage numbskulls, thought they were important. Knew they were. She felt those boys watching, all the time—not just her. All girls were on offer, all the time. We were supposed to be flattered.

I would never have come back to Greenwich if it wasn't for John. I had been away for years by then and glad.

My seatbelt was buckled but I was restless. I wanted to settle my feet into rocky desert sand and get myself together. I asked Gerry to check my phone for new messages.

"You like her," Gerry said.

At Tod's Point, Gerry flashed our beach pass. Like everything in Greenwich, the beach was exclusive. Except during winter months, the beach was for residents only, and you had to prove residency to get a pass. That always struck me as strange and kind of selfish, and over the years many people had complained that it was elitist and unfair, which of course it was, but exclusion was the point.

The air was softer and saltier down here at the beach. It was barely May and still cool enough to keep away the crowds. The air still had a wintery edge, but you could also feel the promise of summer, not too far off—the way the light hit the water and the woods had greened up. I parked, and we took our time getting out. There were miles of trails winding throughout the peninsula and we watched as two women in designer athleisure pushed strollers down one path, talking too loudly and walking at a fitness pace. I retrieved the folding chairs from the trunk. The day before, I went to the Stamford Target I used to go to all the time, where I regularly stocked up on all the crap I now did without and did not miss. The store was bright and shiny and I was dazzled, after a year in the desert. I managed to find a heavy duty, padded camp chair in Sporting Goods. I figured I could help Gerry get in and out of it. It was going to be awkward no matter what, with her two full leg casts. Just one more week, I thought. She would be released.

After the chairs, I grabbed the basket of snacks I'd packed into the backseat. Then I helped Gerry extricate herself from the car.

I kept my pace slow, so I didn't get too far ahead of Gerry. She took extreme care with her crutches on the sandy blacktop. We aimed for the beach's main entrance, just off the parking lot.

Gerry couldn't go far at all once we hit sand, so we stopped where we were, and I set up the chairs. We were practically in the parking lot, still, in the path of beachgoers headed for cheeseburgers and curly fries at the snack stand, but luckily it wasn't open for the season yet. With my help, Gerry was able to lower herself into the camp chair.

We sat together and ate Honeycrisp apples. I was glad my hunch was right, that Gerry might be willing to eat in front of me so long as it was something healthy, like fruit.

Pearl admitted to me, once, that she worried for Gerry, looking like that.

A big girl does not deserve to eat—maybe no one said it, but Gerry heard it and so did I, for a while. We knew big girls were supposed to get small.

I looked at her sitting across from me, settled into her sturdy new chair, and I thought: Gerry was not big but tiny, compared to this beach. Compared with Long Island, its silvery office buildings visible across the water. And, beyond that, the deep, dark blue Atlantic—Gerry was miniscule, compared to that. I wished I could snap my fingers and give my niece permission to eat and exist, take up space and speak her mind—be shamelessly big in all ways, starting now.

Gerry said, "So are you going to tell me about the commune?"

"Oh right," I said. "Well, it wasn't really a commune, more of a community. It amuses me to call it a commune, mostly because it drives your mom crazy. But it was just some like-minded women living together on purpose. Trying something new because we were all in our late twenties and most of us had already fallen into traditional partnerships with men. We saw how it would go. We were supposed to want that, and some of us did. But some of us were open to other suggestions.

"My friend Aria inherited three small houses on some land in Ulster County, in upstate New York, and she invited me and some other women we knew from art school in Manhattan. Aria's father was a contractor and had built the houses on spec, but they hadn't sold by the time he skidded off an icy road and into a telephone pole. I was living in Poughkeepsie, working at a gallery and painting a lot. Several years out of art school, though, and my work still didn't say what I meant. I was frustrated and wanted to quit and apply for graphic design jobs down in the City. The guy I was sort of seeing at the time, a fellow painter, considered himself 'post-New York City.' He said, 'What're you gonna do, get a job in advertising?' Like it was the grossest thing he could think of. He would say stuff like, 'You tell me you're a sell-out and then expect my dick to get hard?'"

"Aunt Paula!" Gerry said, horrified or thinking she should be.

"Sorry," I said. "But he was an asshole. So cool he was cold. He acted like he did not care and, truly, he did not. At some point I found that sexy, I think. It's hard to remember, now. The only thing we agreed on was that we did not want kids. Not with each other, anyway."

"I can see why you dated him," said Gerry.

"Ha!"

Gerry looked beautiful, regal even, in this light, but I saw the thoughts churning behind her eyes and sealed lips. I hoped she noticed the soothing rhythm of waves rising and falling on the beach. I hoped she felt the bedrock beneath all that sand. I took another sip of water and opened a plastic box of grapes, also from Target: a mixture of green and red seedless, plump and juicy.

"Not organic," Gerry noted, when I held out the box to offer some. "Mom says I should only buy organic."

"There are lots of things we should do. According to someone."

"They're not washed," said Gerry, and that was true.

They felt vaguely dusty. I rolled a round, red grape between my fingers and popped it in my mouth.

I said, "My friend Aria wanted us to live in those three houses, make a community of women who were tired, already, by their late twenties. We had art degrees and okay jobs and okay boyfriends we would probably end up marrying if no one better showed up soon. Aria moved in her girlfriend and another lesbian couple arrived together, but most of us showed up alone.

"I thought maybe I would finally write a novel, up there. I thought time and space was all it took to be a writer.

"It was beautiful country, Ulster County. Thick forests and rocky hills cut through with creeks that fed the Hudson River.

"My boyfriend said, 'What are you, gay?'

"About twelve of us moved into the three houses. For a while, it was perfect. We pooled our money for utilities and home maintenance and weekly trips to ShopRite. We shared chores and tools; we hung out on each other's porches and drank instant coffee and smoked the dirt weed I got from the kid at the hardware store. We planted green beans, cauliflower, squash, but nothing much grew. Then Aria's girlfriend left, and other women followed. Aria had to consolidate us into one house and rent the others to anyone who'd pay. The place filled up with strangers, men who looked at us like we were the ones who did not belong. By then, I knew I was not going back to the guy in Poughkeepsie.

I felt strong and independent, and for the first time I didn't care what men thought of me."

"That sounds nice."

"It's a step toward freedom, Gerry. Seriously."

Gerry snapped off a small bunch of green grapes and wiped them with a paper napkin. Then she popped one in her mouth.

I said, "Gerry, I know you probably don't want to talk about it, but I want you to know that I get it—what happened at NYU, I mean. What you did. You don't owe anyone an explanation. Except yourself, I guess. But what's important is that you are okay. You are free now. You know that, right?"

"I wish I was brave like you," she said, closing her eyes and turning her face to the sun.

"You can be. Just decide to be," I said. "Don't waste as many years as I did, letting other people tell you who you are. Especially if they are mediocre dudes."

"Aunt Paula—"

"What did I say about that?"

"Sorry. Paula, did stuff like what you wrote about in your last letter… did that keep happening?"

"I used to drink too much," I said. "Every weekend in high school, junior and senior years, my best friend Melody and I drove down to Port Chester, New York, just over the state line, where the drinking age was eighteen, one year younger than in Connecticut. It was easier for us to get served. We were sixteen and seventeen, but we knew how to play older. If you were cute, or close, certain bars would let you in without even asking to see your shitty homemade fake ID. Everyone knew which bars looked the other way for underage girls. We got to be regulars at one place, and after a while, one of the bartenders started flirting with me. Usually it was Melody who got hit on, because she was blonde and petite. I was as big as a man. But this bartender was interested in me, not Melody. He was kind of old, but cute, I told myself, if you looked at him a certain way."

Gerry was listening but didn't say a word. I broke off another dusty grape and popped it in my mouth. I should have washed them.

I said, "The bartender asked me out and I said sure."

"You were seventeen?" said Gerry.

"Just," I said. "I didn't feel too young, at the time. He suggested we drive into the City for dinner and I thought that was weird, because who drives into the City? Take the train, like a normal person. But he insisted on driving. He said that way we didn't have to worry about getting stuck at Grand Central overnight when we missed the last train at 1:00 AM, when things were just getting good.

"He drove like a maniac into New York, down the West Side Highway, sniffing from a little bullet-shaped thing he had stashed in his car door. I asked him to stop and let me out, several times, but he said, 'You're in more danger, out there.' He parked around the corner from an old diner he'd told me about, which had some meatball sandwich I had to try. He laughed when I said I was not hungry. 'Big girl like you? Who are you kidding?'

"The block we were on was dark and empty. I almost swung open my door and ran away from that car and that man, who was a stranger and high enough to admit that he was forty-one. He told me not to tell him how old I was, because he did not want to know.

"He said, 'You wanna be grown-up so bad?'

"I saw the writing on the wall and decided to do it on my terms. I told him we should get in the backseat. He kept saying, 'I'll be hard as a rock, once I get inside you.' And then he was. On the drive home, I noticed how badly his car stunk of cigarettes and Wild Cherry air freshener. I hated his thick, meaty face.

"I said, 'Mind if I crack the window?'

"'Sure, sweetheart,' he said.

"I rolled the window halfway down and rain blew into the car.

"'Hey,' he yelled, but I pretended I couldn't hear. I let the rain wet my face because it almost felt like crying. He yelled some more, but all I heard was the wind and his tires on the road, which had started to ice over.

"Gerry, what I'm saying is: I know what it is like to walk to the edge and then stumble right the fuck over. You and I, we got hurt and we were not the same, afterwards. But we are here. We made it."

"I don't know what you're—"

"Yes, you do," I said, looking hard at my niece. Her broad forehead was pinking up in the sun.

She said, "I just wish my mom—"

"I know," I said, putting my hand on her arm.

"It's not just her," Gerry said.

"I know," I said, withdrawing my hand. "Believe that you deserve good things. That's all I'm saying."

"Okay, okay," said Gerry.

"Should we get out of here?"

"I'm burning," said Gerry, rubbing her forehead.

"You'll survive," I said, and I got her to her feet.

Before we left the beach, I checked my reflection in the rearview mirror and tried to press my salted, windblown hair back down into something resembling its usual shape, but it was no use. My tangled gray would be an alarming sight to my sister Pearl, probably. I looked like a storybook witch, wild and terrifying, out of control. And old. I should have the decency to hide that, at least.

I drove us straight from the beach to Pearl's condo in Norwalk, relying on Gerry to give me directions. My sister's condo was one in a row of identical one-bedroom, two-story townhomes, in a chic, formerly industrial area near the river with harbor views. I immediately knew which one was Pearl's, by the "Resist Trump" sign she kept in the window.

Pearl opened the door and looked me up and down.

She said, "Aren't you feral."

She let us in, muttering something about a mess, although of course the place was spotless. It was all sleek white surfaces, plumped throw pillows, and old factory-style casement windows. Most of the other residents were younger than Pearl, I noticed.

Pearl stared at her big daughter lumbering in on crutches. She said, "Just one more week on those, right Gerry?"

The tension between them was palpable—I'd never seen it so bad. Maybe it was too much for Pearl, having Gerry in her space again. It seemed like Gerry was right: there was no room for her here or in the house she grew up in.

Pearl directed Gerry and me to a pair of matching club chairs. She returned to her small galley kitchen, behind a wall with a large passthrough.

"I hate to neglect my guests," she said, through the opening.

Pearl went to the same etiquette classes I did, but she loved everything about them: the white gloves, the clear rules, the elegance.

"So what are you two up to, today?" she called.

Gerry said, "We went to Tod's Point."

"I made linguini with clam sauce," said Pearl.

"Did you hear what Gerry said?"

"Pardon?" said Pearl. A kitchen timer started beeping.

Last time I saw my sister, she was at home with Clay, at their house in Greenwich. They hired caterers all the time, even for family dinners, sometimes. Now that house was getting a major renovation that would restore it to its 18th century glory (when houses were cold and uncomfortable, I thought but did not say, when Pearl told me.) Clay was committed to historical accuracy. Pearl admitted that it bothered her, that Clay responded to her leaving by immediately clearing the house of any trace of her. He was supposed to beg her to come back, didn't he know that? Now they did not speak. Pearl told me she was terribly hurt, which was confusing, because for the longest time she seemed pretty sick of her husband.

To Gerry, I said, "You know one cool thing I did at Tod's Point, a long time ago? Jeez, I was, like, fourteen. I did a roller skate-a-thon for Planned Parenthood. They mapped a route around Greenwich Point and closed it to traffic. For weeks beforehand, I walked my precocious self from door to door to gather sponsorship pledges from our neighbors. I followed my old Girl Scout cookie route. This was a harder sell."

"I'll bet," said Gerry. "You were kind of a badass."

"It helped that my best friend Melody was doing it with me. One of the reasons we were friends is because we both called ourselves feminists, although no one cared. The few who listened to us usually said stuff like, "Aren't there more important problems," "Why are you making a big deal out of nothing;" or "No one else is upset." Melody and I gravitated to one another, not because we wanted to talk about that stuff all the time, but because we didn't. We wanted to be able to relax with someone who got it, without explanation. We wanted to be believed."

"That does sound nice," said Gerry.

Pearl came back out from the kitchen, looking harried. Her face was finally starting to show its age, but she steadfastly dyed her hair the same dark brown of her youth. My sister was much shorter than me, but not short by anyone else's standards. She was slim but not skinny. She was normal.

She said, "Lunch is served." We gathered around Pearl's small, square table. "I have white wine, if you like. I know it's the middle of the day, but I'm feeling European."

Gerry rolled her eyes but let her mother fill her glass.

We all dug into our pasta, even Gerry. The food was delicious and the wine was great. It was nice to be with my sister again, even in this unfamiliar condo that looked like someone else's house.

"What did I miss?" Pearl asked.

"I was telling Gerry about the Planned Parenthood skate-a-thon I did at Tod's point that one time."

"Oh my god, I forgot about that. Mom and Dad were beside themselves."

"What? No they weren't."

"Paula. Yes they were. They were mortified—their fourteen-year-old daughter was traipsing around the neighborhood, stirring the pot, talking about this controversial topic like it was no big deal. How do you think that made them look?"

"Like reasonable, modern parents of daughters?"

"You don't just blurt out words like 'abortion.'"

In my peripheral, I saw Gerry's eyes widen.

"You can, though," I said.

"Not in polite company," Pearl continued. "You have to respect people's sensitivities."

Gerry said, "Were Grandma and Grandpa pro-choice?"

That stopped us for a moment.

"Of course," I said, finally.

"No," said Pearl.

"Mom told me once that of course she and Dad would help us 'take care of it,' if either of us 'got in trouble.'"

"No way," said Pearl. "You're lying, right?"

"Yes," I admitted.

Pearl set down her fork and took a long sip of wine.

She said, "I do remember them talking about you and that friend of yours,

Melody. You two were always together. They worried you were gay."

"Worried?" I said. "Melody and I were best friends."

While Melody and I called ourselves feminists, we were also depressed teenagers who wanted to forget that we were not beautiful. We were not pretty like Brooke Shields or hot like Christie Brinkley. But, even so, we had something boys wanted, and that was power. It was a form of power. By then, of course, we knew that we, as girls, were born with less of it. Women started everything at a disadvantage, and yet were encouraged to "have it all." All sounded exhausting. In high school, there were too many boys in the way. Men. Every weekend, there were too many drinks in the way for us to see anything clearly. Melody and I accepted that life was fundamentally unfair to women. Surrendering on purpose felt like power.

We were sluts—that was the secret between Melody and I, not that we were lovers.

I do remember her hair smelled nice.

"Anyway," I said, "That skate-a-thon was a fun day. We raised about $100, I think."

Pearl drained the rest of her glass.

Gerry twirled a tiny bit of linguini with clam sauce onto her fork and brought it to her mouth, then chewed very slowly. She took one forkful for every two of her mother's, I noticed. Would she put her fork down as soon as Pearl did, or before?

Pearl did not notice, or if she did, she did not let on. She was busy talking about all the spineless Senators who, once again, refused to condemn something Trump said.

"I'm sending you home with a stack of postcards to fill out and mail," she said. "We have to vote this motherfucker out."

"Mom!" said Gerry, grinning.

"Patti LuPone called him that," Pearl said with a shrug. "I know it's inappropriate, but it feels so fucking good to say."

"MOM!" said Gerry. Now she was actually laughing.

And Pearl laughed, too. "It really fucking does."

Back at the house, it was finally bedtime or close enough to be acceptable. I was back in the bed of my marriage, the bed I shared with other men, after, when it was clear John was not coming back. I slipped on my reading glasses and checked my phone. There was an email from my realtor: she had scheduled a professional organizer to come by, as well as a handyman, assuming I was ready to tackle that punch list.

"Paula, are you ready to Go For the Sold™?"

I closed the email without responding.

Instead, I texted Sky: "Thanks again for taking care of Alan Alda."

I was grateful for the quiet of texting, tonight. It was a good day with Gerry and Pearl, but I was tired. All I wanted was to talk to Sky.

Sky texted back, "Alan is the best. That old man face! He's seen it all," adding a laughing-face emoji at the end. I loved that she found my cat's bored expression as amusing as I did.

She sent another message, "Forgot to tell u I saw Seth at the motel—with Ruby! Guess all is forgiven."

"Ruby does not shy away from drama," I wrote.

"Did I tell u she had a thing with the guy who owned the Hi-Dez before u?"

"What? Bob Marshall?"

"I helped host a dance marathon he sponsored for wildfire victims. Bob was running 4 State Rep. I told him my roller disco idea & he said Love is love, LOL. Can I call? Tired thumbs…"

"Hi," she said, when I picked up. Her voice sounded like she was right there beside me in bed.

"I won't keep you long; I'll just finish my story," she said. "Bob owns a couple of businesses in town and a few plots of land. He served as a County Supervisor and was running for State Rep. He hired me to help organize this dance marathon, a fundraiser for his campaign, which he said was 'Gay-friendly.' I know that's corny, but the other guy was openly hateful. After about a half hour of watching people dance, Bob and I were both bored. He started talking to me about his lady friend, a poet named Ruby Orr."

"What? She never said anything about knowing Bob or being at the Hi-Dez before she rented from me."

"He said she didn't come to the dance fundraiser because she was mad at him. She was always mad at him, he said. But lots of locals were mad at him.

He'd just sold a piece of pristine desert to Who Gives a Buck for one of their discount stores. It's going in that plot right behind the Hi-Dez—I hope he told you? They've been waiting on permits ever since, but some day they're going to build it."

"I guess that will be convenient."

"Bob lived here for decades; he knew better. But Who Gives a Buck offered him more money than anyone could reasonably expect him to turn down. Problem was, rumor had it that Ruby had counted on Bob giving her that land. He had promised, apparently. And she was pissed. Everyone was pissed. It was the worst dance marathon ever!"

Her laugh, through the telephone, was deep and real, like music.

"And now she's with Seth," I said. "Why didn't Ruby tell me any of this? Why did she act like she was seeing the Hi-Dez for the first time when she showed up to rent a room the very day I opened?"

"Maybe she's just eccentric. Or private. There are a lot of both kinds of people out here."

"Which are you?" I asked.

She was quiet for a moment. "Both, probably. I don't want to talk about Ruby anymore. Or Seth."

"He is apparently irresistible to women," I said.

"You resisted."

"I have made some progress in my middle-age."

"Let's talk about something else. Where are you? What do you see?"

I described my old bedroom to her: the art John and I chose for the walls; the upholstered chair he sat in to put on his socks; the window looking out on the red maple my realtor wanted dead; the empty pillow beside mine.

We talked until we were both too sleepy to follow the conversation. We said goodnight and I fell asleep and had good dreams.

Shades of Gray

Paula

A couple of weeks after I returned to the desert, all the tasks assigned by my Connecticut realtor completed, including renting a storage unit for everything I was not ready to deal with, I was at the table in my room, using fancy pencils to put the finishing touches on Sky's logo. I felt bad it took me this long, with the trip back East getting in the way of my plans to work on it, but Sky said it was fine; she was busy with renovations.

I wanted to get her logo just right. I felt like I had something to prove. Was I the right person to design the logo for a queer roller disco? Probably not. Plus, it was my first design in a while. My first one out here. I wanted to impress Sky.

I did not want to be one of those straight women who thought every lesbian wanted to sleep with her, but by then Sky was openly flirting with me. Wasn't she? The conversations by text, the way she hung out after delivering her baked goods—always one savory, one sweet. Sometimes, lately, I flirted back. We both noticed.

Since I returned from Connecticut, Sky was usually in a hurry to get back to the warehouse. The building's owner was helping her with the renovation, really more of a transformation, financially and with his own elbow grease. I dropped by for a quick hello once in a while but never wanted to be in the way. As busy as she was, Sky often came by the Hi-Dez. A few nights earlier, she kept me company while I did laundry—sheets and towels, as always. She rolled a joint as I moved one load from washer to dryer and started another wash. We smoked the joint back in Room 1. She reminded me to moisturize my hands and massaged in the lotion herself. Then she left.

Every morning, when Sky unwrapped her trays and turned to leave the Hi-Dez, and me, again, I thought—what if? What if I touched her arm? Right now. What was the worst that could happen? Would she jerk her arm away? Feel sorry for me? Tell me I'd misunderstood?

Leave me and never come back?

Maybe Sky believed me when I told her I was straight. I did.

And who said I wasn't? I was frustrated and tired of wondering. I was not sure of anything, much.

A dark blue BMW with Arizona plates pulled into the parking lot. Jasper? So soon? He strode into the office and right to the counter, where he leaned his tall body over to kiss me. But my attention was elsewhere.

"You have a room for me?" he asked.

The truth was, I didn't. "I'm sorry, I've got a group coming this afternoon."

"Then let's go to your room. Can you close up the office for a while?"

"I'm trying to finish this logo," I said, and I showed him my sketchbook.

"You're an artist?" he said.

"Commercial."

"I missed you," he said, reaching out to stroke my neck. "Can't you take a little break?"

I looked down at my sketchbook. Suddenly I was sure I was making a fool of myself, spending my days thinking about Sky, when I was obviously straight and she just wanted to be friends. What, was I seventeen again, waiting for life to happen to me?

I wanted to feel something I knew for sure.

I snatched the office keys from beneath the counter. Jasper and I stumbled down to Room 1. Jasper kissed me like he was angry. He tore off my t-shirt. He was rough and I liked it. I liked it well enough.

Afterwards, I was pissed about my t-shirt. I started to think maybe fifty was too old for that kind of nonsense. What was wrong with me?

"You seem distracted," Jasper said. "Did you meet someone?"

"Maybe."

"You deserve to find real love, Paula."

"So do you, Jasper."

We lay together in silence for a long while. I felt us become strangers again. Maybe we always were. Our heart rates returned to normal and the electricity between us dimmed. Soon there was nothing between us but the past.

———————

I was glad I'd kept myself strong, since moving to California. My legs sang out in protest, but I kept climbing, one boot in front of the other, up Ryan Mountain. The trail was steep and rocky; one thousand feet of incline in a mile and a half. I was winded, but I kept going, following Sky. I knew I would pay for it the next day, but it felt so good to be outside with her, in Joshua Tree National Park. I was grateful for my two middle-aged legs, which kept me upright and moving forward. Of course, Sky bounded up the trail without hesitation. She did not act like someone our age. I paused to catch my breath. Sky tried to talk to me, but I couldn't manage, so we abandoned conversation until we reached the summit: 5,456 feet. From there we had a panoramic view of what looked like a moonscape, vast emptiness punctuated by clusters of rock.

"Listen to that silence," said Sky.

I held my breath, to hear it. Then the wind gusted and broke the spell. We were lucky to be alone at the top, the tourists already gone into town for breakfast after wisely hiking early to avoid the June heat. From this vantage point, I felt like I saw everything clearly.

I said, "This is what I needed. Some perspective. A break from the noise."

The wind blew and I stumbled back, but Sky caught me by the arm. Her boots were planted, her weight settled into her hips.

"Where are you blowing off to?" she said.

Her voice felt like smoke curling into my ear.

She said, "You must be an air sign."

"I'm as earthbound as it gets. Taurus."

"Hmm," said Sky. "There's something windy in you. Something unsettled that might sweep me up if I'm not careful."

Another gust of wind hit, and I said, "I guess we should take care of ourselves."

We hiked back down, enjoying the view of protected desert for miles and miles. She told me she was a Virgo, also an earth sign, and that meant we were both set in our ways and stubborn and might butt heads. We were also sensitive and passionate.

I scrambled to keep up with Sky, who gathered speed as she made her descent. She broke into a run near the bottom, where the trail flattened out. I kept pace, and for a second, it felt like flying.

I panted, breathless, exhilarated from the endorphins, my heart racing from the exercise and heat—it was really hot. But I trusted Sky. I followed where she led.

In the parking lot, when I'd almost caught my breath and we said goodbye, Sky said, "Come by the warehouse again soon, whenever you can get away from the motel."

"I will."

"Consider the invitation open," she said, hugging me just a beat too long.

I was self-conscious about how sweaty I was, but I liked being in her strong arms. I did not want her to let go. Why couldn't I just kiss her? Wasn't that a thing I could do? I had only kissed a couple of girls—maybe more than kissed, a long time ago, in the blurs between men. It never meant much.

This was different. This felt important.

I wanted her to say something. Out loud, so we both had to deal with it. I was afraid I would never be brave enough. I needed Sky to be braver.

She said, "Honestly I would be grateful for your help. My landlord is cool, but he thinks I should have the place open and making money by now."

I said, "Just tell me what to do."

———————

Later that week, I walked into the small warehouse just a few blocks off the main intersection in downtown Joshua Tree. Sky told me that she slept there, on a cot in the back, but I'd never seen it.

I was glad Sky kept the original, bright yellow linoleum in the front. The building was known for it, by locals. She'd added a few upcycled tables and chairs, freshly repainted a cheery, cherry red, and arranged them before a small check-in counter and rental skate cubbies. She told me that it felt like she won the lottery, when she found that old cubby wall at the local swap meet.

Taking up most of the concrete floorspace was a huge, framed oval that was to be the roller rink. There were a number of buckets and floor tools lined up.

"Hey," said Sky, coming over to greet me.

She wore an old blue tank top with a picture of Cher in a sparkly bodysuit and knee-high boots: "Hell on Wheels," printed above. She looked good, strong from all the physical work, lit up with purpose.

"You won't have to get your hands dirty, after all," she said. "I got a couple of friends coming to help me roll on this skate surface stuff."

"I'm not afraid to get my hands dirty," I said.

"Noted," she said, with a smile.

"Aren't we friends?" I asked then, before I could stop myself from sounding like a complete jackass.

"Of course," Sky said. "But you have lots of friends."

"What?"

"Jasper. I'm talking about Jasper. I thought maybe you were done with that guy."

Seth must have said something; Ruby would never.

"Is there somewhere more private?" I asked, as two young men entered, dressed in paint splattered jeans.

"I'll meet you in the back, one second," she said to me, staying behind to give the men instructions on how to get started.

I did not see a cot, but there was a queen-sized futon on a low, wood frame. I sat perched on the edge, hunched over my long legs like some soft, non-threatening gargoyle. I did not touch or look through anything—snooping was never my style. I thought about switching to the much taller desk chair but, in that tiny room, I worried that would put us at a strange disconnect, at such different heights, as if I was trying to get some advantage, or like I didn't want to sit next to her, so low to the ground, on a bed. Her bed.

I was anxious and awkward, feeling hopelessly straight. Why did I default to men, all those years ago? Who could remember. Men were always there, and women were—what? What did I feel for women? Well, love, certainly. I loved looking at and listening to all kinds of women, even the slightly terrifying ones. Especially them. I preferred the company of women because, with them, I could fucking exhale. I felt safe. They did not complain that I talked too much. I was myself.

I told my old friend Aria, more than once, "Believe me, I wish I was a lesbian."

Sky came in and sat down next to me on the futon looking cool but distracted. "I have to go back and help them in a sec," she said.

"About Jasper…" I said. "I guess I just defaulted to what was easy. What I knew."

"I'm just confused about the timing," Sky said.

"I panicked. I have an old loop in my brain: 'You're doing it wrong; You're not enough; You're way too much.' It's loud right now."

"You gotta mute that noise," Sky said, frowning.

It would take too long to explain to her, wouldn't it? Men, all of that. My whole life. At this age, there was so much catching up to do. I wondered if she'd ever wanted kids; if she'd had her heart smashed into pieces. What was her life, before this? Before me.

Sky did not know about my regrets, or how I questioned everything now, because of her. Sky took me at face value, here and now. It occurred to me that Sky might be an honest-to-goodness straightforward person. The kind who did not make assumptions and said what she meant, who did not give passive aggressive digs; or go silent; or speak in code or lie by omission or leave and never come back. Maybe I could let down my guard, a little, with Sky.

I felt a little guilty, because Sky deserved a straightforward person, too, and she would not get that with me.

"The place looks great," I said.

Her mind was elsewhere, on the rink taking shape.

"Thanks," she said, and she led me back into the warehouse.

Back at the Hi-Dez that evening, when the light went peachy-gold and long with shadows, I texted Sky that I was ready to show her the logo. I was giddy with nerves. I wanted so desperately for her to love it.

She texted back: "Have you heard from Fern?"

"Who?" I wrote.

"My ex, Room 5. Not returning calls/texts."

"Maybe she needs time?" I wrote.

"Maybe. On my way. Excited to see."

My heart fluttered and my stomach thumped, or maybe it was the reverse. I dragged a toothbrush around my mouth and did what I could with my hair.

Soon, Sky stood next to me, looking down at the table where my computer was open to a newly digitized version of my sketch: a single Joshua Tree, brown shaggy branches ending in green, which in this case were clusters of small green spotlights. Beneath the tree was a large round shape, like a root ball, but it was a silver roller skate wheel, spinning fast. It reflected a dazzling rainbow of color, plus stripes of black and brown, pale blue and pink—colors of an updated Pride flag I'd found on the internet. I always did research before sketching, and this time especially, because what did I know about queer anything?

"I love it," Sky said, finally.

"I have to be honest, full color is going to be expensive," I said. "But I thought your logo deserved it. I can convert it to black and white—"

"Don't you dare. Shades of gray, maybe, but never black and white. No, full color is perfect. You nailed it. I don't know how to thank you."

I do, I thought. Kiss me.

"I'm glad you like it," I said. I was lightheaded with relief. We stood so close without touching. Her face, when she was joyful, like this, her smile… I could not breathe. I could not see or think about anything else. Her smile was as dazzling as the shiny silver wheel in her logo, reflecting back every beautiful color all at once.

"I'm starving," I said, stepping back from the table.

Sky said, "I heard the gas station across the street has great sushi."

"Surprising but true," I said.

"We'll have a picnic and enjoy this beautiful night. It's nice and cool; let's enjoy it. We can get back to work later."

We walked together in the crosswalk, hands at our sides, not touching, but close. At any moment, one of us could have taken the other's hand.

We got to the gas station and looked into their cooler to see that we had a choice of sushi: Mixed Assortment or Rainbow Roll, which was described as a California roll wrapped in rice and seaweed and topped with strips of red tuna, green avocado, orange salmon, pink yellowtail.

"I can't believe I didn't think of that," Sky said. "The Rainbow Roll. That's what I'll call it."

It took me a second. Then I said, "Oh! Your roller disco."

"I'm glad we were together when the name hit me. I kept hoping the right name would show up eventually. The Rainbow Roll: a queer roller disco in the heart of Joshua Tree."

We waited to cross back across the highway as a long, slow convoy of tan military Jeeps and supply vehicles rolled through, headed east to the base. When we were finally able to cross, we took our Rainbow Rolls, in take-out boxes, down Hart Flat Road, past the motel. Sky held out a packet of cannabis gummies and I took one, because why not?

As we walked, the gummy dissolved in my mouth: syrupy lemon with a skunky aftertaste. My lips were gritty with sugar. We walked until the paved road turned to sand, deep and soft, tough for walking, so we turned for a big boulder not far from the road. It was hard, sharp granite, shot through with quartz, tagged with names and initials. The ground around it was littered with broken beer bottles. From the top, we had a nice view of the dumpster behind Del Taco.

Sky reminded me to drink from my insulated water bottle. "In the desert, you can dehydrate just sitting around."

"Thanks for looking out for me," I said, "It is hard, sometimes, being out here in the desert, alone."

"You're not alone," Sky said, as if people had not said that to me all my life, right before they left. "Are you listening?"

From where we sat on that rock, the view behind Sky, facing east, was beautiful. It reflected the sunset in pinks that cooled to blue even as I watched.

I said, "I'm still getting used to these medical-grade edibles. In

Connecticut, I got by with the occasional dime bag. No one in our circle of friends smoked weed. It just was not something grown-ups did. They joked about 'potheads' and 'druggies.' Of course, several of them were alcoholics. John caught me smoking my little pot pipe, once. He was like, 'Don't writers need to keep their minds sharp?' I told him my mind was plenty sharp."

"Let's eat," said Sky, and she opened her take-out container.

This was one of the reasons I enjoyed Sky's company. She brought me back. I knew I had a habit of wandering off. Maybe because she was a dancer, she was balanced and grounded. I could hold on to her.

We took turns dipping our pieces of sushi into a shared tub of soy sauce. My mouth tingled with wasabi. Sky told me about the roller rink she went to as a kid back in Tampa. She was so good with the details, I wondered if she was a writer, too, as well as a dancer, baker, and the most straightforward person I'd met in a long time, maybe ever. I craved the deep, reassuring tones of her voice. I wanted her to keep talking so I could listen.

Sky said, "You married two men."

"Yes."

"Why?"

"Different reasons."

"Have you been with women?" she asked.

The sky was dark blue. It was harder to see, in the dusk.

I said, "You mean, in a sexual way?"

"In any way."

"A couple times… I mean, not really."

"I'm not the first woman to have a crush on you."

I laughed. "I like sex with men, though. A lot."

"A lot of men?" she asked with a grin.

"I just ended up with men. I only knew straight people, growing up."

"Heteronormative conditioning," said Sky, snapping closed her food container. "That is one persistent bitch."

It was dark now and I knew we should head back to the motel. I took a slug of water and said, "Can I ask you something?"

"Anything."

"Why didn't you tell me you were seeing Fern? I mean, we talked every morning."

"I was a little ashamed, maybe. She is too young for me, I know that. It was obvious. We were all wrong. But she can be charming. And you… were with Jasper."

"Yeah." I knew it was late and we should get going. But it was a perfect moment, there on that boulder, in that desert, far from where I used to be. Far from anything familiar. Maybe it was the edible, or maybe it was the darkness that made me bold.

"I feel it, you know. Whatever this is, between us." I said it quickly, before I could stop myself.

"I know," she said.

"It's just… there has already been a lot of change, lately."

"People need time to adjust their lens, I get it. I'm patient." She reached for my hand.

I leaned forward and kissed her cheek. I was overwhelmed by the softness of it. I could not help but think of the contrast with the rough, male faces I'd kissed, the times I'd come away sore. No, this was different. Sky was different. Her cheeks were firm and smooth, with the finest down where her face met her ear, and I nuzzled against her, giddy and aroused. She took my face in her hands and kissed me and then I knew—because I had wondered—yes, her lips were soft, too. It felt like spinning, tumbling through space, although we were still on that boulder. I hoped we would never stop kissing, but then we did.

Instantly I thought, Did that just happen? Did we kiss? Did I dream it?

But then I looked at Sky, and I knew.

Like Broken Things

Gerry

The smoke from Mr. Patel's cigarette trailed me as I walked down Aunt Paula's street. It was nighttime and dark. I loved feeling invisible. My legs were finally healed. After eight weeks in casts, they came out looking shriveled, hairy, and pale, but I could walk. They got strong again quicker than I would have thought. The physical therapist said I had to trust myself, and I nodded because I knew I should.

I walked down to where I knew I could reach a path along the Mianus River, which passed through these woods on its way to the Long Island Sound, the Atlantic, and everywhere. The banks were leafy and green, thick with trees. I took my time, because I was trying to be more careful now.

That NYU dorm window should not have opened all the way, no matter how hard I pushed. I needed some air, that much was true.

"Why did you push on that window until it was broken?" the cop asked, in the hospital, but before I could say, "Because I am broken, too," I was snatched up by nurses, doctors, an anesthesiologist. They gave me two full leg casts, crutches, instructions, warnings, prescriptions. It was assumed that I wanted to recover.

I hadn't walked far along the river when I saw a guy around my age. He was tall, almost as tall as me, but skinny. He was all glossy black hair and attitude, a collared shirt and expensive jeans his mom bought. I felt it from where I stood in the shadows and watched. He poked around the rocks along the riverbank. He was up to no good, out this late on a school night.

He spotted me and called out, "Don't shoot, Karen."

"My name's Gerry," I called back, before I realized he was trying to be rude. "And I'm barely older than you. What are you, eighteen?"

"Far as you know," he said.

Oh. He was cute.

"I don't care what you're doing," I said, walking closer so we didn't have to shout. I felt bolder, even brave, in the dark.

"What's your name?" I asked.

"Neerav," he said. "It means 'silent.' Isn't that a terrible name to give your child? I go by Rav."

"What are you doing here, Rav?"

"Art. Not that any of these suburban zombies will appreciate it," he said. "They'll get rid of it within a day."

"What kind of art?"

"Art that inconveniences to make a point. I just found this brand-new sawhorse, painted bright red, just sitting at the curb with the garbage. This neighborhood is wasteful. I brought it down here," he said, and pointed to a red sawhorse positioned at the far shore, at a shallow bend in the river, where the water was only about a foot high.

I stepped carefully along the river to get a better look.

"See how the water instantly adapts to the obstruction?" Rav said. "It instantly finds a way around. It changes course and carries on. Already, it is widening the riverbanks. It will affect everything downriver."

"Are you in high school?"

"That's an inappropriate question."

"No, it's not."

"It is when you're responding to someone's art."

"We're like basically the same age. I'm a Freshman at NYU. Or I was. Now I'm watching my aunt's house."

"Must be a fascinating house."

He was gorgeous but I tried not to notice. Also smart.

We both started walking along the river, together, as if we had agreed to walk together for a while.

"When are you going back down to the City?" Rav asked.

"Never," I said. I did not know that for sure until I said it.

"Why would anyone leave New York City to live in this suburban hellhole?" Rav said.

"It's not so bad," I said. "No worse than anywhere else. Lucky for me, my aunt's house is taking a while to sell."

"I bet it's because of those empty fucking McMansions next door. You want to know what I did over there? You cannot tell your aunt."

"I promise."

"It pisses me off that they built all those houses before they even had people who wanted to live in them or could afford to. And now they stand empty while people sleep in the streets. It's not right. Those houses are monuments to ignorant self-indulgence. Corinthian pillars, for fuck's sake. Don't get me started on the landscaping."

"What did you do?" I asked.

"It was just a light fixture. Around the back of one house, by some French doors. It was huge and ornate, like something you'd see on a French chateau. Anyway, I broke it. I hit that ugly piece of junk with a broom handle until the glass shattered and the aluminum bent, and I knew it was damaged beyond repair. I wanted them to think hard about their choices when they replaced it."

"I bet they replaced it with an identical light fixture."

"They did," he said.

"I threw a rock at a glass door on one of those houses," I said. "I thought it would shatter, but it just splintered."

"That was you? Nice work." Something caught his eye across the river. "Shh," he said, pointing at a Great Blue Heron standing absolutely still on the far bank. The huge gray bird lifted one leg, then the other. "You don't see one of those every day," he said.

"Is he okay? Is he hurt?"

"Why would you think he's hurt? I think he's just resting."

I realized that Rav was right. The bird looked pretty chill, actually. He started poking along the riverbank, making his way slowly, on backwards-bending stick legs, his long neck and beak stretching forward, then back, making its own, odd rhythm.

What about broken people? I wanted to ask Rav. How easily are they replaced?

"Sometimes art is a gentle shift," said Rav. "Sometimes it is vandalism."

"I think you just like broken things," I said, and he smiled but did not disagree.

The Rainbow Roll

Paula

"You have to hear this," said Seth, striding into the front office, a copy of the local paper in his hand.

I was closing down breakfast, carefully lifting Sky's leftover blueberry cream cheese Danish into Tupperware. No way was I letting those go to waste. The pastry was flaky and buttery and the cheese was a perfect mix of sweet and tangy. Sky only baked occasionally now, as busy as she was, getting ready to open the Rainbow Roll. I was going to miss these treats.

Seth said, "I saw the headline on my phone and ran across the street to get a print copy," he said. "Holy shit."

"What?"

"Bob goddamn Marshall."

"The guy who sold me the Hi-Dez? What about him?"

"He was the one on fire. That body they found a couple of months ago."

The blackened sand, I remembered.

"They just identified the remains. Guys at the gas station are in shock. They knew Bob for years. He loved their sushi."

"He's dead? Murdered, I guess?"

"Not necessarily, but probably," said Seth, taking a seat at the table. He jabbed his finger at the newspaper. "Paula, it mentions Ruby." He read, "'A little over a year ago, Councilman Robert Marshall enraged Yucca Valley residents with his decision to sell a five-acre plot of commercially zoned land in western Yucca Valley to the notorious discount chain Who Gives a Buck. The land was pristine desert, with several mature stands of yucca, palo verde trees, and a host of other native plants and wildlife. The general consensus was that a fortunate man like Bob Marshall, who did not need the money, should have preserved that land or at least sold it at a discount to someone local. Sources claim that no one was more furious than his ex-paramour, the poet Ruby Orr. She allegedly told friends that Bob promised her the land as a gift.'"

"That writing belongs in a novel, not a newspaper," I said. "Who wrote that?"

Seth squinted at the paper. "Someone calling themselves Terra Firma. Cute picture. But what is she implying about Ruby?"

"Sky told me about this, how angry everyone was. Does the article say anything about suspects?" I asked.

Seth looked at me.

"Ruby? That's absurd."

"He did promise her that land, Paula. Ruby told me. Sounds like she told other people, too. She was angry about it. Bob promised he would sign over that land to her so she could finally have a place of her own to live and write. She said he swore he would keep his promise, whether they stayed together as a couple or not. That's what she told me. And then he sold it to Who Gives a Buck, some Texas-based chain selling cheap, plastic crap made overseas by underpaid women and children. When people noticed he wasn't around anymore, Ruby told me he probably ran off with his sack of money and his tail between his legs."

"Did you know that Ruby and Bob had been a couple? And that she lived here, before?"

"Not until recently," he said. "We don't spend a lot of time on conversation. I know you and Jasper understand." He fixed me with a look. "Although you are full of surprises lately, aren't you?"

"Turns out," I said.

No way was I talking to Seth about Sky. I did not want his gaze or his opinions anywhere near something so exciting and new as whatever this was between me and Sky.

Seth folded up his newspaper again and tucked it under his arm. "Well, I'm off. I think I've got some—"

"—writing in you?"

Seth just shook his head. He grabbed a piece of white bread but didn't bother to stick around and toast it. I clipped the bread bag closed and slipped it back under plexiglass.

I locked the office behind me, checked on Alan Alda, and drove away. No one needed me at the Hi-Dez or anywhere. I drove down the highway to Joshua Tree, fifteen minutes with traffic. I turned onto the downtown block where the Rainbow Roll was in the final stages of renovation.

I hadn't stopped thinking about that kiss on the boulder behind Del Taco. It happened naturally, like it was not even surprising. What was I supposed to make of that?

Sky was up high on a ladder in the middle of the just-completed roller rink, now framed by waist-high, plexiglass boards. I stood below, steadying the ladder's base, while Sky clamped spotlights onto a pipe running the length of the warehouse. They were aimed toward a giant mirror ball.

She said, "Wait till I get the rest of these lights up. I've got multicolor LEDs that will bounce off everything. I want everyone soaked in color, feeling the music, you know? I want them dizzy with joy."

Sky paused while she used her wrench to tighten something a final time, then made her way down the ladder. Her face was sweaty and so was Olivia Newton John's, on the front of Sky's white t-shirt. Olivia had short, blonde hair and wore a white headband. Her head was thrown back in ecstasy.

Sky moved the ladder and climbed back up. I kept holding it, spotting her, although she hardly needed my help. But she asked that I stick with her.

She said, "I want people to skate until they forget their problems and everything but the fact that they feel great, they're having fun. They're free. Pure disco joy, nothing hard, dark, or sad. Just an easy beat, four on the floor. I want this place filled with queer people and our allies, everyone happy and laughing their asses off, not worried about a thing in the world."

When she was finished hanging the lights, we walked together to the front entrance, where a clipboard held a long punch list. We started sorting gently used roller skates into the appropriate cubbies, which were labeled by size.

She said, "You know, I never heard from Fern."

"Who?"

"Paula."

"Oh right, Room 5. Your—"

"I haven't heard from her since that day she moved out of the Hi-Dez and we broke up. Is that weird? I'm not sure if I should be worried."

"You broke up, right?"

"Yes, but—"

"Why are so hot to talk to her?"

Sky smiled at that. "Are we going to talk about it?"

"About what?"

"You know what. The kiss."

"The problem is, I'm straight."

"No, you're not."

"I'm not saying it wasn't a good kiss."

"Great kiss."

"This isn't the first time someone assumed I was gay, or what do you say? Queer."

"Why do you assume you're not?"

"I've always been with men," I said, pausing for a moment while I searched the cubbies for the one labeled Women's size 11. It was down at the very bottom. "I had husbands, Sky. Plural. Lovers and boyfriends and… the rest."

Sky frowned.

"But it was more than that," I said, sliding a pair of size eights into one of several cubbies labeled for that size. "I am talking about a life shaped by men, not just because they ran everything and made all the rules. I grew up knowing how much would be determined by how men saw me. If they wanted me, or if I was too big. It adds up, you know?"

"Not really," Sky said. "For me it was different."

"Tell me."

"You first," Sky said.

"Okay. Well, my dad wasn't around much, and my mom taught Pearl and I to flatter and encourage men, because if we didn't, they might leave. If we were bitchy, we would push men away or push them too far. All of that went sideways for me, pretty early on."

"That sounds awful."

"I bought into all of it. Needing men and resenting them for it."

"You might need to step away from all of that. That whole world."

I shelved a final pair of skates before I looked at Sky. I knew she was watching me.

I said, "I wish it was that easy."

"Do you remember when we met? You had just opened and I came by to try and sell you my baked goods. I had heard that an eccentric, single woman took over the Hi-Dez from Bob."

"Oh god—Bob. Did you hear?"

"I did. That poor bastard."

"Wait, what does that mean, 'an eccentric, single woman'?"

"It means the kind of woman who catches my eye. It means an interesting woman. We connected, Paula. Right off the bat. You know what I'm talking about. But I thought you were sleeping with Seth."

"I wasn't."

"True. You were sleeping with Jasper. Although I never could figure out what you saw in that guy."

I felt a little defensive on Jasper's behalf. I felt tenderness for him, now that we were over.

I said, "It was the best sex of my life."

"So far," Sky said.

———————

Late that afternoon, I closed the motel office again and drove out to my property, past the dry lakebed, past a whole lot of nothing but sand and creosote and a curve of rock. The light was mellowing out.

I unfolded my camp chair and set it at the top of the rise that was part of my two acres. The views were sweeping. Already the sun was behind my little pile of rocks, near the far end of the lot. Mountains in the distance were in shadow. I spotted a rabbit resting beneath a teddy bear cholla. A ground squirrel dashed across open sand, then dove down a hole. All around me, life buzzed.

Maybe I would build a house here one day, but for now it was all possibility and no regret.

I had a notebook and pen in my lap. I planned to watch the sunset and be moved and inspired. I would jot down a few brilliant ideas, then drive directly home to write Chapter One. The entire first chapter of my novel, beginning to end. A rough draft, but complete.

I brought a blanket for when the temperature dropped, because I was no longer hot all the time: twenty-eight weeks since my last period. Twenty-eight weeks was over halfway to a full year, when I would officially be in menopause. I imagined crossing the finish line like the winner of a marathon: I would drop to the ground, cheering with gratitude. Then I would get up, hit the showers, and head out for some big, fancy dinner in a gorgeous, all-white outfit—just because I could, for once, without checking the calendar first.

Maybe I would ask Sky to come out to celebrate with me. Unfortunately, I had a feeling she would suggest we go dancing.

I was at home in my body these days, mostly, but that did not mean I thought I looked anything but ridiculous when I danced. I knew one move, the one I learned as a pre-teen, back in Connecticut, that I would describe as a good-girl shuffle: small steps, bent arms tight to the body. What would Sky, an actual, professional dancer think, and how long would it take her to realize that she had a crush on the wrong girl?

I was leaner as I moved into middle-age. I knew women were supposed to feel better, more at home in their bodies, the smaller they got. But at six feet tall, I would always be big to someone. And I did not want to be small.

The reason I was at home in my body these days, mostly, was because it was bigger, not smaller. My body was bigger than it used to be in how it was capable, strong, and sexual. I was bigger in how open I was to possibility. I had never felt so big in my life.

I was not sure what my novel was going to be about. I had a vague idea, something to do with a woman my age seeing herself in a whole new way and going with it. Transforming or whatever. I would figure it out in the writing.

The wind gusted a little and a family of quail clucked and hurried between creosote bushes. To the west, an egg-yolk sun was drawn under by bloody reds. Across the sky, to the east, pink shimmered against the dark. There was not another person around, just a few lights in the distance. No one would hear me if I screamed.

Sound traveled farther, in the desert, but it also bounced and danced off the rocks and sand. It played tricks. Out here, I could not count on anyone's help if I ran into a man with bad ideas. All my life, I had tried to avoid getting caught alone with a man and his bad idea. Of course, sometimes I did get caught. Most everyone did, sooner or later.

But now, at fifty, I figured I was a less likely target. I knew I couldn't count on that. A man who hated women was capable of anything. Everything. At least my body would not keep a pregnancy, if a man's bad idea involved something like that. Surely my body would expel it, like it did before? And, again, it would be for the best.

My notebook was still closed in my lap when the light went completely, and I made my way back to my SUV. I had nothing written. I had nothing to turn to when I got back to my room and opened that blank Word document, its blinking cursor like a finger tapping. I locked the car doors and turned on the overhead light. I opened my notebook, put on my reading glasses, and wrote:

"Dear Gerry,

"Now that you're back on your feet, I want you to come out here and feel the bigness of this place. You won't believe how different the desert is from Connecticut. The Mojave will make you feel small and as big as everything, Gerry. There is room enough for every idea. I found room for myself here. Maybe you will too."

I looked up, but of course I could not see anything outside the car. I really was making myself a target out here, all lit up in the pitch-dark desert. I turned off the overhead light and let my eyes adjust. A smattering of stars appeared in the darkening sky, a preview of what was to come. I looked around. I could not shake the feeling that I was not alone. This land was layered with ghosts, everyone who'd managed to survive out here for a time: the Cahuilla and Chemehuevi; white homesteaders, miners, ranchers. Then there were the hikers who wandered off trail; the broken-down drivers; the despairing and addicted; the crime victims.

Bob Marshall: that news was still settling over me like a sticky mist. I had never actually met Bob in person, since I bought his motel with a wire transfer and e-signed documents, but from what I'd heard he was a decent guy. Sky thought he was okay.

I turned on the overhead light again and picked up my pen. For a moment I admired the look of it in my hand. I liked the feel and weight of it. I liked the connection I felt between this pen, my hand, and my heart.

"Gerry," I wrote, "you won't believe the stars you can see out here. There are so many more than you realize, but they are always up there. So much exists that you have not yet seen. Most of the time, out here, the sky is blue. But, sometimes, charcoal clouds settle over the rocks, and the wind kicks and screams, and everything is out of our hands. It wrecked my nerves when I first got here, but now I try to appreciate how the wind clears the air.

"I am better out here, is what I'm saying. Maybe you would be, too? I was honored that you shared all that with me, in your last letter. I want you to know that I get it. I want you to remember that you get to choose. You don't have to wait to be chosen. You get to write and rewrite your story infinite times and always be the star. Don't edit yourself to silence."

I stared at the words on the page. If only someone had written something like that to me, when I was Gerry's age, I thought. Maybe I was writing this letter to Gerry and also myself.

I started a new paragraph: "Listen, don't tell your mom—yet, anyway— but I think I am falling for Sky, that woman I told you about."

It looked real, there on the page. It was real.

"I'll tell you all about when you come visit," I wrote, knowing I'd officially crossed into pushy aunt territory. Gerry would see the desert when and if she was ready, like everyone.

I wrote, "There's something else I want to say to you, Gerry. I don't want to make you uncomfortable, but I think sometimes it's okay to be a little uncomfortable, if it means you hear something important. Gerry: you are normal. Your body and everything else. It is your perception that's off. I want you to hear that from me, not some doctor who doesn't get it.

"When your mom and I were kids, I was the heavy one. Grandma caught me with stashes of candy wrappers, hidden in my closet. I was too ashamed to confess. Sometimes I stopped eating altogether. I made excuses and lied about having eaten earlier at Melody's house, anything so that I'd have that exquisite moment, first thing the next morning, when I woke up so hungry I felt like a saint, denied, holy and hollowed out. Thinness became sacred, because it proved restraint. I think that might be how it still is, with your mom.

"You must not make an enemy of your own body, Gerry.

"There will always be people who want you smaller, but you shouldn't be one of them. A woman's big body is just the beginning. We are big when we question traditions. We are big when we stand up and say, 'Fuck you, this is me.' We are big when we dress, live, and love how we feel. We are big when we say the truth out loud, despite everyone telling us to pipe down. We are big when they call us shrill, but we keep talking anyway. We are big when we claim the slurs used against us and all our regrets. When we refuse to settle, insisting on pleasure, or at least some damn peace. We are big when we admit we tried but failed. We are huge in those moments, Gerry. All I want is for you to see how fucking beautiful it is to be a big girl.

"Loving our bigness changes everything," I wrote.

I folded up the letter and put it on the passenger seat. I started up the car and slowly navigated my way back to paved roads. I did not look in the rearview mirror, but I knew they were there: all the old ghosts.

———————

I returned to the Rainbow Roll every few days, whenever I could get away from the motel. Sky and I talked and talked about everything, but we did not kiss again.

One visit, I helped paint the walls. Sky wanted them each a different hue, to offset the entryway's yellow linoleum: hot pink, Kelly green, orange. I wiped baseboards and screwed in lightbulbs and showed the vending machine delivery guy where to go.

I tried not to think too much about how, each time, I was excited to see Sky. How I got that feeling in my chest when she looked right at me, or how disappointed I was when I came by and she was busy interviewing DJs or meeting with her accountant.

Everything in my life was new and I was still adjusting, but I was not confused.

Nothing between me and Sky felt unclear. I just did not have the words for it, yet.

In a few local community groups on Facebook, Sky posted a flyer featuring her bright, rainbow-colored logo: "Sunday June 30! Roller Disco Dance Party! 6-10 PM. FREE entry, 50% off All Skate Rentals; All Ages & Genders Welcome." That last line drew some disrespectful comments and laugh emojis. Sky did not respond, so I did not either, although I sure wanted to. I shared the flyer with the few locals I knew. One replied with a private message: "I didn't know you were gay, Congrats!" An LGBTQ+ center in Palm Springs forwarded the flyer to their mailing list, and Sky was cautiously optimistic about turnout.

We split up the stack of flyers and stapled them to community bulletin boards from Twentynine Palms to Morongo Valley, one of us driving east, the other, west. I asked Seth if he wanted to join me and help spread the word, but he said no thanks.

He said, "You two are getting close."

——————

Finally: sundown, the last night of June, Pride month: the Rainbow Roll's grand opening. I got there right on time. I pulled the handle of the old steel door, freshly painted yellow to match the linoleum. Then I stepped into a dream. Or, not a dream—a party. Sky's dazzling, color-saturated, queer roller disco dance party. A familiar, funky tune drew me into the warehouse: "Ring My Bell." Multi-colored lights splashed across the ceiling and walls, reflected by the spinning, mirrored ball. The music was loud enough to feel. It was pure disco joy, just like Sky said she wanted.

Sky was behind the counter, pulling out her roller skates. She spotted me and waved me over.

No one was skating yet, but some people already had their skates on. They rolled back and forth, waiting, watching, being part of this new experience. I saw a mix of people, mostly in their thirties and older, mostly white, but not all. I noticed this crowd was more diverse than some I'd seen around town. I figured most of them were gay, but what did I know?

"I'm glad you're here," Sky said, when I finally made my way to her. "What's your shoe size?"

"Oh, I'm not skating," I said.

"I knew you would say that. Next time."

I knew she would hold me to it.

I walked to the far end of the building, away from the rink. From there, I watched the front door as the warehouse filled with people, one or two at a time, each person looking around in wonder.

The door opened again and in walked a small woman with a long silver ponytail.

"Ruby!" I called, to get her attention.

When she spotted me, she walked in my direction. I was relieved to see her, someone I knew.

"Hey there, Paula! Nice to see you. This is your partner Sky's place, right?"

"Partner?" I said. "No, why would you—"

"Forgive me, I misunderstood. I thought that's what Seth told me."

"Seth talks too much."

"He noticed the chemistry between you and Sky."

"Sky and I are friends. I don't know if I belong here."

"What? Why on earth?" Ruby frowned.

"Because I'm straight," I said, although, this time, it sounded all wrong.

"Are you?" Ruby asked. "I didn't know what to call myself until a few years ago, when my daughter informed me that I was probably pansexual. She said that had nothing to do with her poor opinion of me."

"Pan—?" I started to ask, but then I noticed Sky had skated out from behind the counter.

"Shining Star" by Earth, Wind & Fire came on. Finally, I saw her full outfit: skintight, gold lamé leggings that showed off her sculpted dancer's legs; a shiny, black, patent leather vest with nothing underneath, looked like. Her strong arms were on full display and her shoulders were dusted with gold powder. She wore a black sequined bowtie at her throat. Her short hair glistened with sweat, already. She was so shiny. She caught the light.

Sky skated over to the DJ booth, partitioned off to the side of the rink.

She moved with a dancer's ease, knees bent, fluid and relaxed. Her skates were black.

The DJ, a curvy blonde, stopped the music and then stepped aside and sat down to let Sky have the mic. It looked a little tight in there, both of them in the booth.

"Hey everyone! Welcome to the Rainbow Roll!" Sky said.

Applause broke out, louder than I expected, because I hadn't noticed how, in the last few minutes, the place had filled up with a crowd. The turnout was amazing. There were all kinds of different people there now and everyone looked happy. I saw it in Sky's eyes: This could really be something.

"Welcome, everyone," she said into the mic. Her voice carried from one end of the warehouse to the other. "Thank you for being here tonight. My name is Sky Silva, and I'm a former and forever dancer. Through the 80s and 90s, I toured with musical acts, mostly boy bands. I had the time of my life, but eventually this aging lesbian got tired of dancing her heart out for boys."

"Whoot!" yelped the DJ from behind Sky.

Sky said, "I've lived in Joshua Tree for a while now. I'm originally from Tampa, Florida. That's where I got into roller skating, as a kid. Every Friday night, we met at the local rink and skated, shoulder to shoulder, with our friends but also people we didn't know, people who came from other neighborhoods. And everybody got along. It was a party. Everybody was there for the music and the fuckin' JOY—"

"Whoot!" called the DJ, again. What was she, a flirt?

"That kind of joy is contagious," Sky continued. "In those moments, you believe it is possible to forget our differences and just be together. Have fun together. I always knew I wanted to try and build a place like that. I call the Rainbow Roll a 'queer roller disco' because, for me, 'queer' is shorthand that includes any and all LGBTQ+ people. I am not interested in our differences—I want to know what we have in common. We are living lives that would have been impossible in our parents' time. We have reclaimed 'queer,' a slur they used to hurt us.

"For me, 'queer' represents a radical perspective, a challenge to the traditional—meaning white—heteronormative, patriarchal, binary bullshit we were all fed by—"

"PREACH, Professor Silva!" shrieked the flirtatious DJ.

Sky said, "What I'm saying is, together we have power. There are still lots of assholes who wake up every day looking to limit other peoples' freedom. Those of us at the margins must skate together, shoulder to shoulder. Just my *dos centavos*."

More applause. Wow, I thought. Listen to her. She is passionate and kind, smart. Look at her, she's… Sky glittered under the lights in her gold and black.

Sky said into the mic, "Wolf, where are you?"

Wolf?

A woman emerged from the crowd and skated onto the rink. Wolf wore a long-sleeved, gold lamé wraparound dress, a match for Sky's leggings.

Sky told the crowd, "Wolf is a dancing buddy of mine from way back. When she left Tampa for L.A., I tagged along until I saw Joshua Tree. Wolf and I are going to perform a little thing we choreographed last night—seriously. Last night. So listen, y'all, be kind! We're dancers, but our feet don't have wheels. But if you're not a little uncomfortable, what's the point, right?"

Sky left the booth and the DJ got back to work. She played Chaka Khan's "I'm Every Woman." Sky hustled over to Wolf and pulled her close. They skated side by side, arms wrapped around each other, legs in tandem. They fell into a rhythm, mirroring each other. Sky pulled, Wolf pushed, then they switched. Sky turned Wolf into a spin and then let Wolf spin her.

Finally, Wolf pulled herself into a tight, solo sit-spin. Her skinny, gold lamé arms raised high above her head like the quivering stamen of a flower. Sky stood perfectly still, balanced on one pointed foot, her other leg straight and braced. Her body was compact, carved like stone. Sometimes, Sky held herself in a more masculine way. At other times, all I saw was the feminine. Masculine, feminine. Suddenly, I didn't know what any of it meant. Right then, in that color soaked, queer disco dream party of Sky's, I believed it was possible for Sky or me or anyone to be many versions of themselves, over the complicated course of a human lifetime.

With a single, pointed toe of her pretty white roller skate, Wolf abruptly halted her spin. She panted as she grinned at Sky. She extended one of those skinny, gold arms and crooked her finger as if to say, "Get over here."

Sky laughed and turned to the crowd, "Everybody in the pool, y'all! Don't make me ask twice."

Skaters applauded and streamed onto the rink to join Sky and Wolf. The next song came on: Donna Summer's "Bad Girls."

"I love this song!" Ruby exclaimed. "Lord, this place takes me back."

Ruby and I started dancing in place. Everyone was dancing, on skates or otherwise. I felt awkward and self-conscious, at first, but I was having a blast. Everyone there was just enjoying themselves, enjoying being part of this, having fun. I looked around. Nothing looked familiar, but it felt like home.

Ruby and I screamed like teenagers as each new song came on and we recognized it. We sang along: "Shake Your Groove Thing;" "I Will Survive."

"If I Can't Have You…" The music downshifted into a slower, romantic ballad, a chance for the couples to have the floor.

I said to Ruby, "Let's get a drink. My treat."

Sky had no plans to serve alcohol at the Rainbow Roll, but the vending machines were stocked with all-natural, cane sugar-sweetened soft drinks. Ruby and I stood by the machines, sipping from glass bottles of ginger beer and celery soda.

Ruby said, "Sky seems like a remarkable person."

"We're not—"

"Sorry, it's none of my business. I'm just jealous, anyway. I wish I had a chance with someone like Sky."

"Aren't you with Seth?"

"No," she said. "Just sometimes. In some ways."

She giggled, and I could imagine teenaged Ruby around the time these songs came out; short-shorts and roller skates and hips swinging from experience to experience.

I said, "There is something sexy about ruined men."

Ruby took another sip.

It was hot in there. Wasn't it? Heat surged up through me. Or was this one final hot flash? Please let it be the final one.

Ruby said, "I wouldn't say Seth is ruined, exactly. Depressed, for sure. Things have not worked out as he planned, but who are we to plan? I am trying to help him see."

"That is nice of you. I hope he's nice back."

"Most of the time," she said. "He's been under a lot of pressure lately."

"Ruby, I have to ask, I mean… the newspaper. Bob Marshall. Why did you act like you were seeing the Hi-Dez for the first time, when you moved in? Why didn't you tell me about your thing with Bob?"

"My 'thing' with Bob? Oh, that man. And now I have to grieve him, too, on top of everything else? I was just attempting to be discreet, Paula. Because I am still married to my husband, technically. I am a private person."

I understood that, of course.

I gave her a hug before we parted. She said Seth was waiting. I could see how it would go between them. Anyone could, but the two of them—how it always was. Both Seth and Ruby deserved to feel good, for as long as they could. Better, at least. Everyone did.

By 9:30, the place started to empty out. By 10:00, Sky had the DJ shut off the music, take her cash and go. I never did catch her name. Then it was just the two of us, shutting off lights and locking up. Outside, we stood together by my SUV on the dark street, in a desert so suddenly quiet my ears rang. Sky was damp with sweat, and I liked her scent. The glitter on her shoulders had migrated down her arms, across her collarbone, onto the point of her chin. This close, it was as if steam rose from Sky, and maybe it did, because she had skated and laughed and danced for hours.

"Did you have fun?" she asked me.

"I did."

"Let's celebrate. Back at the motel, okay?"

Okay.

I said, "I want to tell you something, Sky, how amazing this place is. You absolutely created joy."

She stretched up to press a kiss to my neck.

She said, "Let's go lie down."

———————

I had on my new glasses for nighttime driving, but Sky still followed me in her truck to make sure I was safe. I knew she did not mean to follow so close, but she was excited. She was charged up from the wildly successful, emotional grand opening, everything she had worked for. She wanted to celebrate.

My body felt like dried sweat, dust, and old injuries.

As high with joy as Sky was, I wondered if her body felt the same, the stiffness and soreness creeping in? Or had she stayed in such great shape that she felt fine? What was I thinking, standing and dancing for hours? I was middle-aged. And that probably was a hot flash, earlier.

I wondered about Sky's body and worried about my own.

I would feel better, after a shower. Maybe Sky would want one, too. Luckily I had access to lots of clean towels. I tried to focus on the road instead of what all of this meant: Sky coming back to the Hi-Dez to celebrate. Showers, towels.

As soon as I turned into the Hi-Dez parking lot, I saw Seth and Ruby standing together by her Prius, parked outside Room 4. Things looked tense. Ruby had her car keys in one hand. Seth looked tired and drunk, with a nasty sneer twisting his face.

"Hey Ruby," I called, after I parked by the office. "Glad you got home safe."

"I'm fine," she said.

Behind me, Sky pulled in and parked next to my SUV, outside Room 1. She waited in her truck and looked at her phone, which was probably jammed with congratulatory texts and pictures from the night.

Seth recognized her truck. He looked at me, and he knew.

"Ruby is indignant," Seth said, slurry and mean. "She thought I was flirting with her pretty friend just now."

"Paula," she said, turning to me, "my friend Terra was hoping to talk to you about renting Room 5. She just left."

"Tara?"

"No, Terra, T-e-r-r-a. She is a fairly high-profile journalist. A few years ago, she left the internet and started using the pseudonym Terra Firma after she was doxxed by… I can't remember if it was men's rights activists or white supremacists? I gather there is some crossover. She has a book contract with Simon and Schuster… something about the legal cannabis industry and reparative justice, I believe. I told her to email you."

Seth said, "Ruby is upset because I noticed Terra happens to be young and frankly adorable, on top of being an accomplished writer."

Why couldn't he just be nice? I wondered. I hated when he got like this.

"Right," said Ruby. "I'm off."

She opened her car door, but Seth grabbed her sleeve.

"Get your hands off me," Ruby said.

He let go. "Please get back inside."

"No, Seth."

"Where are you going? You live here."

"I'm going for a drive. I'm going to drive out into the dark desert and roll down my windows and scream at the top of my lungs until I am no longer this goddamned irritated with you, Seth Gladstone."

To me, she said, "Goodnight, Paula."

The silence, when Ruby left, was awkward. Seth didn't say a word and neither did I. Sky still waited outside Room 1. We were supposed to celebrate.

"Bitch," Seth muttered. "Not you, her."

"Go sleep it off, Seth."

"Ruby always has her goddamn keys in her hand, have you noticed? Always one foot out the door. Reminding me she can leave anytime. That little threat, always."

"I thought you two were casual."

"Did she say that?"

"Are you in love with her or something?"

"Something," he said. "But there's no accounting for my taste, is there?" he said. He gave me a hurt look that definitely would have worked on me in the past.

"No one wants me," he said. "The Seth Gladstone show has been canceled mid-run. Ha. I'm sure you'll tell me that's another line for a play."

"No."

"You should go entertain your guest," he said. "You two make a cute couple. If surprising."

"Surprising?"

"Well, to me."

To me too, I thought but did not say aloud. I would not give him that. Seth was being a drunken asshole, and this was none of his business.

In my room, Sky immediately accepted my offer of a shower. I handed her a towel and warned her that the conditioner in the cubby was for curly hair, so she would not need much.

"I wash my hair with soap," she said, running a hand through her buzzcut, forward then back. "Thanks though, babe," she said, closing the bathroom door before I could be sure she'd really said it.

Babe? Did I imagine that?

When Sky finished her shower, she came out wrapped in one of my thin Hi-Dez towels, bright white against smooth, tanned skin. I realized I was staring, so I went to take my shower. I set my glasses on the sink.

As I rinsed conditioner out of my hair, Sky stepped back into the bathroom. She hung up her towel. Through the opaque shower curtain, all I could see was a blurry suggestion of her naked body.

She said, "Mind if I borrow some lotion?"

"Of course not, help yourself," I said. "I have two different kinds, from this cute apothecary in Joshua Tree: Calming and Grounding."

"Tough choice," Sky said with a laugh.

"Up there," I said, peeking from behind the shower curtain to point at the shelf.

She sniffed both, taking her time, then picked Grounding. She bent to massage lotion in slow circles up the length of both legs.

I said, "Sorry if it seems like I'm staring."

"Aren't you?"

I ducked back behind the curtain, glad that she could not see me blush. When I stopped the water, Sky drew back the curtain to hand me a clean towel. I quickly dried myself off. I knew she looked at me. And there was a part of me that wanted her to look: yes, take it all in, my big, weathered, fifty-year-old body that I used to hate but don't anymore. It was a body that hiked in the desert but also sat too much. It was a banged-up body that fell down, over the years, many times, for many reasons.

I wrapped the towel around me and stepped out of the shower.

Sky said, "I have some stuff for your shoulders."

"My shoulders?"

"I can tell they're stiff," Sky said. "The way you hold them. Like you just heard the worst news. Or like you wish you could shrink. What is that about?"

"Old habits."

"I keep this salve in my truck," she said. "It has CBD in it and some other good stuff. Come here," she said, sitting on the bed. "Sit in front of me. You're so tall."

"Sorry."

"I love it."

We sat together on my bed, both of us wrapped in towels. Sky was strong, which was no surprise. She used the heel of her hand to dig the sweet, smoky salve into the knots strung across my shoulder blades.

"Wow, okay… that feels really good," I managed to say. "Never stop, please."

"Okay," said Sky. "If you put on skates and dance with me, next time."

"I promise."

Sky's hands were the softest, strongest, most reassuring hands I had ever felt. In the care of hands like that, I might admit everything: Sky, the truth is, I'm the worst. People leave me, one way or the other. There's your proof. I am too much, too big. The truth is, I do everything wrong. I lead with my heart and figure I'll figure it out later. I don't know what I want until the choice is in front of me, but when I know, I know. And I know I want you.

Thankfully, I kept my mouth shut, until she kissed me. Then I let everything in.

Something Like Hope

Gerry

It was almost midnight and dead quiet on a warm, humid Connecticut summer night. I was on my nightly walk. I walked far these days, out of Aunt Paula's subdivision, down to the river and along it, through the woods, crossing old boundaries every time I climbed over another low stone wall. My legs looked and felt strong, the muscles carved out.

I saw Rav right away, poking around, thinking he was so stealth, but he forgot about his bright white Polo shirt and the new LED bulbs the HOA just installed in all the streetlamps. He carried a backpack on one shoulder: L.L. Bean, hunter green canvas with leather accents. It looked expensive. Rav was out, same as me, most nights, now. Sometimes I offered a timid, "Hi," when we passed in the dark. He was cute and a little full of himself, but he was nice.

Rav headed over to the empty mansions next door. I followed him, staying far enough behind that he didn't see me. Rav scuffed his feet through the carpet of bright pink azalea petals all over the sidewalks, then he walked onto one of the dark green lawns the irrigation system kept alive. The night was clear and the moon full. What would I say if he caught me following him? Maybe I just happened to be walking this way. Rav looked up into the dark branches of oaks, elms, maples, and tulip poplars—I knew what kinds they were because I'd borrowed a book on leaf identification from the Greenwich Library. I'd finally braved the place, which I'd avoided because I knew it would be full of people. Nice, helpful people, probably. That didn't matter.

That was not the point. I did not want to be stared at or even noticed.

"Hi, Gerry."

"I was just—"

"Following me," said Rav, "I know. I don't care."

"Maybe I just happened to be walking this way, too."

"Sure," said Rav. "Or maybe you like my art. Maybe you're curious about what I'll do next."

I was curious about a lot of things. Rav had no idea.

I was hungry for experience. I was not a college student anymore, and I wanted to gorge myself on this new, unexpected, better life I'd stumbled into. Girls were supposed to be satisfied with a taste, just a bite—now I wanted more.

Aunt Paula made me promise I would not live one of those quiet, desperate lives. I had to be brave and reject shame, make whatever changes were necessary to be happy.

I felt like an asshole for not writing back to her yet. I was sure that by now Aunt Paula felt weird about writing all that stuff to me in her letters and getting nothing but silence from me. Especially after I spilled my guts in that one letter. I felt guilty and embarrassed, and it got worse the more time went on. I froze up. I didn't want to talk about stuff like that anymore, I guess. Or for a while. I had to get it out, but then I needed a break.

Rav walked until he reached the house furthest back in the cul-de-sac. He seemed transfixed by the enormous, almost perfectly round fieldstone boulder that sat on a bed of mulch, right in the middle of the home's front lawn. It fell just inside the pool of light cast by a nearby streetlamp. It was the only house in this subdivision that featured a boulder in the middle of the front yard. I decided it was my favorite. Rav took off his backpack, and I saw that his white shirt was damp with sweat. He knelt to unzip the backpack and retrieved a gallon-sized can of white paint.

I said, "What are you doing?"

"Art."

"Does that wash off?"

"It wears off. Eventually."

He pried open the can of white paint. I stepped further back, although

I was already pretty far away. He tipped over the can, slowly and carefully, walking around the boulder to evenly distribute the white paint. Despite his efforts, his nice clothes were splattered. Rav used a fat paintbrush, pulled from his backpack with paint-smeared hands, to spread the paint until the boulder was whitewashed. Then he pulled out tubes of black, brown, and red paint. Rav moved to the side of the boulder that faced the house and, with a smaller brush, painted a single black dot in the center. He encircled it with brown. Then, moving to the back of the boulder, he added spidery red lines. It was a bloodshot eyeball, I realized. It stared directly into the pitch-dark windows of an empty, unsold mansion built on spec. I imagined it also stared at the ghosts of trees that once stood there.

Rav pulled one last item from his backpack: a cheap travel alarm clock. He placed it on the ground, beneath the eye's brown iris, and wedged it securely in mulch.

"It's perfect," I said.

"I don't know about perfect," said Rav, clearly pleased.

It was annoying, how good looking he was. Especially when he smiled.

He pulled his phone out of his back pocket and snapped a picture of his latest art installation.

"Will you send me a copy?" I said.

"I'll need your number."

His iPhone sounded an alert when my contact info arrived.

"You might as well just come out with me next time," he said. "You don't need to hide."

"I just… are you eighteen? You're in high school, and—"

"Don't be a creeper. I turned eighteen a couple months ago. And I'm not in high school anymore," he said. "I graduated. Last weekend." When I didn't say anything in response, he said, "I get it, Gerry. I like being alone, too."

"I guess we could walk around together," I said. "Sometimes."

"Hang out and make art," said Rav.

As he packed everything back into his ruined backpack, I looked at the glistening wet eyeball-boulder that stared, but not at me. I felt something weird and uncomfortable, like hope.

Rav and I walked together that night and the next and every night after that, for a while. He was my first friend since NYU, my first friend in a while.

And he was right: I liked his art, and I was curious.

Strange in His Mouth

Paula

When they finally covered the body, it was mid-morning on an August day in the high desert, forecast to hit 105 degrees. I sat in my SUV, where I'd parked early this morning when I drove out to my property. Something caught my eye in the rocks at the far edge, so I walked over to investigate. Then I called 911.

It was her, I thought. That burst open, picked over, shriveled up corpse they finally covered with a sheet—that was Fern Frankowski, disgraced Twitter poet, my former tenant at the Hi-Dez. Room 5. Sky's ex-girlfriend, or something. That was her.

A San Bernardino County sheriff turned and walked back toward me. He had instructed me to sit tight. I already forgot his name. He said he had questions.

Of course he did.

Here was my question for Deputy Sheriff what's-his-name: How long was I supposed to sit there and sweat?

If I was honest, it wasn't just the desert sun making me sweat, and this time I was pretty sure it wasn't a hot flash. I was sweating because I had nothing in my soft, middle-aged belly but black coffee and a weed gummy, just now kicking in. I should be back at Hi-Dez by now to open the coffee bar, formerly the breakfast buffet. The nightly guests complained about the lack of food, but the writers, even Seth, just accepted the bad news with a slight reduction in rent.

I was so hungry.

I had only intended to come out here for a little while. I wanted some peace and quiet while I tried to write. I worried that the gummy would make me silly or too chatty with this cop. If I was going to be arrested, I reminded myself with relief, at least I was no one's mother.

The sheriff moved like any lean desert creature, eyeing everything, conserving energy.

"You the lucky girl who found our mummy?" he asked, stooping to talk though my driver's-side window. He was all square jaw and shoulders, probably fifteen years my junior.

I said, "She's not a mummy."

"How did you come across the body?"

"I own this lot," I said. "And, in town, the Hi-Dez Motel, have you heard of it?"

"Bob Marshall's place?" he said.

"Not anymore."

"Hmm. You know, he—"

"—I know," I said. "That white fabric flapping from the rocks, was that her shirt?"

"Ma'am—"

"Paula," I reminded him. "Paula Winger. I just want to go back to what you said before. Mummification is a very specific process, whether ceremonial or accidental. She's just… dry. I got into mummies when I was a kid and my mom took my sister and I to see the Treasures of Tutankhamun at the Metropolitan Museum of Art. King Tut was an international celebrity, but I was more interested in the museum's permanent collection. Anytime my mother took us into the City, I wanted to spend time with the mummies. I wondered how they felt, being taken from Egypt to New York and displayed as art." Stop talking, I told myself. Stop talking right now.

"Anything else you noticed?"

"Her hair. It's blonde, but she dyes it gray. I went gray early," I said, pointing to my head. "She's younger than me. I always found that strange."

"Always?"

"Well, I recognized her, despite—"

"You knew the deceased?"

"She rented Room 5 at the Hi-Dez. Most of my rooms I rent to locals, by the week or month. Fern was a poet. Moved out a couple of months ago, without notice. She used to date my girlfriend. We don't talk about her much."

"Do you have her contact info at the motel? We will need to speak to your girlfriend."

I should have called Sky. Texted her, at least. And said what, though? "Sky, your ex is dead. Very dead, and I found her. I took an edible with my morning coffee, and now I'm talking to a cop."

Sky and I had been together for only a couple of months. There was still a lot I didn't know about her and how she might react. The edible was coming on strong. Shit.

The sheriff straightened to his full height. He said, "How 'bout we head over to the Hi-Dez? I'll drive."

His car smelled of sweaty, poly-blend fabric and stale coffee. I did not enjoy riding in the back. I had my phone in my hand, ready to text Sky.

"Why did you buy Bob's old motel?" the sheriff asked, catching my eye in the rearview. He drove slowly to keep the dust down.

"My husband died."

"I thought you had a girlfriend."

"I do," I said, "now."

"Okay."

"John told me he was taking a solo vacation. He hiked and camped alone when he needed time to think. Then he disappeared."

"Never a good idea to hike alone in the desert," said the sheriff.

"John was declared legally dead in absentia, back in Connecticut. I'm not a person of interest," I said, "anymore. They never found a body," I continued, unable to stop. "I just hope"—I remembered the gold chain tucked into the collar of his sand-colored uniform—"and pray that, if they do find him, it's like this." I pointed to the rocks. "I imagine it's easier when a body turns up dry, like that. For everyone. Cops, medical examiner, family. A human body is, what? Water, meat, bacteria—"

"Ma'am."

I felt a bead of sweat dart down my spine. Shit. Stop talking.

I said, "My husband was gone, long before he left. You know?"

No, the sheriff did not know.

"I couldn't stay in Connecticut. John was a local celebrity, sort of. His fans blamed me when he went missing."

"Why?"

"They said I didn't smile enough at WBTW events. They said I didn't even like sports, which was mostly true. Who was I to marry John 'The Elbow' Bowen, a good man with a quick smile who deserved the very best? When I finally got the death certificate and insurance, I bought the Hi-Dez. I thought I could run it and write my novel. That sounded like something other people did, but I decided to try."

Shit. Did I sound high?

"Ma'am—"

"Paula."

"Paula, have you smoked or ingested anything I should know about?"

"Do I have to answer?"

"No," he said.

"I used to answer every question I was asked. Good girls can be fifty years old. Older."

After another couple of miles on sand, we turned onto a paved road and then the main drag.

In the motel office, I gave the sheriff a copy of Fern's lease. Everything she wrote was a lie, from her previous address to her name: Jane Doe. I gave him Sky's cell number. I should have texted her first.

The sheriff told me to wait. He said, "I have more questions."

Of course he did. Shit.

I sat and waited for whatever would happen next. As if I had not fled to this desert to disappear, myself. Some part of me wanted to be reduced to porous bones and dry hair, a scrap of white fabric flapping from my exposed ribcage, a rag or a flag. Finally, surrender.

Shit, I was high. I got up to get myself some water.

I'm not going to pretend I remember every detail of my conversation with Deputy Sheriff Key. That was his name, apparently: Key.

When I asked his name, again, he said, "As in, 'Key-to-your-heart.'"

He handed me his business card and asked where we could sit. I pointed at the breakfast table.

I was settling into the edible's effects, but I worried that I swayed, just a little, as I took my seat across from Deputy Key.

He said, "As you are the reporting party, and an acquaintance of the victim, I'll need to get some more information. This will be an informal interview, okay, Ma'am?"

"Paula. Out here I finally get to be Paula. In Connecticut, I was Ma'am, or Mrs. Bowen. The Hartford Courant captioned a photograph, "John 'The Elbow' Bowen and wife.""

"Okay, Paula," he said. "So, 'Jane Doe'—what was that, a joke?"

"Her name is Fern Frankowski," I said. I retrieved my copy of *Desquamation* from where I'd stashed it at the front desk. "Here's the book that got her in so much trouble. Turned out, several poems had lines stolen from other poets' work. I don't know why she did it."

Deputy Key paged through the slim volume of poems, as if they might offer clues.

I said, "When she signed the lease, she was still pretty spooked. She said she'd had to get off the internet and leave L.A. when an online mob came for her."

"An online poetry mob?" said Officer Key. "I would've guessed that poets were pacifists."

"You might be surprised. I searched for her name on Twitter, after she told me all this. You could feel how angry people still were about what she did. They accused her of intellectual theft, white entitlement, stealing other people's stories, their trauma. Then the criticism got misogynist, like it always does, eventually."

"Sounds like she deserved it," said Deputy Key, as in Key-to-someone's-heart-but-not-mine.

I said, "On Twitter, people tagged every literary journal and small press that had published her poems, plagiarized or not, demanding that her work be deleted from their archives. Editors posted statements condemning Fern. A hashtag started trending: #BurnFern. I could understand why she felt like she needed escape. The desert is good for that."

"Is it?" said Officer Key. "You say Ms. Frankowski rented a room from you? Here at the Hi-Dez, for several months, before abruptly moving out this past April. Correct?"

He knew it was.

"And you believe it was Ms. Frankowski's body you found on your property this morning? Correct?"

"Yes."

"We'll have to wait for the official ID." He leaned in closer. "But if that is your former tenant—"

"It's her."

"Well then, that is uncanny."

Too much time passed before I realized he expected a response. I just sat and stared and maybe swayed. I was stuck on the sound of that word: uncanny. It was strange in his mouth.

Deputy Key walked down to Room 6. He wanted to speak with everyone at the motel, just in case. Just in case what? I wanted to ask but did not. He knocked on Seth's door and then knocked again but there was no response. The room's blackout curtains were drawn against the bright, midday sun, and I knew that, inside Room 6, it was dark as a cave. Maybe Seth found the office locked and dark, so he walked across the highway to grab coffee from the gas station.

Maybe he was drinking enough these days to help him sleep late. I was gone a lot, lately, with Sky. I knew Seth was not happy for me. He was jealous of my happiness. I wished he would focus on Ruby. Ruby deserved better. I think she knew that, but knowing and believing are different things.

Finally, the door to Room 6 opened, and a shirtless Seth stood rubbing his eyes in the bright sunlight. He nodded and the deputy stepped inside. The door closed behind them.

I pulled my phone from my back pocket and texted: "Sky, Fern is dead. I found her."

"Cops called. On my way," she texted back; then nothing.

After Deputy Key left Room 6, I watched him walk a few steps to Room 5 and knock on the door. Terra answered almost immediately. She stepped outside to speak with the deputy. She wore a loose-fitting, off-the-shoulder tee and no bra, which was maybe why she held her crossed arms so tight against her chest. Her shorts were made of what looked like sweatshirt material, the hem curling up from repeated washes and exposing a paler stretch of plump thigh. She kept looking around. Several times, she shook her head No. Then she spoke. Maybe she told Deputy Key about the men who tweeted her home address and cell phone number, along with pictures of her car, because they did not like something she wrote.

Maybe she told him, "Sometimes, Twitter is real life."

Deputy Key returned to the office and asked if I had a minute. This was going to be a long ass day; that was the only thing I knew for sure.

He said, "You were a person of interest in your husband's disappearance?"

"Not anymore."

"Right."

"The police said they received tips about me. Like I said, John's fans hated me. I don't know who they thought was worthy of John, but it was not me. The cops said they knew the tips were bogus, but they still had questions."

"We always do."

I really needed to stop talking. Where was Sky? Still on her way? I wasn't processing any of this fast enough. And Deputy Key-to-my-holding-cell was watching me close.

Just then, thankfully, Sky's white truck pulled into the parking lot. She walked in and removed her sunglasses. When she saw me, she hurried over. She wrapped her arms around me hard.

"It can't be true," she whispered into my neck. "It's too horrible."

Suddenly I was completely, utterly sober.

"I'm so sorry," I said.

It finally hit me: a person had died. Someone I knew. Someone who had been close to Sky, in some ways. A tiny, thin, white crumpled Kleenex of a person. A frightened word thief on the run. Now she would never be able to learn and do better, like we all should get a chance to. Fern was not my friend, but I knew her a little.

"Fern deserved better," Sky said.

She pulled away and wiped her eyes. She looked at Deputy Key.

"I'm Sky Silva, owner of the Rainbow Roll."

"The what?"

"It's a roller rink I opened in Joshua Tree," she said. "Couple of months ago."

"And you are Ms. Winger's girlfriend?"

"Yes," she said.

That thrilled me a little, despite the circumstances. We hadn't used words like "girlfriend" yet. It felt wrong to notice. Fern was here and then she was not. Sky mentioned that she hadn't heard from Fern in a while, but it barely registered. For months, Fern lay forgotten while her ex and I fell in love.

Love? Did I say that? Not out loud, not yet.

There were infinite ways to be yourself, turned out. Change was the only constant, and it was constantly difficult, even when it was great.

Deputy Key said to Sky, "I just spoke to Seth Gladstone, in Room 6. You know him?"

"Sort of," she said.

"Mr. Gladstone said your breakup with Ms. Frankowski was not amicable."

"Did he?"

"He did."

"Did he mention that he slept with my ex the day we broke up? Is he drunk?"

"Not anymore."

"He gets aggressive when he drinks. We've seen him like that with Ruby Orr, in Room 4," Sky said, looking at me.

"No one was in Room 4 when I knocked just now."

I suddenly realized that I could not remember when I last saw Ruby. Was it days?

I said, "Fern snuck back here, after Sky spent all day helping her, hauling her stuff away. She snuck back here and slept with Seth."

"So she's bisexual, too?" said Deputy Key.

Now, that word set me back. Bisexual: was he talking about me? Sky just stared at the man until he stood to go.

Deputy Key said, "Ms. Silva, if you have time right now, I'd like to have you meet me at the station. You might not think you have useful information, but you never know what detail might help us identify that poor soul we found this morning."

"I told you who it was," I said.

"That soul was long gone," said Sky.

Deputy Key said to her, "Let's get out of your girlfriend's hair. Which is great, by the way," he said, turning to me. "I wish my mom would let hers go like that."

———

When they left, I locked up the office and walked down to Room 6. By then, Seth had opened the curtains. I saw him inside, sitting in front of his laptop, which he stared at as if it might tell him what to write.

"You had quite a morning," he said when he opened the door.

"You too, looks like."

"I have a headache," he said.

"Otherwise known as a hangover."

"Okay, Detective Winger. How's your wife?"

"Fine," I said. "How's yours?"

"Ms. Ruby Orr, poetess, is not my wife. We're just… friendly neighbors."

"I realized that I don't think I've seen her for a couple of days," I said. "Have you?"

"Are you suggesting that I drove her away? The answer is, 'Probably.'"

"You're partying too much," I said.

"I haven't been to a party in years, Madam," he said in a theatrical voice. "What you mean is, I'm a drunk. I am turning into an asshole."

"Now that you mention it…"

"I have a lot on my mind," he said. "Usually I write myself clear, but it's not working this time. It hit the *L.A. Times* this morning: an interview with my former student. She was eighteen, but nobody cares about that. It was practically a relationship. On Twitter they're calling me a predator."

"Why did you tell Deputy Key that Sky and Fern had a bad breakup? It's not even true. What's wrong with you?"

"I did not want him to be suspicious of you, Paula. I mean, first John goes missing in Joshua Tree, and now Fern, your tenant…"

"Former tenant."

"I sent Deputy Key in Sky's direction as a favor to you," he said. "You're welcome."

"Get your shit together, Seth," I said, and turned to leave.

"Wait, wait," he said. "Forgive me. I haven't been myself since this news about Fern. I just can't believe it. And you found her? It hasn't hit me, not all the way. She was so young. Too young for me. I mean, over twenty-one, but—"

"She was an adult," I said. "But she was vulnerable."

"And passionate. Every day I heard her banging away at her laptop, like it had done her wrong and she deserved payback. It was almost erotic. We slept together once."

"I know."

"You do?"

"It's a small motel," I said.

"Fern told me Sky hated her poetry. Or, she didn't get it. And she gave Fern a hard time about the plagiarism."

"Of course she did. But Fern was convinced that she was a victim."

"Fern was hypersensitive to criticism," he said. "She had this clenched-jaw need to speak her truth, but she had no idea how to do that, let alone write poetry. I think she worried that the Twitter mob was right. She was a fraud. A thief. She said sometimes she could not remember what poetry was, exactly. She said, 'I want my poetry to be like me, just talking. But in a meaningful way.'"

"Don't be mean," I said.

"You believe me about my former student, right? You know me."

I looked at him because, yes, I knew him. I knew men like him. I knew what it was to be a young woman who let older men make her choices for her. I knew what it was to live with the consequences.

I turned and walked away.

I'm Coming Out

Paula

By late August, the Mojave baked and sizzled and too often burned. Wildfire smoke, carried by strong winds, turned the sky blood-orange. At the Hi-Dez, black ash drifted up against the laundry shed door. Year-round residents of the Morongo Basin woke at dawn to take care of yard work and home repairs before temperatures hit triple digits. Swamp coolers struggled to keep up, especially once the humidity rolled in with monsoon season, when dramatic clouds piled up with a promise of relief that rarely delivered. But, by then, most of the tourists were gone. For a few weeks we had the desert to ourselves, however hot and impossible.

I was alone with Sky at the Rainbow Roll, which was closed until 6:00 PM, when once again she'd start up the lights and music and welcome locals looking for joy. We were in the back, sprawled on her queen-sized futon, tangled in damp sheets. The quilt was in a lump on the floor. She had a box fan pointed at us, which helped a little. She'd pulled her underwear back on to get herself a bottled water from the vending machines, but I was still naked as the day I showed up in this life. With Sky, in bed, I was comfortable. Now, this kind of dancing I could do. I was not always wishing myself smaller. Somehow I understood her body—stronger than mine, but I knew it like my own. I knew what it needed. I loved making Sky smile. Afterwards, we talked for hours, always losing track of time, as if our conversation might never end.

One thing we did not talk about much was the ongoing investigation into Fern's death. Sky was interviewed by Deputy Key and others at the San Bernardino County Sheriff's department. Then she was thanked and sent home, because while it was usually a safe bet to suspect the recent ex, Sky had no motive and they saw that. There was nothing connecting Sky to Fern's disappearance or death. The cops told Sky to tell me that they would be in touch.

Stretching my long arms above my head, I asked, "What made you fall for Fern?"

"Way to ruin the mood, babe," Sky said. "And you know I did not really fall for her. We were just together for a while. Friends, sort of. I guess I like to fix broken things. But that's not love."

"Love?"

"Who would do that to her?" Sky said. "Who would do that to any human being?"

"They don't know for sure that it was foul play. Maybe she got lost out there," I said.

"Fern didn't hike," said Sky. "She called herself 'indoorsy.' Let's change the subject. I have a proposition for you. You know how I said I wanted to make the Rainbow Roll a sort of queer meeting place, in the afternoons before we open? I already have an artist talk scheduled and an all-bodies belly dancing class. I want you to do a reading as a local queer writer."

"Am I a queer writer?"

"Well you are currently naked in my bed, so I would say you are definitely queer."

"I mean, am I a writer? Wouldn't I have to write something first, other than letters to my niece?"

"Babe, I only know one other writer and they said no. Help me out, will ya?"

"What about an open mic instead? I could host it, I guess."

What in the world was I talking about? What made me think I could do that? I remembered an article I read once, in *New York Magazine*, reviewing various open mics around the five boroughs. Maybe I could find the article online.

"As long as you read something, too," Sky said. "Maybe."

"Listening to each other's stories, that's how we build community," she said.

I got up to grab my calendar. Gerry was always offering to help me figure out how to use the one on my phone, but I preferred doing this one thing, if nothing else, the same way I had for years. This spiralbound engagement calendar had glossy, heavyweight paper and full color photographs of Connecticut, a state I never loved until I left it. The photographs featured trees, coastline, sailboats, and horses.

I asked Sky, "When?"

"Two weeks. We'll need to make up flyers and get it in the local paper. Invite anyone with a story. What do you want to call it? How about Out in the Desert?"

"I like that."

"You will read something, right?" "Sky."

"I want to know your story, Paula. Before me. You must have felt something for women."

"I love women. My most meaningful connections were always with women."

"But...?"

"I guess I didn't see women that way. Or maybe I didn't see myself. There were always too many men in the way."

I sat up and put my bra back on, and then Sky took my hand.

I said, "You're staring at me."

"I'm trying to figure you out."

"Good luck."

"I'm afraid I'm going to get hurt," Sky said.

"I won't hurt you," I said. "Not on purpose."

"That's honest."

"I hope you can live with some ambiguity," I said.

"No other way, I guess," she said.

She waited for me to write down the date we chose for the open mic. It seemed way too soon to work up the nerve to stand in front of people like I knew what I was talking about, like I was a local queer writer.

Sky said, "Too much notice and people will forget. Let's keep it simple."

When I was done writing, she took the calendar and pen from my hands and placed them on the floor next to the futon. Then, we both had our hands free.

I took Sky's suggestion and called the open mic Out in the Desert. Local LGBTQ+ writers and dabblers were invited to read their work, for up to four minutes. I made a flyer from a sketch I did of an Avedon photograph I found in one of Sky's books: Diana Ross posed in gold roller skates, legs for days in sparkly gold tights. She lifted the hem of her short gold skirt to give us a peek at its purple lining. Her hair was wild and magnificent, of course, and her rouged face was pure disco-era joy. I drew Diana Ross in the Mojave, framed by rainbow-striped rocks and Joshua Trees, because Sky wanted to be clear that the Rainbow Roll was a roller disco that created joy and welcomed everyone, but was first and always a queer-owned, queer-supporting space.

"Here, queers come first," is something Sky liked to say with a little twist of her smile, because she liked double entendre and was just as flirtatious as that DJ from the grand opening. Sky was a playful flirt, I had learned. I was getting used to how she walked through the world with a confidence that caught the eye of other women. It occurred to me that, for Sky, flirting was just a way to flex certain muscles, keep them strong, like the rest of her.

I was not jealous, because I knew what we had. I knew how she looked at me when we were alone. No one asked me what it was like, being with a woman after a lifetime of men. I would not have known how to answer, and that made me want to try. I just knew that I fell for Sky, like I had fallen for other people, in the past—all men, but that turned out to be coincidence. I fell for Sky like people fall for people, every day.

Sky and I distributed fliers. Once again, we drove the length of the Morongo Basin in opposite directions, pinning them to bulletin boards outside stores that welcomed the rainbows: art galleries, vintage boutiques, a climbing supply shop, vegetarian food places, and a science fiction used bookshop.

As I drove, I realized I did not have it in me, anymore, to pretend that I wanted what Pearl and I were raised to want, what most women were raised to want: marriage and men. We were supposed to bring beauty and brains, and a sweet disposition. Surely I had fallen short of every expectation. It was irrelevant. This was the life I wanted.

Maybe I had lost my mind. Maybe I was making a fool of myself, carrying on out here in the middle of nowhere, a middle-aged lady from Connecticut. Who said I got to run away to the desert, smoke pot, and turn gay, like women can choose whatever life they want?

———————

On the day of the open mic, the air was so hot it burned. I ducked into the darkened cool of the Rainbow Roll at 4:00 PM, ahead of the event's start time of 5:00. Sky had already set up some folding chairs just outside the roller rink. There was a music stand and a microphone and bottles of water and natural sodas in a galvanized tub filled with ice.

I was technically the host, but clearly Sky had a knack for this. She buzzed around the Rainbow Roll in a tight purple t-shirt printed with, "Disco is So Gay," in sparkly, holographic vinyl letters. She looked like she was having the time of her life, creating and recreating this space she made for her community, for people who were not always welcome in other places, maybe even their own homes.

Sky kissed me hello, then went back to unfolding chairs and arranging them in a semi-circle.

"People will only share what they feel comfortable sharing, right?" I asked. I couldn't help it; I was nervous.

"Of course," said Sky.

"And people will listen respectfully? I don't care if only a few people show up, so long as everyone feels heard. That's everything."

"It's going to be great," Sky said. "It's going to be special."

I wanted to impress Sky so badly.

I felt a rush of gratitude when I saw Ruby and Seth walk in. Ruby had returned to the Hi-Dez without an explanation for her absence. I figured she had needed some days away from Seth. And it looked like the time apart did them both good. Ruby gave me a little wave and Seth nodded. They were followed by several small groups of people I did not know. Sky and I looked at each other and I knew she was pleased with the turnout, especially for a literary event at 5:00 on a Tuesday. Sky flashed a smile, and I noticed that her former buzzcut was getting shaggy as it grew out, threaded with more silver all the time. She looked cute as a damn button.

"Hi everyone," I said into the mic as people took their seats.

My voice was shaky. The mic yawned feedback until I backed off.

"Please sign up if you want to read. There is a clipboard going around. Let's keep it to about three or four minutes each, okay? I know that's not much time… I'm sorry…"

I cleared my throat.

I felt like an absolute freak, standing there. Suddenly I was acutely aware of how far I was from Connecticut or anything familiar, anything I knew how to do. I remembered my tasteful logos, my polite marriage, half-frozen and silent. I stood in front of these strangers, like I was a writer, like I was queer. Suddenly, I felt like I was falling, dizzy, tumbling ass over elbow through space. My life had changed so much, too fast. This Taurus just wanted solid ground, meanwhile everything, and everyone, was new. I thought I might throw up or faint or make a run for the door. But it was too late for any of that.

"Thank you all for coming to this special, first meeting of the Out in the Desert open mic," I heard myself say in a bold voice that filled the Rainbow Roll. Whose voice was that?

There was scattered applause. It felt kind.

I said, "Today we are inviting writers who identify as LGBTQ+ to read work on any topic. You can read for up to four minutes, tops."

"How much time do bottoms get?" called a fit young man wearing a Palm Springs Pride tank top.

The laughter broke the tension.

"How about you, Paula? You gonna tell your story?" Sky called, from her seat at one of the tables.

I loved her, although I hadn't said so, yet—but at that moment, I could've killed her.

She grinned because she knew all of that.

Ruby was first at the mic: "My name is Ruby Orr and I am a poet, an old Southern lady, and a slut—the order depends on the day. I should have come of age in Paris, France, 1920s, *les années folles*, with the artists and musicians and free thinkers. But for me, it was late 70s Atlanta, Georgia. Intellectually, I felt isolated, but I sure did have fun going out dancing. Everyone was a little less hopeful than they were in the 60s. That can be liberating. And we had the Pill but no AIDS, yet. For once in our lives, we just had fun, flirting and fucking and—"

"Yes!" Sky whooped.

"I trust my heart's infinite contradictions and fluidity," Ruby continued. "I trust its anger. As a poet, I cannot possibly believe in binaries. I must reject cheap answers to complex questions. I fall in lust, regardless of gender. My poem is called, 'Contrasted.'"

When she was done, Seth stood and approached the mic. This reading was intended for LGBTQ+ writers, but who said Seth was straight just because I'd only ever seen him with women? I realized, now, how much we assumed about other people. How much I assumed, and about myself, too. But we were all a current, temporary version of ourselves, subject to change. There was no telling, by looking at someone, all the different ways they were human.

"I am Seth Gladstone, and I am a disgraced former somebody. I wrote plays that were performed in L.A. and New York, where a few people actually paid money to see them. They featured characters who are now out of fashion, but they were my friends: rich, white, well-educated urbanites. Everyone's favorite villains, these days. But they were also human beings who existed. I'm going to read a monologue from my last play, 'The Seduction of Anger,' which was generally misunderstood by critics. They seemed to think my point, that anger is a destructive emotion that corrodes feminine beauty—not just physical—was somehow a sexist take. From there, it was a slippery slope, as I became yet another victim of the Millennial generation's cancel culture."

"Ok, Boomer," called a Millennial from the back row.

They had introduced themselves to me earlier, name and pronouns: "I.M., they/them." I remained mesmerized by their enormous, magnificent hair. It was a thick, wide, bleached-blonde bob. Real or wig, I could not tell and did not care. They clutched a piece of paper and were due to read next.

"Quiet, children," said Seth. "And, by the way, fuck you—I'm Gen X."

To that, there was finally some laughter.

Seth said, "The monologue I will read is from the second act, where the main character, Amber, is so consumed by radical feminism that her friends give her the nickname Anger. Celibate and furious, she glows with rage, not realizing how irresistible this makes her to men. As she delivers this monologue, she enjoys the afterglow of a rather extraordinary lesbian experience—her first."

Then he read a bunch of porny-sounding stuff, basically Amber with some red-headed barista named Cassandra together in a Starbuck's supply closet performing every possible sex act and position possible between two women, as far as I knew. I could tell he was pissing off some of the older lesbian couples, who had introduced themselves when they arrived and commended us for creating something worth coming into town for. I hoped they did not walk out.

I.M. waited until Seth was all the way back in his seat before they walked up to the mic. I listened hard but could not really follow the words. I liked how they sounded. I remembered some images: a child, sitting alone on a split rail fence in the desert, watching a crow high in the sky, flying back and forth over the fence. There was a lot of alliteration: boundaries, binaries, blueberries, blue tits. I glanced at Ruby, who I figured was a poet and would know if it was any good. She was listening, but her face gave nothing away.

An older man in a rumpled suit introduced himself as "Harmony, formerly Harmon, he/him." He read rhyming couplets to his beloved husband and muse, with him tonight as he was with him always. They had not spent more than a day apart in thirty-two years, he said.

I knew Seth was silently mocking the sentimentality—I could tell by the tilt of his head as he listened. I could see the meanness already congealing in response to this sincerity. I hoped he would keep his mouth shut.

The last name on the clipboard was Sky's. She did not tell me she planned to read. She walked to the mic with her usual confidence, but I saw some tension in her shoulders. Her expression was serious. She stood at the mic with her feet planted.

"Hey, everybody," she said, and we murmured back our hellos.

Softly, looking down at her phone, Sky read: "The ballerina feigns weightlessness. Like a vine, she springs from earth, twirls into the dancer as if he must secure her. But she is rooted. As a girl, she found her footing in dirt. She leapt from boulders and was received by girls like her, impact absorbed.

This dancer may drop her, but she will not fall."

I loved the sound of her voice. I wanted her to read it again, right away. I wanted to consider each word. Just in time, I remembered to clap, as Sky returned to her seat.

The open mic ended a few minutes shy of 6:00, and Sky quickly got the music and lights going so people would stay and skate. She danced in place behind the counter as she rented out skates and made change for the vending machines. Once in a while, she caught my eye and blew me a kiss or winked and everyone noticed.

The old hit "Funky Town" got people on their feet and skating, bouncing, and dancing. Everyone but Ruby and Seth and the husbands in love, who stayed in their seats and watched the action. The place started to fill with locals and a few tourists. One couple was there all the way from Germany.

When there was no longer a line at the skate counter, I went over.

"You going to skate tonight?" Sky asked.

"Sure," I said.

Everything and everyone was new, and my life was so much better.

"What's your shoe size?" she asked.

"Ten. I need long feet to counter-balance my height."

"Well that's just science," Sky said, smiling at me like I was the best thing she'd seen. She reached up to touch my face.

I was not used to public displays of affection, but I liked that.

When I laced up my skates, Sky guided me to the rink while the opening, electronic strains of Chic's "Good Times" soared through the speakers. I tried to keep my limbs loose, knees bent. I found the beat and concentrated. Sky and I moved together, slowly, as I got my feet under me.

It was easier than I'd thought it would be. My legs remembered ice skating on frozen ponds in Connecticut. I was not exactly dancing, but I was moving to the beat. The body remembered, adapted, and evolved, I thought. It was always in flux.

Sky and I were wrapped in color and lights and music and laughter and a rhythm pulsing through a crowd of poets and writers, people who felt deeply and noticed everything, the music uniting us in that way it can, sometimes. We skated in a cluster of people, everyone wanting to be near Sky because she must be magic, to dream something like the Rainbow Roll into being.

And she wanted to be near me.

I hit my stride and we lapped the rink arm in arm, hip to hip, dancing to the beat on roller skates as if we were still the kids we were when these songs came out, as if I didn't have a stiff neck, and Sky didn't have the battered feet of a former professional dancer. After a while, Sky pulled us to the side to rest. She pressed me into the boards with a kiss.

"I love you, by the way," she said.

"I love you, too." I was relieved to finally say it.

I bent to kiss her again, our arms wrapped around each other, slow and easy, as if we were alone. I slipped a little, on my skates, but she held me steady. With Sky, I did not mind being taller. I was not looking for someone to make me feel tiny, not anymore. I knew Sky wanted me to be as big as I could be—big, brave, and honest. She wanted me to be myself.

I felt something shift in me, realizing I was loved like that. I got a glimpse of how big love could be.

Sky took a step back and I saw that there were people all around us.

"I guess I just came out," I said.

She laughed, "Out of what?"

I noticed Seth, watching us from where he sat alone at a table. When did Ruby leave?

When the desert outside grew dark, people turned in their skates and headed home. Soon, it was just me and Sky skating, the lights and color swirling over us and the empty warehouse.

"One more song and then I've got to get back to the motel. I have a load of sheets that need to go in the dryer. I wanted to wait until it was cooler."

The next song came on: Diana Ross, "I'm Coming Out."

"Finally," I said, laughing.

Sky spun me around and around until everything was a dazzling blur.

Show Me What I'm Looking For

Gerry

By the time September rolled around, I was officially withdrawn from NYU. My legs were long healed but the rest of me wasn't there yet.

I got a job as a Brand Ambassador at Big Deal warehouse up near Bridgeport. It was a crazy commute, so I wasn't around Aunt Paula's subdivision much anymore, except to sleep. That gave me an excuse to stop meeting Rav for our nightly walks. They were awkward now, after everything that happened between us. He thought we were cool because I said we were.

"We're still friends, right?" he asked, the last time I saw him.

I was stuck on the word, "still," but I nodded and said, "Sure."

In any case, I walked plenty, all day long, at Big Deal, back and forth across the warehouse, in costume and posing for pictures with customers to promote whatever brand spent the most marketing dollars with us that week. I loved being in costume, hiding in plain sight. My size was actually an asset, because I filled out the taller costumes like the Oscar Meyer wiener, Vlassic pickle, and Heinz ketchup. Rick the Assistant Manager told me that Corporate retired the Dole pineapple when Trump took office—too exotic.

Today was the monthly Fresh Family Farms Day. This time I was a pig, a wooly pink giant on two legs, but the kids seemed to like it. I walked down the paper goods aisle and there was a mother who wanted me to pose with her little girl. We stood in front of the sixty-roll packs of toilet paper. I did what I hoped was a friendly pig pose: one hoof resting lightly on the girl's shoulder, the other on my hip.

A man standing some distance away snapped his fingers to get my attention. He was skinny and short but held himself like a big man. His royal blue Best Buy polo was tucked deep into belted khakis. His face and hair were pale.

"Where do you clowns hide the Meow Munch?" he called to me. "I need Chicken flavor, not Turkey, which is all you got on the shelf. My cat Alexis thinks the Turkey flavor is garbage. I am not going home with fucking Turkey."

The girl's mother fussed with her phone, and the Best Buy guy said to me, "Are you listening?"

Gary—that was his name, I found out later—would end up asking me that a lot, in the months to come: "Are you listening?" He did not like how I was usually off somewhere inside my own head. He was a grump with a heart of gold, I told myself. He loved his cat Alexis, maybe more than me, but that was okay. There were worse men I could hook up with, right? Probably I was too messed up for someone better. Probably Gary was what I deserved.

In my cheeriest cartoon voice, I gave my line: "Oink, oink, the freshest pork comes from Fresh Family Farms."

Gary raised his eyebrows.

Click! Finally, the mom took a picture. I looked down at the girl beside me.

"Oink, oink," I said, hoping for a real smile.

My headpiece tumbled off and smacked her in the forehead. It landed on the floor, near tubs of grape jelly.

She did one of those little-girl shrieks. The Big Deal warehouse went silent. The only sound was the swoosh of automatic doors leading to the parking lot. They opened and in blew the wind and dry leaves.

The mother yanked the girl away, like I was dangerous.

She shouted at me, "What's your name?"

"Gerry."

They stormed off, the mother holding a bag of frozen peas to her daughter's face.

An old playground chant echoed in my ears: "Ger-ry Gi-ant!"

Gary from Best Buy saw everything.

"They got you dressed like a farm animal," he said.

"I didn't—did I? Hurt her?"

"She'll hate pigs for a while, she'll get over it," he said. "I bet it's an interesting story, the one that ends with you working here, dressed like a pig."

"I'm big."

"Compared to what?" he said. "My name's Gary. You gonna show me what I'm looking for?"

Transmission

Paula

Deputy Key made it clear: I was not off the hook. Also, he loved my coffee. He drank most of a carafe at the Hi-Dez without showing any effects—he still moved deliberately, conserving his energy. Seth caught sight of him through the window and turned to walk back down to Room 6.

"I just want to understand," said Deputy Key, "all these connections. Bob Marshall, the man who sold you this motel, turns up dead this spring. On fire, in fact. And your former tenant, Fern Frankowski, your girlfriend's ex, ends up a mummy or something real close out on your land in Joshua Tree. And Joshua Tree is where your husband supposedly went missing."

"Supposedly?"

"It's uncanny."

"So you've said."

"I will have more questions," said Deputy Key.

"You always do."

He left, promising to see me again real soon. He obviously found me suspicious, but of what, exactly? Serial murder, really?

Already it was almost noon. I had lost so much writing time to his unannounced visits over these last couple of weeks. Otherwise, after the success of the open mic, surely I would have made progress on my novel. Without Deputy Key breathing down my neck, I would have figured out the plot, the characters, and what I was trying to say.

I could see why he had questions, but he had to remember that this desert was a place bodies turned up now and then, long before I got here.

The dull truth was that I was innocent. I had nothing to do with anything.

The phone rang at the front desk.

"Hi-Dez Motel," I said when I picked up.

"My name is Darcy Orr and my mother Ruby is a tenant of yours," said a woman with a Southern accent. "I have not heard from her in almost two weeks."

"Oh, I thought you two were estranged," I said, before I could stop myself.

"We are. Doesn't mean we don't talk."

I tried to remember but couldn't be sure—had I seen Ruby since the open mic?

"I'm flying from Atlanta tomorrow. Have you seen her? Do you check in with your tenants periodically?"

"No, I—"

"Where in God's name could she have run off to, this time? What kind of a mother makes her child worry like this?"

"The worst kind," I said.

———————

The next morning, Seth and I were alone in the Hi-Dez front office when Darcy entered, looking cool in a preppy, Southern way, if a little rumpled from the flight to Palm Springs. Her blond hair was smoothed off her face by a polka-dotted headband. She wore white capri slacks and rhinestone-encrusted flip-flops. Her toenails were polished pink.

Seth got up to offer us the table, but instead of leaving and heading back down to Room 6, he took my seat behind the front desk. Was he looking out for me, or had Darcy caught his eye?

Darcy and I sat, and I noticed Seth's toast crumbs and a smudge of butter. Darcy did not see it, though, and rested both pink elbows on the table.

"My mother is selfish," Darcy began, "but this time she has really upset my poor Daddy. Honestly, she has put him through enough. I would like to go to her room and see if I can figure out where she is."

"Sure, I guess," I said, getting up to reach past Seth to the desk drawer with all the room keys.

"I'm just having a hard time understanding how you could go almost two weeks without noticing that one of your tenants is missing."

"I'm not a housemother," I said.

I was no one's mother.

I heard Seth shift in his seat. My seat.

The truth was, I had not been around the Hi-Dez as much, lately. Maybe I had not been around enough. I was usually with Sky at the Rainbow Roll, neglecting everything else, like a lot of us do, at first, when they fall in love. I ignored emails and let the motel's front office sit dark and locked. I got a couple of bad reviews for that on some new "hip rustic motels" site, but I did not care. I was already thinking of converting the whole place to long-term housing for local writers so it would officially be a sort of writers' community. A writers' community hosted by a graphic artist who intended to write a novel but might never. A community like what Aria tried in upstate New York. Maybe, like Aria's place, it would be great for a while.

Lately, when I got tired of washing sheets and towels; waiting around for deliveries of coffee, toilet paper, and bleach; being the person everyone called when their old wall ACs froze up, or when ants, scorpions, or tarantulas got into their rooms; when I got tired of all that, I thought about selling the motel. I could just walk away, I reminded myself. I could walk away from this motel, this desert, this whole absurd, embarrassing idea of starting all over at midlife. I came out here to run a motel and write a novel, nothing I knew how to do. It must have been the wine I substituted for weed, back in Connecticut, that made it seem like a good idea.

Darcy said, "I've been in contact with a San Bernardino County sheriff—Deputy Key, do you know him?"

"As a matter of fact."

We walked down to Room 4. Beside the door was a line of small, peachy-tan rocks, all of them vaguely heart-shaped, all of them collected by Ruby on her walks. I wondered if Ruby ever took me up on my offer to visit my property.

I wished I could remember if I'd seen Ruby since the open mic. I was ashamed that I'd been too busy, too wrapped up in new love to notice much.

As I turned the key to Room 4, I thought about what Ruby, or any of us, owed family. What did we owe family who disapproved of us, who called us ridiculous? Did Darcy deserve to be let into her mother's room without permission, just because she was worried?

I stood in the doorway as Darcy went through her mother's things. She seemed irritated by the clutter, like she was the mother inspecting her teenaged daughter's room. It sent me right back to Connecticut and all the conflict I had with my mother, growing up. It always started with my room, a chaotic mess compared to Pearl's. The state of my room was a symptom, I knew that, even then. I wanted her to see: this was how it was, inside me. I wanted my mother to ask me, "Are you okay?"

I knew Gerry wanted the same, from her mother.

In Ruby's room, books and papers were stacked on both sides of the bed and on the dining table. There were dirty teacups in the bathroom sink. But the bureau was cleared off, save for one overstuffed manilla folder of poems, secured by a thin, green rubber band. Tucked beneath the band was a sticky note that read, "Transmission: New Poems by Ruby Orr."

Darcy did not bother reading the poems, but she looked at everything else. She pawed through papers strewn here and there, mostly Ruby's scribbled notes to herself. There were stacks of poetry collections, anthologies, and pamphlets—work by Ruby and other poets alive and long dead.

"Everything is research, to her," said Darcy.

I think she meant it as criticism.

"Your mom is great," I said.

"She does not behave like she is someone's mother."

"What does that mean?" I asked. "How should she behave? Are mothers supposed to be quiet and disappear?"

"I'd settle for quiet," Darcy said.

Darcy opened every drawer in the bureau. They were mostly empty. Something in the bathroom made her say, "You have got to be joking."

She would not say what she found.

"Her Prius isn't here, obviously," she said, "and neither are her keys. I can't find a wallet or anything to suggest she is coming back."

"This looks like a finished manuscript," I said, pointing to the folder on the table. "She wouldn't leave that behind, would she?"

"You might be surprised what my mother will do for dramatic effect. Especially if it could boost book sales. My mother is brilliant but vain. She has a mean streak – most people don't see it. She left this behind on purpose, for me. I'm supposed to mail it to her publisher. They will know how to market this as her final manuscript, found abandoned in a shabby motel by a rebellious poet-activist, lost to the desert."

"Lost?"

"My mother has a history of leaving when things get dull or difficult. I'm sure she is just fine."

Darcy stood before a corkboard on one of Ruby's walls and examined everything pinned to it: articles from science journals about mutating viruses; full-color printouts of microscope slides. I skimmed them and got the gist: The CDC is closely monitoring... On alert... A matter of time. Climate change, and not for the better. We encroached on wilderness and wildlife and now we pay the price.

"Sometimes, it is hard to see our mothers as women," I said. "It's hard to forgive them for that."

Darcy did not say anything right away. Finally she said, "I just want my mom. I want the mom I need."

"Of course you do," I said.

Darcy took a deep breath and looked around the room. "Maybe she will come back."

"I can give you one of my nightly rooms, no charge."

"I'm down the road in the better—I mean, bigger—motel, she said. You know, the chain one. I had points," she said, not meeting my eye.

"I get it," I said.

No one should stay where they would rather not be.

When I returned to the office, Seth was still at my desk. He got up to give me the chair and returned to his usual seat at the table. He was worried about something; I could tell by the way he raked his hand through his hair.

"Paula, I had no idea you kept our room keys in an unlocked drawer like that. Anyone could break into these rooms. Did Ruby know about that drawer?"

"What? Why?"

"I think maybe she was angrier than she admitted, about me and Fern. Hell hath no fury and all that. Ruby confronted Fern outside my room, the night Fern and I were together. I'm surprised you didn't hear."

I remembered standing silent in the dark, a few rooms down, eavesdropping in my own motel. I heard.

"What are you suggesting, Seth?"

"Maybe Ruby stole the key to Room 5 and let herself in and… did something. Hurt her."

"'Hurt her?' Jesus, Seth. Ruby?"

"I don't think you realize how high and inflexible her expectations are. For other people."

I said, "That doesn't mean she is capable of violence. She is a tender-hearted poet. Remember how she defended Fern when you criticized her? She said she was drawn to wounded creatures. And anyway, Ruby is tiny and has to be in her early sixties. You think she murdered Fern, hoisted her body into her Prius, drove out to my property, where she then dragged Fern's body into the rocks?"

"Maybe she lured Fern out there. Maybe Ruby had a weapon."

"Oh come on. You think Ruby was jealous of Fern because Fern slept with you? Once?"

"Maybe Ruby couldn't get past what Fern did: stealing poetry. Intellectual theft. She took that sort of thing very seriously, I'm telling you. Ruby has lots of friends in this town. She has lived here a long time. I think it's likely that she is behind what happened to Bob Marshall, too."

"Seth," I said. "Bob Marshall sold land to a discount chain. It was a dick move, yes, but come on. From what I heard, Bob was otherwise an okay guy. Ruby loved him, didn't she?"

Pain flickered across Seth's face.

"How can you have been involved with Ruby and not know who she is?" I asked. "Ruby is a sweet, empathetic, curious, and expansive woman, liberated before her time. She is a good enough poet that she doesn't care what the bad ones are up to. She knows that she gets to have her say in her poems. She's had lots of lovers and you and Bob Marshall were just two of them. You did not change who she is. Ruby Orr does not need to kill people."

"You don't know anything about her," Seth said. "Not really. Ruby knew that Fern desperately wanted to be a real poet. She knew that Fern wanted her forgiveness, not so much for sleeping with me, but as a poet. For existing, for writing anything at all. Maybe she found herself in a spiteful mood one night and invited Fern along for a drive. Ruby drives out to your property all the time—you know that, right? I mean, you did say it was okay. She described the silence out there as 'so heavy it is erotic'."

"Now that sounds like Ruby," I said.

———————

Darcy filed a missing person's report and sure enough, the next day, Deputy Key was back.

"We meet again, Ms. Winger," he said, when he showed up with a younger deputy and a forensics guy looking to search Ruby's room. "In regards to yet another missing person associated with this motel and/or its current owner. It is downright—"

"Uncanny?" I asked, opening the desk drawer to retrieve the key to Room 4.

The forensics guy noticed what he thought might be blood on one of Ruby's heart-shaped rocks and took all the rocks as evidence.

The police soon determined that it was not blood on the rock, but a sunbaked squirt of Del Taco's Del Inferno hot sauce. They were irritated that we disturbed the room, but like Fern's room, Ruby's showed no signs of foul play. The women were here and then they vanished.

Seth said I did not really know Ruby, but I had read her poems. Had he? Ruby's poems questioned everything. They made it clear: she meant no harm but knew she had caused it. Over the course of our lives, we each caused harm, hopefully not on purpose. Ruby's new poems were bound together in an empty room, unread by her daughter. I doubted Darcy had read much if any of her mother's work. Darcy could not try to understand her mother, because if she did, she might have to forgive her.

Now Deputy Key was back again. And again, he enjoyed the free Hi-Dez coffee. He added a packet of sugar to his cup, and then another, and another. He stirred with a wooden stick until the crystals melted and he took a short, careful sip. He stared straight ahead, long legs tucked beneath the table. His walkie talkie beeped and crackled.

He said, "Ruby has not made contact with her husband."

"I thought they we separated."

Deputy Key blew on his coffee. "Still, it seems odd."

"I don't think so."

"You don't think it's odd?"

"Not for them. Ruby is… unconventional."

"So I've heard," he said, taking a careful sip.

"What does that mean?"

"She sleeps around," he said. "All due respect to my elders."

What a dick, I thought but obviously did not say.

Seth came in, looking somewhat more pulled together than usual. He cleared his throat and approached Deputy Key.

He said, "I have some information I would like to give. Formally."

"This is about as formal as I get," said Deputy Key. "Why don't you sit down?"

Seth poured himself a cup of coffee and sat down across from Deputy Key.

He said, "You already know that I slept with Fern Frankowski, and that sent Ruby into a jealous rage."

"Okay," said Deputy Key.

"It is always terrifying when a woman finally reveals her true self—you know what I'm saying, sheriff?"

No, the sheriff did not know.

"Somehow, I'd thought the great poet and activist Ruby Orr would be above petty jealousy. But she lost her mind when she found out about Fern. Ruby could not stand that girl. What might even Ruby be capable of, in a moment of humiliated rage? Of course, I hope I'm wrong; I hope Ruby did not lash out because I broke her heart. I will take some responsibility for that. But she gave me the power to hurt her."

Seth talked to Deputy Key for a long while. More than anything, I think, Seth wanted someone to talk to. Deputy Key was silent as he scribbled notes, which was perfect, because Seth just wanted to talk.

———————

That night, Jasper's familiar, dark blue BMW rolled back into the Hi-Dez parking lot, and I was filled with dread. I did not want to hurt his feelings. We were good for each other, for a while. That was it. Why would be come back again now? Couldn't he feel how far apart we were?

"Relax," he said, when he walked into the office. "I know you're with someone else."

"A woman," I said.

He raised his eyebrows. "Well now. Actually, that does not completely surprise me."

"Really?"

"Why? Does it surprise you?"

"A little. I don't know if 'surprise' is the right word."

"Listen, I just wanted to tell you in person that I won't be driving back and forth to Riverside anymore. My dad and his lady friend broke up and he's moving back to Phoenix. I'm on my way to help him pack."

I did not expect it, but I was sad. Jasper and I were not meant to be, but he was always kind. He was always safe. He reminded me that there were options besides mute, touchless marriage and anonymous flings. There was a sexy haven between lust and love that could hold a person just long enough to remember herself and relearn trust. How could someone in your life be that important and then suddenly gone?

I said, "I'm going to miss you. A lot."

"I'm going to miss you too, Paula. It was good for a while, right?"

"Really good. Jasper, I will always—"

"I know," he said, and a rare blush bloomed through his dark stubble.

"Can you stay for a cup of coffee?"

"Dad's expecting me."

"Shit, so this really is goodbye?"

He nodded.

"Shit," I said again.

I hugged him hard. We held onto each other like that for a minute, and then we let go.

———

Seth found me at the laundry shed, folding towels as usual. They were getting awfully thin, and I meant to replace them, soon, with better ones. I had all kinds of plans to improve the Hi-Dez.

I was a little high from my morning writing session and the half a joint I'd smoked in the process. I wasn't writing a novel, but I wrote other things. Some mornings. All sorts of things: I wrote a very short story about a middle-aged woman who walks into the wrong room. I wrote fragments of erotica and monologues from characters who preferred to keep things private. I wrote plot-thickening banter, and old-fashioned letters between characters, like Gerry and I wrote. I stopped questioning whether it added up to anything. I knew it did not. But I kept going anyway. I decided to trust whatever this compulsion was that kept me wishing and trying. Whatever words arrived, I wrote them down.

Seth said, "Terra has another article in today's paper."

He had the local newspaper's front page open on his phone. He read, "'As reported this summer, the burning body discovered on property belonging to the Bureau of Land Management, northwest of Joshua Tree's dry lakebed, was identified as Robert (Bob) Marshall, longtime Yucca Valley resident and former owner of Joshua Tree's Hi-Dez Motel, currently operating under new management.'"

"Wasn't she supposed to be writing a book about pot?" I said.

"'Sources in the San Bernardino County sheriff's department confirmed that, approximately one year ago, shortly before Mr. Marshall sold the Hi-Dez and various land parcels, he was under investigation by their Vice team for suspected felony pimping and pandering.'"

"What?" I said, dropping the towel I'd been folding. "Say what now?"

"'Charges were eventually dropped when investigators concluded that Mr. Marshall was, at worst, guilty of looking the other way as sex workers rented rooms for the purpose of prostitution.'"

"This won't be good for business."

"Are you even bothering with those two nightly rooms anymore?"

"Not really," I admitted.

He returned to his phone: "'While the public was not made aware of the investigation, the pressure obviously took its toll on Bob Marshall. He reportedly developed a dependence on alcohol. He lashed out at family and friends and wrote a letter to the editor of this newspaper that went viral. It is reprinted here in part:

"'I thought I lived in the American West where a Man was still free to make a dollar without being scolded by a bunch of hypocritical Whiners. I've lived here forever, longer than most of you people, and I did my part guarding my acres of pristine desert habitat. For years I kept it out of the hands of you L.A. types who build overdesigned boxes with too much glass to rent to tourists for $600 a night so they can take selfies. And when it wasn't you rich posers, it was the corporate jerks, offering to pay me whatever I wanted so they could build another drive thru. But at the end of the day, you can't ask me not to retire, which I can actually do now, thanks to Who Gives a Buck. As for any party with their nose out of joint about alleged promises of land or anything else—I don't know what to tell you. Women hear what they want to hear.'"

Seth lowered the paper. "I forgot about that letter to the editor. That old prick. Now we know why he was in such a rush to sell the motel and get out. He knew he was in trouble. When nobody saw him for a while, we all assumed he'd finally fucked off to Nevada or Arizona."

"I guess he never made it," I said.

Seth looked surprised. "I guess not."

I started folding towels again. I only had a few more. Then I would load them on the supply cart and deliver them door to door, like I was trying to be someone's mother.

Whatever this motel was before, it was good now.

Seth said, "Ruby must have known what was going on here at the motel. She lived here."

"There has to be an explanation."

"The explanation is that people present a sanitized, summarized version of themselves, but there is a deep darkness in all of us."

"Does the paper say how Bob died?"

Seth skimmed it and then read aloud: "Exact cause of death remains undetermined, but because the body was tampered with post-mortem, Bob Marshall's cause of death was recorded as a Homicide."

"I guess the 'how' doesn't really matter. It doesn't change anything."

"I'm sure it matters to his family."

"Do they mention his family?"

Seth looked back at the article, then read: "'Mr. Marshall is survived by four ex-wives and five children, none of whom claimed his physical remains when contacted by the county coroner."

There were all kinds of reasons a person might end up alone in the desert, lost in their own deep darkness.

————————

When we got back to the front office, Deputy Key was sitting at the table. He'd helped himself to coffee.

"Two bodies and now a missing person, Paula," he said. "Bob Marshall, Fern Frankowski—"

"I thought you were waiting for the official ID," I said.

"—and Ruby Orr. Your second tenant in less than a year. And then there's your husband."

His tone pissed me off. After a half century as a woman on this planet, I was tired of men's veiled threats.

"It's like the Hi-Dez is some sort of magnet for trouble," Deputy Key continued. "Or maybe you are the magnet. What did you have against those people, is my question."

"Nothing. I don't hurt people. Not on purpose."

"I assume you are following the paper's investigative series on Bob Marshall, written by that tenant of yours, Terra Firma?"

"She was supposed to be writing a book about pot."

And in walked Terra Firma, a stack of newspapers under her arm.

"Thought your guests might like copies of today's paper," she said, placing them in a neat stack on the former breakfast buffet. "Free of charge. I bought them across the street, at the gas station. It's owned by a lovely immigrant family. You should shop there."

"We do," I said. "They have great sushi."

"Eew, really?" said Terra. "Sushi? Anyway, I wanted to be up front about my latest freelancing gig, for the local paper. I'm actually writing about Bob Marshall—"

"Deputy Key was just telling me."

"I'm sorry, Paula. It all came together very quickly. I did not mean to blindside you. I don't think having the Hi-Dez in the news is necessarily a bad thing, though. I make it clear that the motel has a new owner."

"I thought you were writing a book about pot."

"Yes, that too. Technically it's about the legal cannabis trade, the movement to purge all past nonviolent convictions, and police reform."

"Well, ladies, I will leave you to it," said Deputy Key, and he stood and walked away.

As soon as he was gone, Terra said, "Tomorrow's paper will report that Ruby Orr, your tenant and Bob Marshall's former lover, is a person of interest in his murder. Apparently Ruby was the last person to be in contact with Bob, and they were having a lover's quarrel shortly before he disappeared. I'm just saying—she had motive. You'll have to read the rest in tomorrow's paper."

"Let me ask you something: How would Ruby possibly manage to kill and—for God's sake—burn a big man like Bob Marshall? She had every right to be mad at him. It is always worse when good men let us down. But an angry woman is not necessarily dangerous, and she probably isn't crazy, either."

Terra said, "There are several people of interest. I guess the San Bernardino County sheriff's department has some questions for you, too."

"Okay, Terra Firma, I'm closing up the office, so…" I picked up her newspapers, put them in her arms, and followed her to the door.

"Your husband disappeared out here, too, right, Paula? Is that why you moved out here? To look for him?"

"No," I said, closing and locking the door behind her. "The cops out here already know my story," I said through the glass.

"There's always more to know!" she said, smiling and turning away, walking back to Room 5.

I regretted renting her a room. But Terra was just observant, like any good writer, I imagined. She was curious. She watched and listened and remembered.

Another Version of Myself

Paula

Sky and I lay across her futon where we'd ended up, sweaty and spent. The room was dark except for twinkle lights around the window and the moonlight streaming in.

I'd filled her in on Ruby's disappearance, Darcy's visit, and the questions about Ruby—the insinuations—from Terra Firma and Deputy Key. I did not mention my final visit from Jasper. She took it all in, and I knew it was a lot. She nodded as I talked, listening hard. When I was done, I wondered if she would have questions for me, too, but she just leaned in for a kiss.

Now she rolled over to the upturned crate that was her nightstand and retrieved a small paperback book.

"Check this out," she said.

The cover was an x-ray of someone's neck. The vertebrae were twisted and out of alignment. Printed across the cover, in a font meant to resemble a doctor's messy handwriting, was the title, Blue, and the author's name: I.M.

"I.M. is that poet who came to the open mic, the one with the big, blonde hair? It's their first book, a mini collection—a chapbook, I think they called it? Their publisher wants to rent the Rainbow Roll for a reading and launch party. Isn't that cool?"

"Very cool," I said, opening the book.

The poems were just a few lines each, the words spaced across the page, as if the desert winds blew around and between them. I flipped through, reading lines here and there that caught my eye. The child sitting alone on a split rail fence was back and watching.

"It's a queer publishing collective in the Coachella Valley and it sounds like they could help us draw younger skaters from down the hill."

I said, "Well, the desert is everywhere in these poems. And it's queer because I.M. is, I guess?"

"Not just because of that."

"I don't get the book's connection to roller disco."

"I think they just want to have a party. Share the joy."

"Maybe that's it," I said. "I don't get the book's connection to joy."

"That's her neck, on the cover," said Sky. "Shit, I mean their neck. I need to do better with pronouns. The young queers are impatient with their elders, not like I blame them. What do you think?" she asked. "I.M. wants to do a short reading and signing. I figure that's your department."

"Why?" I said, sitting up.

"Because you are my favorite local queer writer."

"I'm not a—"

"Maybe you need to give yourself permission to be imperfect. To do it wrong, or messily, or too slowly."

"To do what?"

"Everything," she said. "Give yourself permission to do, say, and be everything wrong."

I looked at her, and I realized I was searching her face for the withheld truth, the bad news, the announcement that she was leaving me, just like I knew she would.

I said, "It's not just that I feel dishonest, calling myself a writer."

"I figured."

"You keep calling me queer."

"Yes."

"For all my life, I called myself straight."

"You're still worrying about this?" She reached out to stroke my arm. "Babe, you are definitely not straight. Not anymore. What will help you accept that?"

Why was I having trouble? Did some small part of me not want to be gay, or bisexual, or whatever I was now? No, truly. That wasn't it.

"I think it's about identity. About having to move into a whole new identity at age fifty, just when I was settling in for the long haul, thinking I knew myself a little. Something like this makes me wonder if I knew anything."

I thought of all the different women I had been, over the years: artist; aunt; women's community member; wife to men. Almost mother. Why had I assumed I would stop changing at some point?

In Sky's bathroom, I looked into the mirror and whispered, "Queer. Paula, you are queer." I repeated it a few times, to get myself used to the sound of it.

It felt…okay. Clearly I could not go around calling myself straight anymore. "Queer" felt closer to the right word for myself—if a word must be found—than "lesbian." Hadn't I disqualified myself from that? I could not see myself using Ruby's word, pansexual, since I'd only just learned what it meant. To me, it felt grandiose. I was just a fifty-year-old woman, with a past full of men, who fell in love with a woman. "Bisexual" seemed old-fashioned, like people were one thing or another, but I had long since stopped believing that anything was black or white. Everything was shades of gray. Or hues on a spectrum. Fifty years of life had made me humble. Maybe each of us was a blend, in varying proportions, of everything a person could be.

Queer it was, then.

I could not resist the smile on Sky's sweet face. She watched as my thoughts churned. She waited and stroked my arm. Sky trusted me when she had every reason not to. How could she not worry that I was a straight lady having a midlife crisis? Experimenting or taking a temporary break from men, toying with her heart? And then there was Deputy Key with all his questions, implying that I was guilty of being something worse than what I was: a middle-aged woman who fell short of expectations.

I wondered then if I had made it clear enough to Sky, how much I appreciated her trust, how deeply I felt about her. How sure I was. I vowed to treat her like a queen and never leave her.

(She would leave me—that much I knew. Eventually I would make her leave me, like the others before. Until then, I would enjoy every moment.)

I said, "I.M. could read from the book for, say, twenty minutes. Give us some context, the backstory, how she—"

"They."

"Shit, sorry. How they came to write these poems, the inspiration for the collection, and then we could get into their thoughts about the high desert's gay scene—"

"Don't say 'gay scene,'" said Sky, trying not to laugh.

"Okay, what it's like to be a queer person in the high desert. And then maybe we could have an open mic and invite people to—"

"It all sounds perfect. This is your thing, Babe. I want you to do it your way. I'll take care of the skate party afterwards."

I snuggled up close to this woman I loved, who took it for granted that I was capable of things I had never imagined, of being someone new. My heart flopped around, every time I was near her. I felt like I understood Sky, and she understood me. And she loved me, anyway.

It made me uncomfortable, sometimes, how she searched my face for the girl I once was, before men looked at me and I felt them looking, before I let them make my choices, before I hitched shame to my belt loops and let it drag me down.

I wanted to say, "That girl died before she was born."

Sky had danced beside men all her life, and her feelings about them were less complicated.

With Sky, I was another version of myself, again. We talked about how it was, to be women in a man's world. To be diminished. We talked about definitions and labels and how sometimes a person just wants to be, as they are, without explanation.

"Thank you, Sky," I said, grabbing her hand and bringing it to my lips for a kiss. "I mean it. For seeing me the way you do. I never would have dreamed. I'm having so much—"

"Fun?"

I nodded.

"Right on," she said.

"You're opening up new worlds for me," I said.

"Speaking of opening up…"

She reached for me, and we kissed, and I was gone.

Sky trusted me, so I would trust her, and this, how my body responded, how my heart flopped around. Again, despite everything, I would trust this hope I felt.

I Am a Pink Bath Bomb

Gerry

Gary and I became a couple pretty quick. He hated driving all the way to Aunt Paula's house in Greenwich, so I moved into his studio apartment near the Bridgeport train station, which was closer to Big Deal anyway. It was above an old hamburger joint, and everything stunk like grease.

Mom said I should get an office job because it would look better to NYU when I reapplied. I did not plan to reapply, but she didn't know that yet. So now I had an office job, Assistant Buyer for *the country's #2 bath & body retailer.* Mom wanted me to quit Big Deal, but I kept a couple of weekend shifts a month. I was still happiest in those costumes.

Gary and Gerry: I knew it sounded dopey. I knew we looked dopey when we went out together. He was tiny and I was big—big as a man, while he was small as… what? A woman? I was always relieved when we lay down.

Gary said I was a weirdo and uptight. He didn't like me talking to other guys. He knew what happened at NYU because I told him. I regretted telling him, afterwards. He made a face and looked at me like I was crazy. "Crazy" was a word he used a lot, about me. He said I was lucky he was a patient man..

Gary did not want to hear about my "college-girl problems," as he called them, but he was very interested in the two full leg casts I'd worn. He ran his fingers through my leg hair, which I'd left long and soft ever since the casts were removed. He wanted every detail: Did the plaster chafe? Itch? How did it feel to be completely incapacitated? Weighed down. Were my legs braced by a horizontal bar? He wanted me to describe my legs when they first emerged. He was less interested in how strong they were now.

It was just so hot, he said, the idea of me helpless like that.

I left him playing video games and closed the bathroom door to start a bath. I stuck the rubber stopper in the drain.

I had a pink bath bomb that I planned to toss in, once the water ran hot. It was sitting on the edge of the sink, swaddled in hot pink tissue, trimmed in gold and printed with the name of my new employer. This was not one of the free samples I got as a perk, sometimes. This was part of a retail package valued at roughly $35.00 that I stole from the warehouse when I was down there looking for the Receiving supervisor. I was known for my big, baggy clothes.

I unwrapped the bomb and slipped it underwater. The water blushed as it fell apart. The bomb had a red core, turned out. Once it dissolved, I lowered myself into pink water, careful not to slosh any over the sides as my large body displaced it. My leg hair waved underwater like kelp. Red swirled around my legs which, if anything, were bigger than before, certainly stronger.

The water's surface was skimmed with oil, and the air was scented rose and pomegranate. Salt settled to the bottom. I massaged some into my shoulders, chest, legs, and arms. Anywhere I felt dead skin.

The week after I moved out of Aunt Paula's, someone made an offer on the house. Below ask but not insulting. Something Aunt Paula could live with and be free.

I sent her some stuff I stole from *the country's #2 bath and body retailer*, although she always said the only thing she wanted was for me to come visit. I wanted to see the desert; I did. I did not know why I didn't just make plans and do it. For Aunt Paula's last birthday, I sent her a set of floral hand lotions with a card saying I would visit soon.

Was I always a liar? I was not always a thief. I started out with good intentions. I was hired as an Assistant Buyer Level II, meaning I placed replenishment orders for low to moderately priced items with steady, flat, year-round demand. I educated myself on the industry to improve my predictive skills. I researched the slip-and-fall concerns with bath oils, and the branding challenges of bath salts (what with a street drug of the same name). I formed well-founded opinions about whether traditional bubble bath would ever make a comeback, really, and if the scent of lavender-vanilla was iconic or a mass-marketed cliché.

At home, I made dollhouse furniture. Gary worried about my lack of ambition, and so did my mom. Gary was practical, and I needed that.

He said, "Everything I needed to know in life I learned on the sales floor. Like: tell people what they want, because they don't know."

He said big women intimidated men, but it would help if I smiled more.

I liked building a miniature world within a dollhouse, where I was in charge and decided what went where. I worked in a flimsy chair meant for the beach, at a table on our screened-in porch, the smell of meat rising into my nose from the hamburger grill downstairs. I bought bags of raw pine beads from the craft store and carved dozens of them into tiny apples. I was capable of more intricate carvings, but the apples kept my hands busy so my mind could wander. When I laid them out on screens and painted them red, they looked like drops of blood

All day and into the night, trains rattled past, to and from New York City, a place I was not ready to go back to. I wanted to stay here in Connecticut and make art, like Rav.

Some nights, after Gary fell asleep, I left the apartment and walked alone through the dark, city streets of downtown Bridgeport. I liked walking after it had rained and pulled down more autumn leaves. From a distance, I knew I looked like a man. I counted on that to keep me safe.

One night, I walked past a fancy French restaurant, and I saw by its candlelight that it was decorated throughout with enormous glass bowls filled with ripe, red apples; yellow lemons; green pears. Real food, posed in abundance, as décor.

At the end of the week, I saw all that of that uneaten fruit was in the dumpster in the alley behind the restaurant. What would Rav do, I wondered?

The next morning, when a prep cook arrived to open up, he was surprised to find the doorway strewn with dozens of tiny, red, wooden apples. I watched from across the street as he stepped over them to get to the front door. I hoped this qualified as an inconvenience that made a point. And that Rav would approve.

Aunt Paula thanked me for my stolen gifts with handwritten letters where she rambled on and on. She wrote them over a bunch of days, using different pens. The paper smelled like sage.

Keeping my hands dry, above the bathwater, I reached for Aunt Paula's letter from where I left it on the closed toilet lid. So far I'd only read the first half. It seemed like Aunt Paula was a lesbian now? Although she never actually said that. She did say her relationship with Sky had nothing to do with her experiences with men, but that they were on her mind. I re-read the last few paragraphs, to make sure I understood—that guy Jasper made it possible for her to love Sky? It kind of sounded like Aunt Paula had lost her marbles, out there in the desert. She was becoming strange in ways I knew would freak out my mom. I would not say a word.

I kind of wanted to be Aunt Paula. I mean, I wanted to be like her, when I got old.

"Love doesn't always show up looking like what you expected, or what you are told to want," Aunt Paula wrote. "Expectations are problematic in general, wouldn't you say? Gerry, will you die of embarrassment if I write about sex? Something happened between me and Uncle John toward the end of our marriage. Or rather, something stopped happening. It was not my choice. We lost a baby, or the promise of one. Maybe that was the reason he would not touch me, or one of them. All I know is, it messed me up. For years I was convinced that I was unlovable, or at least unfuckable. John let me keep on believing it, as if it really was my fault. I don't think he meant to be cruel, but he was a coward. John 'Elbow' Bowen, beloved local TV newscaster and everyone's friend, had secrets. Like we all do. And one of John's secrets was that he was a coward. He could not forgive me for causing him pain, or for seeing him hurt, or for asking him to talk about it. He retreated further into himself until he was barely a shadow. Then he left and never came home.

"Sex saved me," Aunt Paula wrote. "Men I didn't know helped me recover from the men I did. They reminded me that I existed, when I had started to doubt, because they saw me perfectly well, waiting for them in the produce section of Whole Foods."

I flipped through the rest of the letter to see how much more was left. Good grief, Aunt Paula. Go write your novel already. FYI, the genre is Gritty Mature LGBTQ+ Western Feminist Romance or something, so good luck finding a publisher. But for your own sake, you should write it.

Aunt Paula wasn't the only one better at giving than taking advice.

I skipped ahead a couple of paragraphs:

"…Jasper gave me the chance to reconnect with my deeply passionate nature. It was neglected by the time I met him. And at times before, it was abused. I was at mid-life and taking stock, I guess. And because Jasper and I expected nothing from each other but honesty and great sex—"

I stopped reading and skipped ahead, again. I flipped over the page:

"We push stuff to the back of our minds to remain open to men, romantically and sexually. We have to. Good guys forget we can't spot them at a glance. Anyway, my point is—"

At last, her point.

"Gerry, you must stay open to love without expectation. Stay flexible and willing to transform. People can and will change you. In good ways."

I put the letter back on top of the toilet seat and shifted lower in the tub until my head was submerged in pink water. My knees stuck straight up and steamed in the cold air of the bathroom.

"Home is what holds you," Aunt Paula told me once, a long time ago.

I didn't really get what she meant.

I wished I could float away from my body, but I was wedged in tight. I wanted it to dissolve like the pink bath bomb, now nothing but oil and salt. But there was no escaping this body. It would always take up space. It would always be big.

But this body was mine, and, at least tonight, it was warm and soft and scented rose and pomegranate. I stood and pulled the plug. The bathtub drained noisily, with a slurping sound, which was good because then Gary would not hear me crying.

He would not ask, "What now?"

When I got out of the bath, Gary was deep into *Call of Duty*. I sat on the bed with my lap desk and stationery and favorite pen to reply to Aunt Paula.

"It's funny that we write real letters, like we're pen pals," I wrote. "Do you like this stationery? I had no idea where people bought this stuff, but I found it at Big Deal. Don't tell mom, but I still work there twice a month. You know I'm not really into talking about personal stuff, but thanks for telling me all that about you and Jasper. It's not like that with me and Gary. I mean, we have sex, don't get me wrong. But not like that. It's not making anything possible for me or whatever. Gary is always telling me he could do better. He doesn't really mean it, but it hurts my feelings. I'm too sensitive. I'm glad you like this woman Sky. I hope I get to meet her when I come visit, which will be soon, I promise!"

I signed my name and immediately wished I had a do-over. The "y" in my name had an exaggerated, open loop that looked, to me, like a greedy, needy mouth.

I shoved it in an envelope anyway, sealed it, addressed it to Aunt Paula and stamped it, so I would have to follow through and mail it.

Everything New and Possible

Paula

The house in Greenwich sold to a nice, normal family, the kind that would keep up with the yardwork. They insisted the red maple be cut down before closing, exactly as my realtor predicted. Gerry was long moved out, now living in Bridgeport with some guy she met at Big Deal. I did not like the sound of him, but my niece said she was okay.

In a few months it would be 2020, and it felt like everyone was ready for a fresh start. In just over a year, we got to vote for President again and maybe undo some damage. Somewhere, far from the desert, candidates debated. It felt safe to feel optimistic.

It was dawn when Sky shook me awake. "Babe, there is some new article by Terra Firma in today's paper, some kind of print exclusive. I just got a notification on my phone. I want to run across the street to get a copy before the gas station sells out."

"What?" I said.

Half awake, I felt around my nightstand for my phone. I accidentally knocked it to the floor and there I left it.

"Let's take advantage of the early morning," Sky said. "We are together in this magnificent place. We are so lucky. We can't take anything for granted."

She put down her phone to get dressed. I forced myself upright and out of bed. I walked to the bathroom.

Sky called, "You know, they say there are electromagnetic aberrations in the Park that become portals."

"Portals to what?" I called.

"I don't know," she said.

Sky sat on the end of the bed and pulled a pair of clean socks from the drawer I had cleared for her things. She wore jeans with a tank top. She shrugged on a long-sleeved shirt before I could touch her bare arms.

"Portals to another world, I guess," she said.

"Maybe John slipped into a portal."

"Let's hope," said Sky.

She left, and I shuffled to the kitchen. I ran water into Alan Alda's food bowl to soak off the remains of last night's Meow Munch.

I went to the closet for something to wear so I could join Sky on her spontaneous adventure. We were lucky; she was right. The joy I felt was terrifying. I vowed to do anything to keep a smile on Sky's beautiful face, even believe her when she said she would never leave.

Sky returned with the paper. "She's not implying anything about you," she said, relief in her voice. "We can look at it more closely when we get to the Park, but it sounds like all the attention is on Ruby, now. Obviously you had no reason to hurt Bob Marshall or Fern, for God's sake. I know how kind you were to Fern."

I wanted to say, "Sky, you have to believe me when I tell you I don't make people disappear. They turn and walk away."

I wanted to say, "I'm sorry I found Fern and that I was flip about it at first—not just because I was high, but because I was shocked." I wanted to tell her that I did love John, very much, for a long time. Even if did not sound like it, now.

I followed Sky to the front office, so we could make the coffee and get going, into the Park.

I wanted to say, "Sky, I grieve for Fern and all of us lost before anyone noticed we were missing." But it was early yet.

"Let's go," Sky said.

She drove and I chewed a cannabis gummy, because I wanted to relax and enjoy the Park with Sky, who knew me, even if others did not.

"People need time to adjust their lens," Sky had said, that night of our first kiss on a boulder behind Del Taco.

It was getting harder to remember how I used to see things.

Sky drove us in her truck up the long road to the ranger station at the Park's West entrance. She waved her annual pass and drove us through and then we were in it. The view opened up and I swooned, as I did, every time, from the vastness. On both sides of the car were endless, surreal variations of rock, rounded forms cut with jagged, geometric breaks, Joshua trees and yucca, cholla and all the other plants I did not yet know the names of. I was dazzled.

"It did not have anything to do with John," I said, out loud, to my own surprise.

"What didn't?" Sky said.

"My decision to move here. I mean, we both loved this place, but for our own reasons. I came here for a new life."

I remembered that when John and I first hiked these trails, I knew I was home. I did not tell John. I stopped to let him hike on ahead and then I listened to the pristine quiet, so absolute it was as if I had returned to the womb, the whole world muted. One by one, I let the sounds back in: the cactus wren, like a motor, trying to turn over; families of squabbling quail; coyote singing their welcome to the dark. In the shapes of these boulders, John said he saw eagles and men. I saw bellies, swollen with possibility. I saw the earth's formerly molten state, proof that phenomenal transformation was possible. It was natural. I wondered if maybe, someday, the desert would deconstruct me, as it deconstructed everything—wood, leather, steel, and even sound.

I said to Sky, "I came here alone and now I get a reboot."

"Rebirth," said Sky.

I let that word, rebirth, be what lingered in the air between us. I said nothing more as Sky drove us through Joshua Tree National Park.

 For years, I came out here alone, in different seasons, wanting to know this place better. I learned that bitter wind sometimes roared across this desert, and I could make friends with it or leave. I learned that it was a tough place to live, sometimes, but if it called you, you listened.

Sky parked at Cap Rock and we were in luck; there were not many people there. We sat at an open picnic table at the base of a large, freestanding mound of boulders. The largest was capped by a flattened rock, like a beret.

It was warm in the sun, but in the shadows, it was icy cold. The wind gusted and I was glad I'd brought a jacket. We sat and sipped coffee from our travel mugs. It was still piping hot, and I blew on mine as Sky read from the newspaper's front page:

"'Newly discovered text communications between Bob Marshall, whose body was found ablaze in north Joshua Tree this past April, and the poet Ruby Orr reveal that Ms. Orr was well aware of the illegal sex work occurring at the Hi-Dez Motel, and she did not care.'"

"Now under new management," I said, taking a sip too soon. I burned my tongue.

"'These text messages reveal that Ms. Orr did know that the motel's other residents, all younger females, were engaged in prostitution—contrary to what she told investigators at the time. She reportedly told Mr. Marshall that so long as they were all consenting adults, and Bob was not a client, she had no issues. She fundamentally disagreed with the criminalization of sex work. But she was not above using the information to her advantage.'"

"Terra is the one who should write a novel," I said.

Sky continued, "'Ms. Orr offered her silence in exchange for a small plot of land in Yucca Valley, owned by Mr. Marshall. She told Mr. Marshall that she wanted to build herself a small home and writing studio. Then, as many locals are aware, Bob Marshall sold the promised plot of land to the Who Gives a Buck Corporation.'

"'In Ms. Orr's last text message to Bob Marshall, sent shortly before he was seen alive for the last time, she accused him of playing her for a fool. According to sources at the San Bernardino County Sheriff's Department, who spoke to this reporter on condition of anonymity, Mr. Marshall's last known words were in the form of a reply text to Ms. Orr: 'That land was never yours, and neither was I. Best o'luck from your old pal Bob.'

"'Sources say Ms. Orr was incandescent with rage.'"

"Oh Terra," I said.

"'Now, with Ruby Orr missing, gone without a trace, her daughter Darcy and her husband—to whom she is still legally married, and who still resides in their marital home in Decatur, Georgia—are left to ask: Where did you go, Ruby Orr?'

"'Join us for a new, six-part podcast, "Where Did You Go, Ruby Orr," which'—oh, wait," Sky said. "That last part was an ad."

"Maybe Terra is too busy publishing articles to decide if she's a serious journalist or a tabloid hack," I said.

I tried another sip. Perfect. It woke me right up. I took in the desert views for miles in every direction. Then I closed my eyes and, as usual, realized I'd been holding my breath. I drew a deep inhale, "filling my belly with it," like they taught me at that Berkshires yoga retreat.

You would think, by fifty, I would know how to breathe.

"This does sound bad for Ruby," I finally said. "Wherever she is." I looked at Sky, the vast desert and blue sky behind her. "The Hi-Dez is going to have a sleazy reputation for a while."

Sky said. "It has nothing to do with you."

"The Hi-Dez has everything to do with me," I said.

Maybe Ruby was guilty of something, but I was innocent. Or, not innocent—I was still a big, bad woman, and someone would always be suspicious. Because I was divorced, or had gray hair, or because I made two husbands fall out of love with me. Because I had no kids. Because I let men do things they should not. Because I smoked pot and slept around. And now, because I was a lesbian or bisexual or whatever I was. Queer. Because I had sex at all, at my age. How embarrassing. Because I was too big to fit into other people's expectations or my own.

What kind of woman behaved that way?

The worst kind.

I said to Sky, "I know people see the Hi-Dez and judge it for looking cheap and a little run down. I can relate, you know?"

And Sky did know. She laughed and shook her head in protest, but she knew.

————————

It was a Mojave morning as easy and pleasant as the desert ever was—a nice surprise, since we were now deep into November. I was indoors, restocking the coffee bar. The Hi-Dez housed just me, Seth, and Terra. I wanted to fill the other rooms with writers who needed a place to stay, cheap and long term. I really was going to try and make this a writer's commune—or, not a commune, a writer's community. I did not know why I thought I could do something like that, but everything in my life felt new and suddenly possible.

It was quieter around the motel. Seth spent most of his time in his room. I felt him pulling away. It felt like we had hiked the same trail for a while, but now I wanted to set up camp and explore, and he'd turned off onto a loop that would bring him right back where he started.

I charged the lowest rent I could while still covering my mortgage and food for me and Alan Alda. I knew my tenants struggled to scrape together a few hundred dollars every month. I was not looking to get rich.

"I am a writer," I told myself in the bathroom mirror, trying to get comfortable with it, like I did with "queer." Sometimes I believed.

In my old life, in Connecticut with John, I usually ended up wishing I'd kept my big mouth shut. But now I had a lot to say.

This morning, Terra was first to stop by for coffee. She filled two coffee thermoses and stuffed stevia packets into the fanny pack she had slung across her chest. One cup in each hand, she nodded "thanks" and somehow used her elbow to gracefully open the office door and exit.

I heard her typing, all day long, every day. Every damn day.

Seth came in a few minutes later. He would not make eye contact.

"Oh shit, I forgot," he said, when he saw the former breakfast buffet empty except for the coffee carafes.

"Are you okay, Seth?"

"Nothing tastes right," he said. "Except coffee." He went over to pour himself a cup.

"And booze?"

"Not for a couple of days, actually," he said.

With his back to me, he said, "I have to leave. Move out, I mean. I'm sorry."

"Look at me, Seth," I said, and finally he turned around.

He looked like he might cry, like he had already cried today.

"Where are you going?"

"I got a job," he said. "I'm going to be a high school English teacher."

"High school?"

"Don't worry," he said. "I know better now. No students."

"Yeah, I'd say that's a good baseline rule."

"A college buddy of mine just opened a new charter school outside Atlanta. They have a lot more flexibility when it comes to hiring teachers with, you know. Baggage."

"Seth—"

"I just need to quit drinking and I will make good decisions. I know what will happen if I don't; I'll get crucified on the internet. I'll never get another play produced."

"I'm not sure that's the most honorable motivation, but you know what? Whatever works."

"There's another reason for taking this job; my daughter Patty and her mom live in New Jersey, so at least I'll be on the same coast."

"Will you be able to visit her?"

"That's up to my ex. But whatever happens, I'm glad I'll be closer."

Seth was a father; I almost forgot. "When do you start?"

"January," he said. "Let's go for a drive."

He put down his coffee and came over to where I sat at the front desk. He hugged me hard.

"I'm sorry," he breathed into my neck.

Seth knew the way, so we took his truck. I think he liked driving because he could talk without making eye contact. On our drives, I'd heard stories of triumphant opening nights, good reviews, critical acclaim. Once upon a time, he was noticed by important people.

"I was so close to being somebody," he said, on a long, hot drive out to Amboy, where we climbed inside a long-dead crater, all that remained of a one-time, red-hot eruption.

Today we were headed for Giant Rock. Seth drove north, away from Yucca Valley, away from the highway, through open desert framed in the distance, always, by rocks. It reminded me of the surface of the moon or Mars. How I imagined they looked. Seth slowed down when the road turned to sand, thick and sloppy. Goat Mountain rose high and sudden, and we passed it. I rolled down my window and let wind spit sand into my face, through my hair, which whipped around, obscuring my view as if I'd passed into a silver cloud.

I could not see, and I did not care. In my mind, I was sixteen again, tearing down some narrow, leafy road in backcountry Greenwich, Connecticut, too fast in my beat-up Chevy Chevette. It wasn't Seth beside me but my best friend Melody, our brand-new driver's licenses tucked into our LeSportsac purses that also held fake IDs, Binaca spray, and condoms. I sped around town, too fast, my little brown suitcase of cassette tapes open on Melody's lap. As each tape ended, she had the next ready to go: Mötley Crüe; Blue Oyster Cult; Def Leppard; Judas Priest; Quiet Riot. Van Halen. Ozzy. To me (and maybe Melody too?), heavy metal felt like sex, like screaming in a way that was okay, even for a couple of white girls from Connecticut. Melody liked guys with big hair and eyeliner. I liked guys with a mean look in their eyes. We never slowed down for the old farts in their Oldsmobiles and Mercedes, but swerved around them, honking as we passed to give them a jolt. I wanted to be as tough, cool, and beautiful as Nikki Sixx, or at least one of the models he dated.

Now, though, there was Seth, a man I could have slept with but did not, for once. In that moment, I was happy. I was ageless.

"How are you and Sky?" he asked.

I thought about how much fun I had with Sky, how we laughed and talked about everything, always losing track of time; how, when we danced, I was graceful; how I swooned when she looked at me; how I wanted to be with her all the time.

"Things are good," I said.

Seth stopped the car because we had arrived. There was no confusion as to which rock was Giant Rock: in the middle of a sandy clearing stood a single, enormous boulder, seven stories high. Beside it sat the chunk that spontaneously cleaved and fell away some twenty years ago. Some said it had been the world's largest freestanding boulder, until that happened. The sand was littered with broken beer-bottle glass and blackened campfire coals. Giant Rock was tagged with layers of graffiti, which spilled onto the smaller, surrounding rocks: names, hearts, dates. One rock had "MAGA 2020" scrawled in red.

I said to Seth, "Why do people do that? They see some amazing natural wonder and their first impulse is to deface it."

"They want to claim it," Seth said.

"We want to feel superior to everything else on earth," I said, "but this shit just proves the opposite. It's a damn shame," I said, looking around.

"Look closer," said Seth.

He put both hands on Giant Rock and moved in close, as if listening. He closed his eyes, so I closed mine too. I put my palms against the rough, sharp rock that I had learned, from another of John's guidebooks, was igneous quartz monzonite. It was considered sacred or magic (was there a difference?), and who was I to say it was not true, because I could have sworn I felt a jolt from where my hands made contact, up through my arms, into my chest. Did I really feel that? I kept my hand where it was on the rock, to be sure. I had heard that this was a special place, supposedly a spiritual vortex at the intersection of "ley lines," whatever those were. An access point for extraterrestrials, if you believed in that sort of thing. I liked the idea of believing in aliens, but life on Earth was wild enough for me.

Seth opened his eyes and walked some distance away. He sat down in the sand and kept still in the rock's long shadow. After a while I walked over to join him.

He dug a joint and lighter out of his pants pocket. He wore a pair of Dickies work pants he'd picked up at a thrift store, splattered with someone else's white paint. He got the joint going and passed it to me. It smelled delicious and strong, and it was: I drew the smoke into my lungs and held it and then exhaled through my nose, slowly. I sat in the sand and enjoyed the feeling of surfing this moonscape without leaving the ground. I was where I belonged.

All my questions, fears, regrets; my shame… I drew them with the smoke into my lungs, my body, until I could no longer bear the pressure. Then I expelled everything with a deep exhale.

Seth said, "Some people live and die without ever hearing silence this complete."

A jet came into view overhead, tiny in the far distance, a long delay between sight and sound.

Seth laughed. "Well, there you go," he said, stretching out carefully so he didn't cut himself on the green and brown shards sticking up from the sand. He propped himself up on his elbows.

Squinting up at the sky, he said, "I should have listened when you said

I was drinking too much. All my life, I have listened to the wrong people. Starting with myself."

I said, "Fuck, I love this rock so much." I was high and suddenly emotional. "She is so breathtakingly, astonishingly big. She is so big that she is sacred. She is huge, enormous. She gets stared at. She couldn't blend in if she tried. Of course some people treat her like shit. They treat her like something to scrawl their names on or smash bottles against."

"You think Giant Rock is female?"

"Oh yes," I said.

———

Somehow it was December already. I sat in my room at the Hi-Dez and watched though the window as the bulldozer arrived on a flatbed truck. It pulled around back, to the empty lot that maybe got Bob Marshall killed. Someone had decked out the bulldozer with reindeer antlers. The lot was dense with cholla and creosote, and I expected they would clear it down to bare sand. Who Gives a Buck built roomy, stand-alone stores. This would be the 299th Who Gives a Buck. They'd already filed permit applications for the 300th, ten miles down the road in Joshua Tree.

Hart Flat Road and the side entrance to the Hi-Dez parking lot was partially closed to traffic, which would have been inconvenient if I still had nightly guests checking in and out. I looked out my window and thought about how, from now on, I would always see traffic along that formerly quiet dirt road. Discount shoppers would drive up and down all day. Nothing would be the same, here or anywhere. There was no getting back to normal, because the only normal was change. It seemed there was no returning to anything, in life.

I tried not to dread what was coming or hate the man who operated the bulldozer or blame him for what its claw pulled from the earth and tossed aside. My tenants would probably find it convenient, having a Who Gives a Buck in their backyard. I tried to be glad for that. That land was someone else's story. I had to hope this desert would survive us – us, meaning people.

I turned from the window to my computer, open on the table. My novel was finally in progress. Every morning, lately, with a fresh, hot cup of coffee, a glass of ice water, and maybe a couple of puffs on a joint, I added more words. It was my story, but only abstractly. Only emotionally. Every morning, I put on my reading glasses and wrote my way through my old life. My old lives. Slowly but surely, I wrote my way to the future.

Gerry and I mostly texted, now, communicating more often than before. I tried not to ask too many questions. I knew how badly she wanted to trust me. I knew she wanted me to be someone she could tell the truth, all the stuff she kept to herself because she did not want to upset anyone, or bore them, or irritate them, because how could she think she had problems, compared to other people? She did not want anyone to think she was crazy, weak, sad, or lost. I thought about the weight Gerry carried like saddle bags, like a yoke—I knew the burden and comfort of weight like that. It was grounding, some defense against the darkness we did not want to bother anyone by mentioning. I wanted Gerry to bother me.

Gerry could not trust Gary, not completely, that much I knew. Whatever it was she saw in that small man, I could not see it from here.

Gerry wrote that she was back full-time at Big Deal warehouse. *The country's #2 bath and body retailer* fired her when she was caught stealing merchandise from the warehouse floor. I did not ask if she was guilty as charged. I remembered the fancy lotions and bath bombs.

We texted about politics, a little.

Once, she texted out of the blue, "Aunt Paula, I hope you don't mind me asking, but how do you identify, now? Did you turn gay or were you always?"

"LOL, don't say 'turn gay,'" I wrote back.

But I did not want to scare her off, now that she was talking. I texted that I did not know how to answer her question, but I would try. I told her how I arrived at "queer," and that every person's experience was different. My path might be less common, but it was not strange. Maybe I was always queer and just had not met the right girl. Maybe I was not always queer, but things changed, like things always changed. I told Gerry that I did not mind living with unanswered questions. And anyway, as soon as I was sure about anything, it shifted and became something new.

I opened the door to the Rainbow Roll feeling excited. I'd expected to be nervous, but I wasn't. Tonight was I.M.'s book launch and I felt almost confident about hosting. It helped that Sky would be there, catching my eye, flashing that smile. It helped that the desert was my home now. These were my people. I had not realized they were missing, but I found them.

The Rainbow Roll felt a little more serious with the house lights up. The yellow linoleum at the front showed its scuffs, all that history. It felt right for a literary event. Sky had already set up folding chairs in three short rows around the podium.

"This is perfect," I said. "Enough chairs to make it look inviting, but not so many that it will be embarrassing if we get a low turnout."

"We won't," Sky said.

I took my time reading the copy of *Blue* that I.M. gave Sky, and now I understood what I.M. was trying to say in those poems they read at the open mic back in August. The poems were part of a larger series, or story: a lifelong, psychic conversation between crow and human child, who did not stay sitting on a split rail fence but retreated indoors and almost died from despair. Thankfully they could always hear the crow, a shrewd scavenger who recognized opportunity, who recognized the child, neither boy nor girl, all through their growing up. The crow soared unbothered over split rail fences, walls, all boundaries. It told the child to fly away, because we get to be who we are in this life, not what others expect.

"Please help me welcome I.M., who is here to celebrate the publication of their debut poetry collection, *Blue*," I said, standing at a mic before the crowd who filled the chairs just right, leaving a couple free for latecomers. The audience listened with respectful attention.

I continued, "It is a semi-autobiographical fable constructed of queer, desert poems that are both poignant and defiant," I said. "I mean, that's what I got from it."

I.M. nodded gratefully from the audience before coming up to take my place at the mic. They looked good up there, and something else... peaceful? The audience was a mix of Rainbow Roll regulars, friends of I.M., and some younger queer writers and their friends up from the Coachella Valley, curious about any poetry reading in a place calling itself a queer roller disco. Some members of the publishing collective that produced the book were there. Terra Firma showed up to cover the event for the paper.

I.M. read beautifully, taking care with each word without getting precious about it. They read the spare, plainspoken lines, free of meter or rhyme, in a voice high and clear, a blurring of pitch. It was obvious they listened carefully to the words they read. They remembered why they wrote them.

Afterwards, the audience clapped enthusiastically and then I.M. opened the floor to questions.

"Who or what is the crow?" I asked.

"Exactly," they answered.

Murmurs of appreciation for that answer rippled through the Rainbow Roll. Hands shot up with more questions. Terra stood and headed for the door. Afterwards, several people bought a copy of *Blue*: $16.00, cash only, with half the proceeds pledged to a local mutual aid society. I.M. was elated.

A couple of people came up to tell me they hoped the Rainbow Roll would have more literary events. As everyone drifted away with their signed copies, Sky got the lights and music spinning: ABBA's "Take a Chance on Me." Nostalgia and an easy beat got a surprising number of poets and their friends laced up in roller skates and out onto the rink. I.M. brought their own skates from home: battered silver that reflected the Rainbow Roll's swirling colors. The skates had pom poms and wheels that lit up. I.M. skated with friends and kind strangers who had listened and heard. I looked for Sky in the crowd of skaters. I found her looping the rink alone, skating up to and chatting with one group of people and then another, checking in with everyone to make sure they were all having fun.

Sky was probably too good for me, I had decided. But I was not about to tell her that, which only proved I was the worst.

I walked over to the rink and I.M. skated up to say thank you.

"I can't believe it! Is it okay if I give you a hug?"

They were a little unsteady on their roller skates, reaching across the rink's plexiglass boards, but I anchored us both. Their body was small in my arms.

I could do this, I thought, for writers like me. I could help other people tell their stories, and I could tell mine.

"I wanted to ask if you had any vacancies at the Hi-Dez Motel," I.M. said.

"The owner of the house I share with a few other people gave us notice that he's turning it into a vacation rental. They all found places, but I—"

"Room 3 is yours," I said. "The Hi-Dez is glad to have you."

When I.M. skated off to rejoin their friends, I looked up to see Sky watching me from across the rink. She smiled because, although she could not hear what I.M. and I said to each other, she could see I.M.'s joy. And mine.

"Everything was perfect," I said later. "Wasn't it?"

"It was," Sky said. "Are you surprised?"

"Yes. And one of my empty rooms was filled by a local writer who needs it."

"A local, queer writer," she clarified. "Like you."

Sky told me to sit as she wrangled a couple of people to help her stack the remaining chairs. It made me uneasy, to sit while others worked, but I was tired, suddenly very tired. I was exhausted from the adrenaline spike and now, the crash. I'd felt high while I hosted the event, standing up there in front of everyone like I knew what I was doing, inviting them all to look at me, like I did not know I should hide.

It was hard to believe, just a few hours later, back at the Hi-Dez. I looked at myself in the bathroom mirror and thought, Who is this person who looks and sounds like me but is happy?

I remembered the child in I.M.'s book, and the crow, and I thought that maybe I was flying now, too, above fences and everything else, in a clear blue sky that looked even more beautiful up here than it did from the ground.

ID, Please

Paula

January arrived, election year, and 2020 had me giddy with hope. Love and happiness coursed through me like a new drug. I was finally writing the novel in earnest. When I was deep in it, it felt like exploring underground, excavating my own past while writing the stories of characters who showed up fully formed, or nearly. With Sky by my side, in this new place, this new life, anything was possible. We could move past Fern's death and Sky's complicated grief. We could accept Ruby's disappearance and what she maybe got away with. I could forgive those who found me suspicious.

Nothing smelled like hope like clean laundry. I rolled the cart, stacked high with fresh sheets, blankets, and towels still warm from the dryer. I was on my way down to Room 6 and from there I'd work my way back up. Room 6 was now home to Daniella, a recent high school graduate from somewhere in the Midwest, whose family told her she was not welcome so long as she insisted on using that name or wearing those clothes. I knew she was intensely private, and I tried not to bother her much, but I always loved when she answered the door and gave me a glimpse of what she had done with the place: Seth's old dark cave was somehow transformed into a bright, clean, airy studio, with bamboo mats, succulents, twinkle lights, and gauzy curtains.

Daniella wore a figure-hugging, pale-yellow tracksuit that set off her dark skin. I stole a look at the bright, sparkling room behind her.

"I'll change it back when I move out," she said.

"Please don't," I said. "I wish you could do this for the other rooms."

"Oh, I would do each room differently," she said, taking a stack of linens from the cart and ducking back inside.

"We should talk," I called through the closed door.

Daniella opened the door again quickly. The stack of linens was on the round table.

"I'll bring the dirty ones to the laundry shed."

"I'm serious, I want you to spiff up the other rooms," I said. "If you're interested, I mean. I can pay you a little and of course provide materials."

"Yeah, maybe," she said, and closed the door.

The Hi-Dez felt strangely different, with Seth gone. Not necessarily in a bad way. I missed my friend, such as he was. I hoped he wasn't doing anything stupid at that charter high school outside Atlanta, anything I could not forgive. I missed the familiarity of his routine, but I was learning to live without familiarity in general, these days. I told I.M. to put out the word that I had another room available for a writer in need of cheap, simple housing with clean sheets, blankets, and towels included.

I pushed the cart up to Room 5 and heard Terra tapping away at her laptop. She came to the door looking distracted if not dazed, her attention turned deeply inward, how she always looked when she was writing.

"It's unbelievable, right?" she said.

Terra lifted a stack of linens from the cart and clutched them to her chest, propping open the door with her hip. Behind her, Room 5 was clean as always, laptop on the round table, bed neatly made. On the bureau, she had fresh flowers and ripening avocadoes. I looked at the wall where Fern once stacked cartons of her unsellable books.

"Unbelievable?" I asked.

"Oh, I thought you read my article? In today's paper, about Fern?"

I shook my head.

"Anyway," Terra said, "they found Fern's car a couple of days ago, abandoned way out in the Mojave National Preserve. They asked me not to make that public until today, so they could process the evidence they managed to get. But the car was stripped: catalytic converter, stereo, even the doors, all four tires, the leather seats! What no one took was Fern's book, *Desquamation*. Investigators found it on the floor on the passenger side. It was signed and dated by Fern and the cover gave the cops a usable fingerprint. Well, today I reported that the fingerprint was a match for one notoriously abrasive L.A. poet, very active on Twitter. He was one of the first to get the #BurnFern hashtag going. He had a quill pen as his profile picture, so no one knew what he looked like. They just arrested him at a cigar lounge in San Diego, where he barely made it out the door before tearfully confessing. First degree murder. They say he convinced her to take him for a drive because he was a fan with a crush. Apparently he told her he had always wanted to see Joshua Tree, but in fact he was quite familiar with the area."

"He killed her because she plagiarized some poetry?"

"He had a long history of threats toward women, on and off the internet, and apparently he had become increasingly violent."

"Same old story," I said.

"Yes."

I knew this was why Terra went by a pseudonym, fearing for her safety because men on the internet disagreed with her, or disliked her because she corrected them. Now Terra had to report on Fern's murder, with all the details of how Fern was lied to and lured to a place where no one heard her scream. Terra knew it could be her, one day, tossed onto a pile of rocks, if she ever let down her guard.

"Terra, I know that you also—"

"I don't discuss it," she said.

"At least now you know this had nothing to do with Ruby. Or me."

Terra shifted her weight. The sheets and towels in her arms were getting heavy.

I said, "Someone should tell Deputy Key: not all women are liars."

Terra said, "There are still lots of questions about Bob Marshall. And, you know, Ruby's husband is missing, now, too. Some of their neighbors in Decatur, Georgia, told me they think Ruby probably surprised him out of the blue and used her feminine wiles to convince him to flee the country with her."

"Isn't 'feminine wiles' kind of sexist?"

"I guess so."

"I'll let you get back to work."

"Thanks, I'm swamped. I just got word that Doubleday wants me to write a book about Bob Marshall and Ruby, based on my series for the paper."

"Congrats," I said.

"Thanks," she said, watching me in case I was being sarcastic.

But I wasn't. Of course I was jealous as hell, but I admired Terra Firma, or whatever her name was.

She said, "That is, assuming I can figure out how to write the conclusion to a murder mystery with the main suspect gone missing in action. Meanwhile, are you tracking these reports out of Asia? This new virus?"

"What?" I said.

"Read a newspaper," she said, taking her door in hand, about to close it. "They sell them at the gas station across the highway."

She shut the door in my face. I had to admit, Terra was growing on me.

———————

"Last Night a DJ Saved My Life" bopped from the speakers as I entered the Rainbow Roll. The house lights were up; Sky was the only one there. The music was loud and she did not hear me come in. She was on roller skates, setting up chairs, grabbing each from a stack and twirling it around like a partner before setting it down gently on its four legs. Sky looked as powerful as always, beautiful and handsome. She wore jeans and a black shirt with rainbow lettering: "You Make Me Feel Mighty Real." Her jacket lay draped over one of the chairs, which she was setting up in rows around the podium, for the second Out in the Desert open mic. It created a sense of intimacy, even in this big, empty, high-ceilinged space.

Every once in a while, it occurred to me what a risk love was. How some of that falling at the beginning was realizing how badly you could get hurt. Love changes everything, and not everyone loves change. Real love was terrifying but worth it.

I loved Sky so much.

"Fuck!" she yelled, turning to see me standing there. "Babe, you scared me. Get over here."

She picked up a remote and turned down the music. It shifted into "Night Fever" by the Bee Gees. Sky drew me into her arms and we danced a little. She spun me, then pulled me in for a kiss.

She nuzzled her face into my neck and said, "You're going to read something tonight, right? You promised."

"Maybe," I said.

I was amazed by how Sky endlessly reconfigured the place to accommodate different events. She liked how the Rainbow Roll's daytime events were going: her dance classes; the Know Your Rights sessions; the short workshops and shows by local and visiting queer activists, singers, and dancers, everyone wanting to connect.

In my purse was a folded sheet of paper printed with something I had written late the night before. I was revising it up to an hour earlier. I was not sure I would read it or should.

"Did you see the news about Fern?" I asked Sky.

"Yeah, I saw the paper. It's so awful. She knew she'd fucked up. She hid herself away out here, but that wasn't enough for them. She knew no one would forgive her, but did she deserve this?"

"Of course not," I said.

"I feel like such an asshole. She should be mourned by someone who loved her."

"What about her parents?" I said, walking to the stack of chairs to help Sky finish setting up.

"They claimed her remains, that's all I know."

I said, "I read some of the things the suspect tweeted about Fern when her scandal first hit. The intensity of his hate was shocking."

"Men like him love having a reason to pile on," Sky said. "Nothing is more delicious to a misogynist than a woman who actually fucked up. A disgraced woman is an easy target."

"It's like she gave him an excuse."

"No," Sky said, "Fern is not to blame. That man who tricked and murdered her, he's the one to scrutinize."

"You're right."

Sky said, "I think about it, sometimes, all those days and nights Fern's body lay out there alone, exposed to sun and wind.

He left her out there like trash and didn't even have the decency to take the book he tricked her into signing."

"She wanted to believe she still had a fan," I said.

"Or that someone forgave her. Anyone. Fuck, I was hard on her."

Sky sank into one of the chairs. She checked the time on her phone: still a few minutes before people started showing up for the open mic. She exhaled and put her head in her hands.

"We are not responsible for everyone we date," I said.

"They had already silenced her."

"I know."

The front door opened, and it was all my tenants from the Hi-Dez: Daniella, I.M., and Terra Firma. It made me happy to see them hanging out together, although Terra was clearly the odd one out—or, more accurately, the straight one out. Daniella and I.M. were nonconforming in every way.

The sign-up sheet filled quickly with nine readers, including I.M. and Daniella.

"What about you, Terra?" I asked.

"I'm covering the event for the paper," she said. "I'm writing a review."

"Of course you are," I said.

Menopause had made me blunt. I'd passed the one-year mark and then some: my periods were over and done. I could not remember my last hot flash. I could not remember the last time I broke out in zits or was overwhelmed with emotion, like a teenager again. I no longer walked around feeling simultaneously angry, sentimental, and horny. Fuck, I was grateful to be done. I might never get back around to watching my mouth.

Two people passed us to take their seats, and I took the opportunity to excuse myself. There were a few new people who sat in the back rows, there to listen but not read, not yet. The first reader walked up to the mic in a shirt that rippled with blousy, poofy layers of pale blue satin.

"I like your shirt," yelled someone from the audience.

"Thanks, I made it. To accompany my poem," they said. Among all that pale blue, their face was white as the moon. "It's called, 'I Wander Lovely as the Clouds,' with apologies to William Wordsworth.'"

I realized I should decide whether I was going to read the piece I wrote. I was not at all sure I was ready. Why would I invite a bunch of stares, when all I wanted was to be invisible?

Because that was a lie. The truth was, I wanted to be seen. I wanted to see myself.

Daniella performed a powerful spoken word piece from memory. Her words felt like a confrontation. She was beautiful and furious and also sad, and I could not take my eyes off her.

I.M. read a poem from *Blue*, as well as a new poem told from the perspective of a single chunk of million-year-old monzogranite that had been knocked around by earthquakes, exposed by wind and water. When I.M. was done, the audience erupted in applause. I.M. was quickly becoming a local favorite among Rainbow Roll regulars.

After all nine readers took their turns, I stepped up to the mic and asked, "Does anyone mind if I read something?"

There were murmurs of "course not," and, "go ahead." Sky smiled at me from where she stood behind the last row of chairs.

I opened the paper clutched in my hand.

"I wrote this recently and decided to read it here, today, before I lost my nerve. The title is, 'ID, please.'"

I looked up from my piece of paper, at the audience, strangers who felt like my people. Everyone was respectfully quiet, mostly paying attention. Behind them was the dark, hushed roller rink, a noisy place gone quiet.

I swallowed and began to read:

"'How do you identify?' is a question I was asked, recently. It had not come up before. "Were you always gay?" they asked, and I had to take a moment to consider.

"I fled to the desert from a life of men to live out my days alone, and instead fell in love with a woman. What did it mean? Had I changed? Were there rules?

"I asked myself, "Well? How do I identify?'

"I identify as an animal, hominid, advanced primate.

"I identify as a creature of base impulses, and I identify as a highly moral person.

"I identify as a socialized human being who used to try harder to do things the 'right' way. I identify as an ex-wife, ex-slut, legal widow, happy girlfriend. I identify as a motel owner and commercial artist. Maybe a writer, too. I identify as someone who used to think she was too big.

"I identify as someone who distrusts easy answers.

"I identify as a woman who recognizes the woman in any human being who claims it.

"I identify as a human being with female reproductive parts, who has known the relief and agony of blood, who desperately wanted and did not want to be pregnant, at different times. I identify as no one's mother.

"I identify as someone who believes a woman's body is entirely her own business. Everyone's body is entirely their own damn business.

"I identify as someone who called herself straight, who said, 'Believe me, I wish I was a lesbian.'

"So, now, if I must, should, or want to identify myself with a letter from the expanded but still limited menu, I choose Q. The letter Q looks like a big friendly face with a jaunty moustache, an oval roomy enough to hold us all as we move together toward a better future, because progress may be slow and too often thwarted, but it is inevitable.

"I identify as a reclaimed slur.

"And with love, and hope, and fear, and courage, and more, so much more. Just like everyone else."

It wasn't until I was finished and people clapped that I realized how quiet the Rainbow Roll had been as I read. I'd felt the audience with me from beginning to end. Now I was light-headed, like my knees might buckle and I might fall. But I did not.

Before I returned to my seat, I invited everyone to stay for the Rainbow Roll's General Skate, 7:00-10:00 PM, starting in just a few minutes. As soon as everyone stood up to stretch and talk, Sky came over and wrapped her strong arms around me. She held me like that for a moment, and I almost cried into her short, silky hair. Then she stretched up to kiss my cheek.

"I'm proud of you," she whispered.

Terra came over to join us. "Very nice. Heartfelt."

"Thanks," I said.

Daniella and I.M. both stopped by before heading over to change into roller skates. They both said they would come to the next Out in the Desert, if there was one. Sky beamed at me.

"I liked your new poem, I.M.," I said. "I thought maybe you were saying we are each alone, together."

"I don't know that I was saying anything so much as asking questions. But I like your take."

"I'm gonna go hit the lights," Sky said, skating off to create more magic, another celebration of joy.

As much as I wanted to, I would never ask her to stay put beside me when she could fly like that. My heart clutched at the sight of her skating away. She moved away from me with grace and confidence. I lost my breath, like I'd been punched in the gut. Love is always a risk.

Later, when I told Sky I was headed back to the motel, she asked, "Should I come by after I close?"

"It's late; I'll see you tomorrow."

I could tell she was relieved. "Cool, babe, that actually works, because this guy just introduced me to his friends who dance, and they want to talk about doing a workshop for—"

"I love you, Sky."

"Oh babe, I love you too," she said, and she took me back in her arms for a long while. Hopefully, Sky would not become another person who left. How would I ever recover?

Back at the Hi-Dez, I pulled into the parking space right outside Room 1. I.M. had the door to Room 2 wide open. Daniella sat on I.M.'s neatly made-up bed, across from I.M., with Terra sitting stiffly at the table. Some sort of moody, ethereal music played from I.M.'s thrift store turntable. Terra spotted me first and waved me over.

I stepped into the room and saw that they each had a take-out container of sushi from the gas station. Daniella and I.M. had theirs carefully balanced between them on the bed. Daniella had a bottle of water, but I.M. and Terra drank glasses of the same boxed red wine Seth used to like.

Seth. How could someone be your friend, part of your everyday life, and then suddenly disappear and become a stranger? Did anything last? Could I lean on anything in this life and know for sure it would hold? Was there any solid ground, or was that another illusion? Some childish idea I should have outgrown before I was Gerry's age?

"Have a glass of wine," said I.M., pointing to the box on the table.

"I'm not much of a drinker," I said. "But I have a joint if you're interested."

I.M. smiled broadly. "My Connecticut mom smokes pot?"

"She does all kinds of stuff," I said. I did not add that I was no one's mom. "Do you have an ashtray?"

I.M. got up to fetch a small, round ashtray, amber glass with fluted edges. When I took it and looked more closely, I saw that it was very old, with a Hi-Dez Motel logo that must have been from before Bob Marshall's time. "Hi-Dez Motel" was printed in an Old West font, and the "t" in "Motel" was the silhouette of a Joshua tree.

"Ha! Where did you find this?" I asked I.M.

"That thrift store on the highway, same place I got the record player. Everything there is still old and cheap, not 'vintage.'"

"I love that logo," I said. "I design corporate logos. I mean, I used to."

Wrong life, I thought. This is your new life.

"I thought you were a writer," said Daniella.

"Sometimes," I said.

"You are a writer," said Terra. She stared at me with smug confidence, like she had studied me and had my number. "I hear you typing," she said. "I see that far-off look in your eye, like half of you, at least, is somewhere else, digging around in that manuscript, probably, oblivious to everything else. Yup, you're a writer."

I lit the joint and drew the smoke into my lungs. I'd looked forward to this since leaving the Rainbow Roll.

"Is that how I seem?" I asked.

"It's not a criticism," Terra said. "Just the opposite."

Exhaling, I passed the joint to I.M., who took a drag before passing it on to Daniella, who hesitated.

"Okay," she said, finally. "One little puff."

Daniella coughed as she exhaled and got up to bring the joint to Terra at the table.

"Would you like some, Ms. Firma?" Daniella said, holding out the joint which was smoky and burning too fast. I hoped Terra made a quick decision.

"Call me Terra. And no thank you," she said, holding up a hand. "I would, but I'm thinking of getting into politics."

"Really?" I asked.

"I like to keep my options open," she said.

I took the joint from Daniella before it turned entirely to ash. I drew more smoke into me and felt my body relax, unspool. I'd felt more anxious, more hormonal, as the day went on. I'd assumed it was nerves about reading my piece at the open mic, but now… If I didn't know better, I would say I had PMS.

I felt oddly disconnected, like I was watching myself from the outside. There I was, sitting and chatting with friends, strangers to me just a short time ago. I had just read something very personal, out loud, to a roomful of them. Now I sat in a Mojave Desert motel that was mine, somehow, where I lived in a single room and wrote daily and no longer bled monthly. I was disoriented but felt at home.

I.M. removed their platinum bob wig, revealing a shaved head underneath. They smoothed the wig over a wooden, egg-shaped wig rest. I handed them the joint for another hit.

Terra said to me, "There was a reported sighting of Ruby in Puerta Vallarta, did I tell you that?"

"Really?"

"Nothing came of it. Just her, they said. No husband."

I looked at Terra, leaning into her elbows on the table, beside the sushi take-out container she had re-closed to keep her leftovers fresh.

I said, "Why are you so sure that Ruby isn't a victim too? Not of murder but of rumors and innuendo."

"That's what she wants you to think," said Terra. "Ruby Orr is no one's victim."

But we are all someone's victim, I thought. Aren't we? And someone else is ours.

Back in my room, I changed into my warmest pajamas and washed and moisturized my face. Here in the desert, my skin was drier than it had ever been, maybe because of the rough winter winds, or maybe that was yet another thing I could chalk up to menopause. I'd felt myself withering a bit, lately. Shriveling into something left out in the weather. I was about to slip between my sheets when the phone rang. It was Pearl. What time was it in Connecticut? The middle of the night.

"I'm worried about Gerry," she said when I picked up. I could not remember the last time she'd called. "I have no idea what she needs," Pearl said.

My sister sounded desperate. I got up and wrapped a robe around me.

"She is so unhappy, Paula. She thinks I don't care enough to notice, but I do. I know she is unhappy with this Gary person—I mean, what was she thinking?—but she is also just miserable in general. I think maybe she always was. She was always so quiet."

"What does she say when you try to get her to talk?"

"Oh, I don't want to pry. If she wanted to tell me something, she would. Wouldn't she? Has she said anything to you?"

"I can't share what she tells me in private," I said, bending to stir Alan Alda's Meow Munch, to lure him back to the bowl. Lately he was losing weight, becoming angular and old. Alan rubbed up against me, then went to eat some more.

I said, "Gerry is doing better lately, I do believe that. She will be okay. I want to get her out here for a visit, though. I think she might like the desert. It might be good for her."

"Good for her, how? Oh, before I forget—I need to give you contact info for your old friend Aria. We ran into each other at the club and she asked me to pass it on. You know, Clay and I talked about whether you might be a lesbian, back when you moved onto Aria's commune or whatever that was."

My sister missed her husband. I could tell because, ever since she moved out, she had not mentioned Clay. Finally, she missed him. Pearl was lonely. It was after 1:00 in the morning, her time.

I let the word "lesbian" echo between us and then drop, ignored. My sister thought she had guessed right back then, and I decided to let her.

But my life of men was not erased by my love for Sky. My past was full of regret but not denial. For better and worse, it was all true.

"Aria wants to ask if her daughter can rent a room from you. Her name is Andante and she just finished college in northern California but already has a three-book deal with HarperCollins, writing 'queer YA,' is how Aria put it. She wants a quiet place to write while she gets over a breakup. With a girl," she added.

"Thanks, Pearl," I said. "I will call her in the morning."

"I'm trying to get used to all this, Paula."

"I know."

We stayed on the phone together for a little while longer, despite how late it was.

"I have one last thing to tell you," said Pearl. "I almost don't want to."

"What is it?"

"It's about John," she said. "A friend of a friend heard a rumor that someone thinks they saw him, alive and well, that son of a bitch, in some tiny town in northern Maine. Walking with some woman."

Oof.

"Do you want to hire someone? A private investigator?"

I felt a stab of grief, like nothing I had felt yet for John, a dull, rusty blade shoved deep into heart muscle. The idea, that he might have faked his... that he might have wanted out so badly...

No, it was unthinkable.

I tossed the phone aside as a soundless sob clutched my whole body. My sister stayed on the line, waiting for me.

No, what this was, was unlikely. John loved being a public figure. He would never give it up for me.

"This is just a rumor!" I heard Pearl call from where I'd tossed the phone.

John never wanted to cause a scene. Or be the bad guy. He would tell himself he was being considerate.

"If it turns out John is not dead after all," I said to Pearl, finally, bringing the phone back up to my ear, "I'm not sure I want to know. To me, he is dead. I mean, I have legal proof."

Dead or alive, John was gone.

The Worst Girl's Best Day

Gerry

February in Connecticut was icy and frigid and the month I wished I lived anywhere else. The Mojave Desert, for example. In her last text, Aunt Paula made another push for me to come out there and stay with her for a while.

"Not forever," she wrote.

I'd told her I'd lost my so-called "real" job at *the country's #2 bath and body retailer*, and that I was back in costumes at Big Deal. She knew I spent my free time hunched over dollhouse miniatures, which was a perfectly fine creative outlet, except that, for me, it was also about control, and Aunt Paula knew it. I made these tiny things exactly the way I wanted them, and then I held them tight in my fist. Aunt Paula knew things with Gary were not bad, exactly, but they weren't good enough.

She said she had one last empty room at the Hi-Dez. Apparently, the place had changed with the new tenants. The energy had shifted, for the better, is what Aunt Paula said. Deputy Key finally backed off and there were no other alleged sightings of Ruby in Puerta Vallarta or anywhere. Ruby was gone, in the wind, as they said on those cop shows, probably getting away with murder. Terra Firma was as busy as ever, but she lost her book deal with Doubleday, because what good was a murder mystery without a murderer? It wasn't like she could just make one up.

One Saturday evening we spoke by phone. "Remember I told you about my old friend Aria?" she said.

"The one with the lesbian commune in upstate New York?"

"It wasn't… yes. Anyway, she has a daughter, Andante, who is a writer and only a couple of years older than you. She just moved into Room 4."

"Wasn't that Ruby Orr's room?"

"And a lot of other peoples' before it was hers. Andante writes queer YA fiction," Paula said. "I think she has a crush on I.M., who does have a certain magnetism. I already told both of them that it's none of my business, they can do whatever they want, but they need to keep me out of any drama. I need 2020 to be the year things calm down at the Hi-Dez. I need to catch my breath after all this change."

When Aunt Paula announced that she was leaving Connecticut and moving to California to run some old desert motel, my mom thought her sister had finally lost her mind. I guess Mom could not understand what the Mojave Desert had to do with our family. Or how Paula could be happy living in a place that looked nothing like Connecticut. Didn't she get homesick? Now Paula was dating a woman. Mom thought maybe it was the agonizing not-knowing, for sure, what happened to John, that made Paula go crazy. Or maybe it was just menopause or a plain old midlife crisis that made Paula think it was normal to suddenly change so completely, her own family did not recognize her.

Aunt Paula's head might be spinning a little, but she was definitely happy. She drove herself from one life to another, with just an old cat for company. My aunt was brave, if crazy.

"I'm just saying, Gerry. There are younger people here who could be your friends."

"I don't really have friends," I said, but then I thought of Rav. I said, "I have to go soon. Gary will be home any second. I just wanted to say that I think you're right. I want to come to the desert. I know I need a big change, one way or the other. I don't want things to build up again to where something happens."

"Again," said Aunt Paula.

I pretended not to hear.

I said, "Maybe I could move out there for a little while? Not forever. I'm so sick of Gary and this tiny place. Maybe I should be where there is a little more room."

"That's great, Gerry. Let me know when you have a date in mind. Have you heard about this virus?"

"Of course," I said. "It's all over the news."

"Are you scared?" she asked.

That surprised me—my tough, independent Aunt Paula.

In my car, before driving home, I texted Rav: "I can't think of a good lie, so here is the truth: I am texting you out of the blue because I miss you. If you miss me, too, text back."

Before I could even reverse out of the parking space, his reply text pinged: "What are we, in high school?"

"How are you?" I wrote, rolling my car back into the space and setting the brake.

I saw the three little bouncing dots as he typed his response, proof he was on the other end of the line, that he was there, with me. I just had to be patient. I was so happy I almost cried.

March 4, 2020, was the day Governor Gavin Newsom declared a state of emergency in California due to Covid-19 and it was also the day I got my goddamn period. Again! After more than a year without. I thought I was officially, finally in menopause and now I was in a different state of emergency, because I had given away all my tampons. Months ago, I put the box on the supply cart and invited my tenants to help themselves. That was how sure I was that I was done.

I howled with dismay at the sight of blood, that old nemesis. So much for my newfound freedom. I ran across the highway to the gas station for whatever dusty package of pads they had jammed between car air fresheners and Pepto Bismol.

Damn it, I was pissed.

Soon there was talk of a stay-at-home order on the horizon. Everyone had to pull together, shelter in place, flatten the curve. The virus was set to roll across the U.S. and we all had to get inside. I was glad I'd already switched over the Hi-Dez to long-term housing, as motels and other short-term rentals were probably going to be forced to shut down for a while. I felt a sick dread in my gut that was probably cramps.

Suddenly, everything felt dire.

I could not risk Gerry getting stuck in Connecticut or shut out of California. I could not risk her getting stuck with a man like Gary. She thought Gary was the best she deserved. She told me he made fun of her sometimes, like when she worried too much. He slept while she walked the dark city streets at night and made art. He did not love her enough to realize how sad she was, or he did not care. He did not know how to help Gerry, and that was not his job, anyway. But maybe it could be mine.

It was now or never, if I wanted to do something for that girl.

I drove over to the Rainbow Roll to see Sky. I was flying out of Palm

Springs first thing the next morning. One brief layover and then I would land at La Guardia and drive a rental up to Connecticut. I planned to meet her at Big Deal, rather than Gary's apartment. In Bridgeport I would return the rental car, and Gerry and I would load what we could into her Hyundai hatchback before hightailing it to California. My carry on, my only luggage, was already packed with the maximum three ounces allowed of hand sanitizer, some anti-bacterial wipes, snacks for the road, (so we wouldn't have to stop much), and a handful of disposable masks. It seemed like planes might be grounded soon, so I had to go now. This new coronavirus was so contagious, so deadly. They said the hospitals might not have enough ventilators.

Whatever did not fit in her car, Gerry did not need. If this moment brought anything into focus, it was that some things were essential, but most stuff was not. I just needed her to come with me. I needed her to let me help.

I pulled into the Rainbow Roll and was surprised to find it dark and quiet. Sky's truck was the only vehicle parked outside.

"I decided to shut down, temporarily," she said when I went inside. "I couldn't figure out how to keep everyone far enough apart, and the more I thought about it, the more if just seemed like an unnecessary risk. Roller disco should be fun and easy, and it can wait."

"I think you made the right decision."

"So long as this doesn't go on for more than a couple of weeks," she said. "I'm about ready to lock up. Should I follow you back to the Hi-Dez? Then I can be there in the morning to feed Alan while you get on the road."

"Thanks for taking care of my old man," I said.

She laughed and kissed me, which suddenly felt like a risky act. We were supposed to keep six feet from anyone outside our immediate household, but I realized she was moving into the Hi-Dez while I brought my niece home to live there, too, so maybe we already were an immediate household, on our way to being family.

Early the next morning, we stood together in the Hi-Dez parking lot, my SUV packed with supplies. Sky put her arms around me, and I put mine around her. I absorbed her steady, strong energy, her love and joy, all of which I felt through her arms, and in her breath on my neck. I drew in as much of it as I could before I let her let go.

She said, "Just get yourself back to me safe and sound."

I promised.

Maybe the two of us would build something, someday, on that land beyond the dry lakebed. We would keep the native flora but clear off the ghosts. But for now, the world felt too unsettled. Everything was soaked through with vague, existential dread.

"What do you know for sure?" I asked myself as I drove away. It was an old trick for when I got too deep in my own thoughts. I reminded myself to recommend it to Gerry. What I knew for sure was that I loved Sky. And I really did not care what that meant or did not mean about past versions of me. At fifty, I had seen too many exceptions to every rule, too many contrasting, coexisting truths, to ever limit myself to one definition.

What I knew for sure was that my home was not Connecticut, the Hi-Dez Motel, or even Joshua Tree National Park. My home was Sky.

It was my last shift at Big Deal, because Aunt Paula was kidnapping me later. I made that joke to her when we planned it on the phone, but she didn't see the humor. Things at Big Deal were pretty much the same, despite all this Covid stuff. Some of the shoppers were weirdly frantic and we were already running low on stuff like toilet paper, Clorox wipes, and rubbing alcohol. Rick told us to keep one set of sliding glass doors open, so there was some fresh, cold air. Now all the cashiers wore parkas, woolly hats, and gloves. Rick wrote a memo that he tacked up on the employee memo board announcing that a jumbo-sized bottle of hand sanitizer had been purchased at management's expense and was installed in the employee break room FREE OF CHARGE because Big Deal Cares™.

Once again, it was Fresh Family Farms Day, but this time I was a spring lamb. The costume was roomy and white with polyester batting that I guessed was supposed to be my wooly coat. It attracted all kinds of dirt.

Rick was recently promoted to Acting General Manager, while Corporate conducted a nationwide search for someone better. For some reason, everyone (but me) loved Rick, and rumor had it the job would soon be his for real.

"Baa, baa, the freshest lamb comes from Fresh Family Farms," I called out to no one as I strolled the wide, mostly empty aisles. I made my way to the back of the store because I was due for my fifteen-minute break. I stepped out back and removed my lamb headpiece and put it on the picnic table. I unzipped my costume enough to get to my back pocket, where I had a pack of cigarettes and a lighter. Yes, I was a smoker now. Dumbest habit ever, obviously, but I was not interested in hearing that from anyone. It helped with my nerves. And it stopped me from eating.

Out back, it was bright and cold. There was one tree just starting to break out in pink blossoms. I sat down and lit a Marlboro. I took a deep drag and then exhaled smoke and everything else that was bugging me: Gary, our apartment, my job, Rick, and how I was done with college but still wanted to learn things, but every day was just more of what I already knew.

I stubbed out my cigarette in the melamine ashtray someone boosted from Camping & Outdoor when I heard someone approach. I turned and it took me a second… Aunt Paula? I wasn't expecting her until the end of my shift.

We stood awkwardly six feet apart, at first, and then, since we were going to be together in the car, anyway, we hugged. Aunt Paula was almost as tall as me but not as fat. I held onto her and the idea that someday I might be less.

"That costume does not smell great," Aunt Paula said, when I finally let go.

"Nothing here does," I said.

"You're smoking, now?" she asked, but I just shrugged. "I don't have a membership, so they wouldn't let me in," she said. "I've been parked out back, hoping you'd eventually come out for a break. Listen, we need to get out of here. Everyone should be somewhere they don't mind being stuck for a while. We need to hunker down."

"Hunker down?" I repeated. Aunt Paula could be so corny.

"I don't want you to get stuck here," she said.

"I don't mind this job."

"I'm not talking about the job," she said.

I put my lamb's head back on and opened the door with my employee ID. Aunt Paula put on a fabric mask and slipped in behind me. Immediately I saw Rick coming around the corner from Automotive, and I knew he'd spotted us.

"Gerry? Who is this?" he called, his mask slung beneath his chin.

I stopped walking and let him catch up. Aunt Paula stood silently beside me, and I could tell she planned to let me do the talking.

"For real this time," I said to Rick. "I quit."

"You're not really Big Deal material, are you, Gerry?" Rick said, scowling up into my lamb face.

"Let's hope not," I said. "I'll hang up the costume in the employee lounge."

"That thing looks like shit," he hissed, this time keeping his voice low.

"It smells like shit, too," I whispered back.

As Aunt Paula and I headed for the employee lounge, a customer tried to get me to stop and take a picture with her squirming toddler in a sparkly tutu, but I pretended not to hear. I kept walking. I saw a tall, dark-haired guy watching me from the endcap in Kitchen & Home. He wore a paper face mask over his nose and mouth, but I knew who it was.

"Rav," I called.

"Gerry? Is that you?"

I pulled off my lamb's head so he could see me. He walked over, stopping six feet away.

I said, "What are you doing here?"

"Looking for you. I heard Big Deal wasn't taking Covid seriously. I wanted to make sure you were—"

"I just quit," I said. "This job, and also Connecticut. My whole life, I think."

"What about your boyfriend?"

"I'm about to head home and quit him, too," I said.

"I'm heading out to my car," said Aunt Paula, resting her hand on my wooly white back for a moment. "Take your time."

"This is Rav," I said.

"Hi Rav, I'm Paula. We were neighbors, right?"

"For a while."

We watched Paula walk away, and then he said, "Were you going to tell me you're leaving? I don't want to fall out of touch."

Touch: the word lingered between us.

"Me neither," I said.

Seeing Rav in person, I realized how much I'd missed him. I wondered if he'd missed me.

"I'm moving to California," I finally managed. "Just until this Covid stuff is over, probably. The timing is kind of good, anyway. Paula wants me in California so we can hunker down."

"Hunker down?" he repeated with a smirk that was gone as swiftly as it appeared. "California?"

"I need a big change. It worked for Paula."

"Maybe I'll move to California then, too. Not like I have anything to stay here for. I recently stopping going to class, so…"

"Really?"

"I hate college," he said. "I don't want to be taught how to think. I just want to make art that makes sense to me and hopefully a few other people. One person would be enough."

"Your art makes sense to me," I said.

In the employee lounge, I hung up the costume to await the next Big Deal Brand Ambassador. It looked limp and filthy. Sometimes it was easy to walk away.

Rav and I walked out the open set of doors at the front. I was blinded by the sun reflected off old snow along the curb.

Rav said, again, "I don't want to lose touch."

"We won't," I said. "We can't."

I saw Aunt Paula sitting in some shiny red sedan, her rental, I guessed, which she'd parked next to my Hyundai hatchback. I asked her for one of her business cards and then I gave it to Rav.

He read: "The Hi-Dez Motel, Yucca Valley, California."

"That's where I will be," I said. "Come visit."

"I will."

"Promise."

He looked at me, and I knew.

"I will miss walking dark city streets," Gerry said, as she drove us away from Gary's studio apartment.

We left Gary where we found him, on the couch playing a video game Gerry later told me was *Call of Duty*. He did not put up a fight, in the end, when Gerry introduced me and announced that she was leaving.

"For good, Gary," she said.

"Good," he said, not taking his eyes off the game.

I suspected that Gerry was a little embarrassed that he did not object, or even notice, really, as she packed and loaded her car. Gary was relieved, maybe. Grateful that she had the courage to end it, because he did not.

"And I will miss the woods," Gerry said. She steered us through a modest neighborhood where roofs sagged with old snow and windows displayed red hearts leftover from Valentine's Day, even this close to Easter. "But otherwise I'm looking forward to the desert."

We hit a pothole and my gray spirals bounced.

Gerry said, "My favorite part of living at your house was how close it was to the Mianus River."

She followed signs to I-95 South.

"I thought maybe your favorite part was meeting Rav Patel," I said.

Gerry rolled her eyes, like that was the corniest thing she'd heard, so I knew I was right.

I would miss the Mianus River, too. I thought about a plastic grocery bag I once found snagged along its banks. This was back when John was alive. I hated that the bag was there, that nowhere was spared human garbage. I tried to remove it, but the bag was tangled in tree roots. It might still be stuck there.

"I think Rav will like the desert," Gerry said.

I looked at my niece and I knew: she was not okay, but she would be.

Gerry steered us south, then west, and then we really were on our way home.

I said, "When we stop for gas, remember I have a tub of bleach wipes for the keypad and gel sanitizer for your hands."

"Rav said I should wear a mask."

"I have those, too. We're going to be okay, Gerry."

"Maybe this is what it took to make us all stop and pay attention."

"To what?" I asked.

"Everything," she said. "Anything."

We paid the toll at the Delaware Water Gap Bridge and drove through deeply green Pennsylvania, climbing up into the Poconos.

"Tell me about your art," I said.

"I'm thinking of taking a break from miniatures," Gerry said. "Maybe I'll learn how to build furniture for real people. What about you?" she said. "How's the writing going?"

"It's going," I said, and it was.

"Tell me about Sky," Gerry said.

I said, "She is light on her feet but grounded. She is playful and fun and deadly serious about the stuff she cares about. She loves me and does not expect me to make sense. She just lets me be. I'm glad you're finally going to meet her."

"Is it different, with a woman?"

"It's different with her," I said.

Crossing the Mississippi, in view of the St. Louis Arch, I spotted a slippery patch of ice up ahead but told Gerry to keep going, keep her foot off the brake.

"Let momentum work for you," I told my niece.

By Oklahoma, Gerry told me that when she was young, she was teased on the playground with chants of, "Ger-ry Gi-ant."

I said, "It's time to stop punishing yourself for being who you are."

She did not respond, but she heard me. Eventually, she agreed to let me call Pearl.

"Our girl is going to be okay," I told my sister, and I heard her stifle a sob of relief.

Gerry said she already missed those costumes.

"No more hiding," I said.

When we got back into the car after stopping to see Cadillac Ranch, along the highway outside Amarillo, Texas, I said, "I won't feel sorry for you, but when you are ready to tell me the whole story of what happened at NYU, how you fell… I would like to hear it."

"Where would I start?" she said. "How far back would I go?"

"All the way," I said.

Gerry's words bubbled up and I could see how it lightened her, to release them, to have them heard. Afterwards, Gerry seemed happy. Happier.

"Maybe the desert will deconstruct you, too," I said. It was my turn to drive. Pulling back onto I-40 West, I said, "Once you finally fall apart, you get to decide who you are."

I drove us toward whatever was next—to everything we could not know. We were headed for the middle of the Mojave Desert, nowhere really, some rundown motel with worn out beds and a bad reputation—like me. The worst.

I drove us home, as the past shrank to nothing in the rearview.

ACKNOWLEDGMENTS

Thanks to everyone who shared work at the feminist, queer, and "otherwise radical" Desert Split Open Mic, and to the 35 contributors to *Feckless Cunt: A Feminist Anthology*. Also inspirational to *The Worst Kind of Girl* was the #MeToo movement. I appreciate every woman who told the truth about her life.*

*Thank you, as always, Muriel Rukeyser.

I am deeply grateful to Jennifer Lewis, brilliant writer and founder of Red Light Lit, for giving this book a second chance to find its readers. Her support helped make this book possible – not once, but twice.

Big hugs and thank yous to Gayle Brandeis, Gina Frangello, and Jen Michalski, authors I admire greatly, for taking the time to write nice things about *The Worst Kind of Girl*.

I appreciate the encouragement from editors who recognized early versions of the manuscript:
- Santa Fe Writers Project (Shortlist, 2022 Literary Awards)
- Black Lawrence Press (Finalist, 2022 Big Moose Prize)
- Dzanc Books (Longlist, 2022 Prize for Fiction)

Several chapters of this book grew from seeds planted in previously published work. Thanks to the journals who found something to love as this story evolved:
- Cholla Needles #45, "Timeline for Decomposition;" #33, "Desert, Mother, Home"
- Mojave He[art] Review, "I Was a Pink Bath Bomb"
- Luna Luna, "Things Break Easily in My Big Hands"
- Necessary Fiction, "The Worst Girl's Best Day"

So much was synthesized to become *The Worst Kind of Girl*. I am grateful for all of it.

Susan Rukeyser writes and lives in Joshua Tree, California. She created the Desert Split Open to amplify literary work that is feminist, queer, and otherwise radical, and publishes select titles as World Split Open Press, including *Feckless Cunt: A Feminist Anthology*. She is the author of one previous novel, *Not On Fire, Only Dying* (Twisted Road Publications). Her short work appears in many wonderful places, online and in print, and is collected most recently in *Utility Location* (Bottlecap Press) and *Whatever Feels Like Home* (above/ground press). www.susanrukeyser.com

9 780999 889558